Deep Song: *Cante Jondo*

A Novel

by

Laurel Mae Hislop

Manna Mark

Published in Canada by Manna Mark Books

Vancouver, British Columbia

Library and Archives Canada Cataloguing in Publication

Hislop, Laurel Mae, 1953-

Deep Song: *Cante Jondo* / Laurel Mae Hislop

A Novel

ISBN 978-0-9938237-5-6

For Raquel

Raquel Garcia Varela
25 September 1943
-
03 August 2021
Drawn by Raquel 02 August 2021

Prologue

'It is song without landscape, withdrawn into itself and terrible in the dark.'

Federico García Lorca on *Cante Jondo*

Early on a sun-filled afternoon in July of 1979 a crowd gathered near the *Cuevas del Sacromonte* in the Spanish province of Andalusia. Someone famous was to visit that day. A string of fourteen brightly painted caravans known as *vardos* were lined up blocking the traffic on the *Camino del Sacromonte.*

The store fronts, in this archaic section of the city of Granada, served as facades over cave entrances. Behind them, smoke coiled up from chimneys, protruding from the craggy landscape like canons pointed to the sky.

A human menagerie, decked out in vibrant apparel, lolled about the sidewalk cafés. The fetor of fried fish streamed from the flue of the cafes and settled over the gathering. It was hot, no breeze.

People could also be seen on dirt paths leading to more caves high above the main street. With no facades, the upper caves resembled bat holes in the sandstone face of the hill. But from up there, a spectacular view of the Alhambra unfurled, an ancient crimson castle emblazoned against the Sierra Nevada Mountains.

Amongst those gathered on the street that day were: a couple in their thirties, two teenage boys and a four-year-old. The four-year-old yearned to run and play with the children who were squealing in and around the *vardos*. But he was dressed in his best white shirt and shiny black shoes and knew he couldn't. That's about all he knew.

He wasn't aware that the cave dwelling behind him, the place he came every night with this troupe of musicians, was once the home of his grandmother. She died before he was born. She'd been the most famous *flamenco* performer ever born in the Caves of *Sacromonte*.

He didn't remember his *mamá* or *papá* either, who had both been killed in a motorcycle accident when he was two. He did know that if his white shirt became dirty he wouldn't be allowed to go on stage with the band. And he knew also, if he was quiet and didn't complain, someone would pass him his *requinto* once the music started. Then he'd be allowed to strum along in time to the clacking of shoes, the snap of fingers and clicking of tongues. And the boy would rather do this than anything else in the world. So, he made himself content to sit and watch the other children.

The child didn't know that these caves had once been the primary dwellings of the *Romany* people, who had populated this hamlet for hundreds of years, or that the *Roma* were his ancestors. Few people lived here anymore. Some of the caves had been reconstructed into a domestic museum to show how they would have been used years ago as homes. These days, the business operators and performers in Andalusia were still predominantly *Gitano.* Almost everyone worked in tourism.

The boy didn't even know his people preferred to be called *Roma,* but were sneeringly called *Gitano* in this part of the world, Gypsies or Tinkers in other places. He didn't know about the *lungo drom,* the long road that led his people from India to where he stood. Nor was he aware of the persecution suffered by his ancestors, in most recent times under Franco and the Nazis. Or that the Spanish government had been tolerant of the *Gitano* since the Second World War, nurturing an artistic community of which the boy was unknowingly a part.

He *did* know that someone very important was to visit the Caves that day. He knew this because he heard the adults talking about it.

One woman said, "I've heard that a man died of sorrow once, while listening to her song."

"She has even made a movie in Hollywood," said another.

The women discussing this were dressed, as were all the females, in flamboyant, tight-fitting *flamenco* dresses they would wear on stage later. Many of the men had on hats and suit jackets and wore shiny shoes or boots even though it was sweltering.

The four-year-old was the first one to notice the old woman coming down the hill from the bat-hole cave where she lived above the village. Using a cane to dig into the dirt in front of her, she sidled downward along the path, her back bowed with a curve like his uncle's *bandurria.* She was *drabarni,* the oldest fortune teller in the community. The boy was scared of her. She had no teeth.

The sun was beginning to set by the time she stopped and leaned against a wooden fence one tier above the *Camino del Sacromonte.*

She addressed the gathering in a raspy voice. "The woman you wait for will not come." Everyone quit talking and looked up at the ancient fortune teller. "In a vision this afternoon I saw this woman you hope to see." Her hand shook and one bent finger pointed up to the sky. A quaver crept into her voice. "An owl was dead at her feet."

The crowd gave a collective gasp. Everyone knew that a dead owl signified something terrible had happened, or would soon happen, to the person in her vision. The *drabarni* stared into the crowd intently, tipped her head back, closed her eyes for a moment and then turned to start her slow journey back up the hill.

Shows were cancelled and the performers filtered into a single club that night. Every chair along the wall was taken. Most of the women and all the children had to sit on the floor. Even with an audience that was largely *Romany,* the atmosphere was subdued. The boy sat between his aunt and another woman. He liked to be close to the women, because they smelled like flowers.

"The owl curse; I hope it's not her new baby," his aunt said.

The other woman nodded. "Me too. So many things can go wrong when they're newly born."

That night, the musicians played the slower songs. His aunt

stood up and sang *cante jondo,* or deep song, a type known as *una siquiriva,* not usually performed in the *Zambra* of *Sacromonte.* It made him think about the newly born baby. He hoped nothing bad had happened to it.

Part One

Birthdays

It's June 15, 2012, my guesstimated thirty-third birthday, and when I wake it feels like any other day. I used to think birthdays were significant, a time to review the previous year and make plans for the future. At some point, I realised the future is never any different from the past, and so your date of birth means nothing. Besides, when you don't know the actual day you were born, it's absurd to celebrate.

It's Monday and my day off. I have a doctor's appointment. I get up, slip on my tatty robe, throw back the curtains, and push the window wide open. An ocean breeze brings in a musty hint of seaweed. I decide to bail on the doctor. What good would it do? I identified my affliction months ago. It matches the images on the WebMD site.

But the clinic charges for missed appointments, so I call and cancel. "I'm unwell today," I say. "It may be the flu, and you would not want me in your office. I'll re-schedule when I'm better."

I do not intend to re-book. Our family doctor is so dull, you could be high on coke and he'd still put you to sleep. And why I made the appointment on my birthday baffles me. I'm not sure why I decided to go at all. I guess it was to confirm what I already know. There's no treatment for vitiligo, and over time it will get worse.

I watch as the residents of Kitsilano wake. Zeus, the golden Lab from next door, herds his elfin owner out for her morning walk. Two all-night party girls stagger arm in arm up the stairs of the King's Head Pub. Their face piercings glitter in the sun, lending a festive air, and I think of Erin. We never went to nightclubs, but I miss that arm-in-arm camaraderie.

During my morning shower, I sing Whitney Houston's "I Have Nothing" with abandon. I only ever sing in the shower. A mirror, affixed to the tiles, fogs up, and I wipe it with a facecloth and pump out the chorus. After a rigorous lather and a quick icy rinse, I push open the bathroom door and step out through a cloud of steam.

A few months ago I moved my antique vanity away from the window, into the centre of the apartment. I live in a single room

—a bachelor suite, but I have plenty of space. Still damp and wrapped in a towel, I patter barefoot across the hardwood floor, stop in front of its large oval mirror, and inspect my back. Even though I know it's futile, I pray to see improvement. I look and cringe. Even in the dimmer light, it's as if someone's hit me with white paintballs. A new patch has emerged on my shoulder blade, a ghostly splat creeping up the dark skin en route to my neck. I suppose I should be thankful it's not yet reached my face.

The padded bench lets out a whoosh of air when I sit. Leaning forward, I squint at the mirror and comb my heavy eyebrows with a fingernail. Mother used to nag me to pluck. "They're like caterpillars." Then she'd get that look, like some bug was crawling up her arm.

I turn and see letters scattered near the mail slot. I squat and reach for a brown envelope that's drifted under the umbrella stand. It's from the guy in Amsterdam I've hired to find my birth parents, the man who claims to be a detective of genealogy.

He's written my name with a heavy hand, To Halca Visser, a thick awkward scrawl that indents the paper. The envelope doesn't feel any thicker than the previous invoices he's sent. I prefer not to spoil my birthday, so I toss it on top of the fridge with the other bills. He can wait for his money.

So far, the only information Mr. Vanderburg has produced is how many dead ends he's run into and how much I owe him. The last time he passed on any actual news was over two months ago. The orphanage in Holland had a flood, he explained. They lost all the records. None of the nuns remember a baby abandoned at the Roosendaal train station in 1979.

I throw my robe back on, go to my computer, and find a website that claims vitamin B12 is a cure for vitiligo. They recommend a strict regime for a year or two. I'll have to pick some up. Vitiligo isn't life threatening, the article says, and I'm aware of this, but it is hereditary and that concerns me. Who knows what other nasty surprises lurk in my gene pool? I glance at my stack of bills and frown. Besides the gene pool worry, it reminds me I haven't written to Erin in over three weeks. I dig in the drawer for a pen and paper. I wish I could email her, but she's a complete Luddite and doesn't even own a computer, so our letters travel back and forth by snail mail.

Dear Erin

Just a quick note today. It's my birthday and Mother has summoned me home for a celebratory dinner. You know how much I enjoy those.

I told you about hiring the genealogy detective, and no, before you ask, I will not tell Mother about it. I considered telling Dad, but have decided against it for now. If he ever digs up any information, I'll reconsider. I'd hate to upset Dad for nothing. The investigator has been useless, and why I ever hired him is a mystery. I'm sure it surprised you. Remember years ago when you wrote me and asked, "Aren't you curious?" I wasn't then, and I'm still not. But in a way, it's because of you I've changed my mind. I think of your struggles with Crohn's and your aunt and three cousins who also have it. You said the doctors diagnosed it right away because of your family's history. They've kept it under control too. I hope you're getting the same excellent treatment in Ireland.

So, I'm not after details of my real parents. I'm sure that's a gruesome story that I'm better off not hearing. It's the family history of disease I'm keen to know—cancer, heart disorder, Parkinson's, mental illness. We all have the right to answers, don't we?

I hope everything's okay. I worry because you've not replied to my last three letters. Please write soon. I miss you.

Love always and forever,

Hally

I didn't mention the vitiligo to Erin. She'd only stress. I grab an envelope, scribble Erin's address, and affix it with an international stamp. If I don't hear back, I'll try phoning next month. I can't afford it, but it's not like Erin to ignore me. I curl up on the sofa with a magazine and mimic a sloth for the remainder of the day.

When I drag myself off the couch, it's four o'clock. I locate my mother-visit costume, a pair of grey slacks and a cream knit top. I dress quickly, find and insert the pearl studs that were last year's birthday present, knot my hair in a bun, take out the make-up remover and wipe away the smudges of mascara under my eyes. When I'm presentable, I head outside and stroll to the car.

The garage door is open when I pull into my parents' driveway. Dad is leaning over a workhorse, tinkering with a long piece of metal that has a house fan welded to the end. Another invention, no doubt. Since selling his building contract business, this is how he spends his time. I'd love to see the working result of one of his gadgets someday.

Dad doesn't fit the image of an inventor, no frenzied clutter, no unkempt hair. He's a lanky man, built like a Hollander. When he moves, it seems his arm and leg bones are trying to escape his skin. I'm always amazed by his work area. Behind him, tools aligned on a pegboard cover one entire wall. On the counter, with military precision, he's arranged speckless glass jars of nails and screws, and sorted them by type and size.

I cut the engine and open the car door.

He looks up and grins. "You're early." The order around him melts with that goofy smile.

I check my phone. "Only two minutes."

"It's okay. I think Mother is ready."

As I head to the entrance, an unusual scent blows up from where he's working. It's like walking through The Bay cosmetics department. I glance back and he's bent across his contraption again.

Inside, the kitchen is bare and clean, clean, clean as always. In the middle of the table, a birthday cake with sculpted white swirls rests on a pedestal plate. This is Mother's traditional vanilla cream. It will be baked to perfection, moist, and finely textured. I appreciate her efforts, but prefer Black Forest. My mother, Lieke Visser, knows this but she's never made me one.

"Is that you?" Her voice comes from the end of the hall. "You're early."

"No, I'm not." I peer into the dining room at the golden carriage clock on the mantle. "It's five-thirty, on the nose." Footsteps sound and she appears in the doorway. She's always reminded me of a doll from the Netherlands, the type brought home by tourists. Her hair is blonde and thick-bobbed, with straight-cut bangs halfway up her pale forehead.

"You're tired. Have you been reading all night again?" She inspects me up and down.

"No, I feel fine."

She places one hand on each of my shoulders, dispenses a stiff hug, and steps back. "How is work?"

"It's the same. Ulla says hello."

Ulla is the owner of *Der Schwarze Koffer* Fashion and my boss. She and Mother have been friends forever. Ulla gives Mother and I something to talk about.

"She is still trying to sell the store?" Mother plucks a starched tea towel off the stove door, spreads it on the table, re-folds it, and hangs it back up.

"Yes, didn't she tell you? It looks like she might've found a buyer."

"What will you do then?" Her face is expressionless, but she eyeballs me with her 'so disappointing' look.

"I don't know."

"You should go to school. There is a course offered at the college this summer in Business Management. Then you could run your own place."

"I don't want to run a store." This truth pummels me, because that's exactly what I do. I run Ulla's shop for her, and I hate it.

Mother shakes her head. Just then the afternoon sun streaks in and lights up her eyes. Normally you don't notice her different coloured eyes, but now her green and blue eyes flash with wintry brilliance.

"Well, the water isn't worth the cabbage. I will call in your father now." She heads for the door. "You could move back home. Then you could afford college."

I should nip this conversation in the bud, but I'm speechless. Why is she always butting into my life? My life is fine. And why does she think I avoided college fifteen years ago? Return to this house? Never—it was worse than a prison. I shake my head.

Mother leans out the door. "Janz, come in and wash for dinner." She does an about-turn, marches to the sink, picks up a dishcloth and wipes her spotless counter. "Well, consider it. A woman of your age can still return to school. Selling dresses is not a career."

This school business will be the focus of conversation all evening. Lieke is always ready and willing to plot out my future, but she's never once offered information about my past or delved into an emotional issue. I have the urge to ask her how it feels to celebrate the birth of an adopted daughter. Does she yearn for what might have been, wonder how different she'd feel if I'd grown from her body and looked like her? How often does she wish I wasn't a dark-skinned, dark-haired alien?

"I have heard the instructors at Langara College are the best in the city."

"I'm sure they're fine." I clear my throat and gaze out the window. I'm no imbecile. If I was interested in school, I'd do it on my own.

"They have many other classes." She hoofs to the countertop and scratches at an imaginary spatter.

Dad steps into the room.

"Have you washed up?" Mother asks.

He holds his hands out for inspection. Then he walks across the kitchen, and kisses my forehead. "Happy birthday, Hally."

Thank God for dad.

"Come, we should eat now." Mother points to the clock. "It's after five-thirty."

In the dining room, she has the black lacquered table set with her good bone-white china on grey place mats. As we sit, she lifts the lid on the silver warming tray and a puff of steam escapes over pasty potatoes, yellow wax beans and pale sliced pork smothered in onions. Mother has something against colour. Even a carrot or two would liven up this spread. I wonder about the red tablecloth I bought her for Christmas a few years ago. I've never seen it since.

"Pass me your plate, Janz. Halca is considering about Langara College." She spoons food out for him.

"Good for you." He gives me an appreciative look. Dad's always pleased when Mother gets her way. He would agree to anything for a quiet life.

"What's the latest invention, Dad?"

His eyes spark. He lifts his fork and wands it through the air.

"It will attach to the clothesline in the laundry room and dry the clothes. I suspended it on a rail. It will hook to the top line. A motor powered by a battery will move the fan back and forth alongside the clothes." His forehead wrinkles in concentration. "The start works, but I have not yet mastered the stop and reverse." He raises one eyebrow and flashes me the hint of a smile. "It will give the clothes a gentle breeze, like a spring day. I may add a scent too. I am on a search for the correct fragrance."

"That's what that smell was." I chuckle.

"I can't even open windows on that side of the house." Mother plugs her nose. "Such a terrible stink."

"Dad, wouldn't it be easier to put a clothesline up in the back yard?"

Mother drops her knife with a clang. "And let the neighbours gawk at our underclothes?"

She spends the next fifteen minutes gossiping about the neighbours, with extra emphasis on Frieda's daughter who's gone back to school to study law. This is all very difficult to digest with pork, but somehow I manage to clean my plate as expected.

"Go, bring the present," she orders Dad when we've finished the main course. "I'll get the cake."

They leave the room and I ponder how long I'll be expected to stay after the present opening and cake.

When Dad gets back, he sets a wrapped parcel on the chair next to me while Mother surgically slices the birthday cake with a wide knife. She deposits equal-size pieces on square dessert plates. The present is huge and I try to imagine how it'll fit in the back of the closet with the gifts of previous years, which include: a set of Val D'Or china still in the box, a book entitled "Black and White, Interior Decorating with Class," and a pathetic photo album of my baby pictures. Each snapshot depicts a dark-skinned baby clinging desperately to her cool blonde mother. I separate the white bow and navy wrapping from this year's gift. It's a black leather briefcase.

"Thank you. This is lovely leather." I run one hand down the side of the case. A brochure from the college pokes from an exterior flap. I slip it out.

Mother leans over and taps one finger on the flyer. "If Business Management does not interest you, there is another course, to be a Certified General Accountant."

I take a mouthful of cake and look at the brochure. "Here's something interesting. I should sign up for this belly dancing class."

A cup and saucer clatters. All eyes turn to dad. Spilled coffee soaks the front of his beige shirt.

"Oh, Janz, you clumsy oaf. Look at the ugly stain."

When did Mother develop such repugnance for brown? Did it always disgust her or did it begin years ago when her adopted baby's skin began to darken too much?

The Black Suitcase

Der Schwarze Koffer Fashion, translated as "The Black Suitcase," is situated off 4th Avenue six blocks up from Kits Beach. I always try to arrive precisely at nine, not a moment earlier. Over the shop door, on brass hooks, a pretentious sign with gold lettering sways in the breeze.

I insert my key in the first lock, then the second lock, click open the third lock and squat to unlatch the extra lock at the bottom near my foot. Ulla, obsesses over security.

An ocean breeze whips hair into my eyes as I swing the door open.

The air inside blisters with the essence of ripe cheese. I once thought expensive clothes should smell like perfume, but the garments in this store arrive with the odour of their origin. European seamstresses sweating over hemlines, probably can't afford deodorant.

Three boxes sit outside the change room, past the racks of colour-coordinated pants, blouses, and skirts. The dresses from Germany have arrived. I'm relieved because this will keep me busy. Mornings are always dead. It's rare to see a customer before noon.

From the back I drag a rack we use to steam clothes and set it up in the aisle between the glass jewellery cabinet and sweater shelves. If Ulla were here, she'd insist I do it in the claustrophobic cubicle of the storeroom. But she's not in yet. Sometimes she doesn't appear before two o'clock. Most days I'd rather she stayed home, because Ulla does nothing. I do the purchase orders, the cash, the inventory, and as far as she's concerned it's always wrong, especially the ordering.

Last week she scratched off an order I put in for a line of summer blouses with a trendy Empire waistline.

"We sell classics," she snarled.

"But, they are classic." It was useless to argue, but I had to say something. "The Empire waistline dates back to the early nineteenth century."

"We do not peddle the latest trend." Ulla's thin lips tightened to a reedy line. As always, I took a big breath and gulped down a cranky retort that I knew would only result in days of stilted silence.

When Ulla approves an order, it's my job to enter it into the database. Last year I tried to save a step and get her to sign a form printed off the computer, but she refused. She makes me handwrite each item on the standard paper form, the one she has always used, including the convoluted full addresses of the European designers, complete with details of colour, fabric and sizes. Then, I have to retype every detail into the store catalogue. Only then can I place an order on the vendor's website. It's inefficient, but she pays me to do it, so I've learned to keep my mouth shut.

I plug in the steamer, slice through the packing tape of the top box, drape the first dress and begin steaming. By noon there's not a wrinkle in any of the new dresses. They're organised on the garment rack per Ulla's demand, not touching, not crammed together, colour-coded, grey with grey and black with black. 'This is not a Salvation Army thrift store.' My boss brings this to my attention at least once a week.

The cheesy odour in the air around the steamer bowls me over. I pick up a metal cylinder next to the cash register and spritz some lavender mist, Ulla favourite fragrance. Maybe, when she gets in, the scent will calm her.

Not one customer has crossed the threshold in three hours. The clothes are pricey, but I often wonder how the business keeps running. Last winter, I suggested a sandwich board on 4th Avenue. "A sandwich board?" You'd think I'd asked her to strip and run naked through the streets. "We are not a delicatessen." Could've fooled me with the smell of this place.

At 12:30 I toss out the remnants of the salad I brought for lunch and sit at the computer, one eye on the entrance. My Google search for tarot card meanings yields 512 results. Overwhelming, but it'll keep me occupied. I'm aware that horoscopes, psychic readings, and other-worldly topics have no basis in reality, but they fascinate me. In fact, I've booked a reading for tomorrow afternoon at that little upstairs room on Main and 23rd. They say Madam Lavinia is the best clairvoyant in the city.

At two o'clock, I'm still engrossed in my research. I don't notice the customer standing less than three feet away until the woman clears her throat. I jerk to attention. She's middle-aged, size fourteen or better, with blonde, blowsy hair framing her face. The hairstyle might compliment a twenty-year-old, but on this lady, it pings of eccentricity.

"Excuse me. Are you open?"

"Yes, of course, sorry."

The woman tugs on the hem of her too-tight paisley top and glances around the store. "I'm looking for a skirt."

I direct her to the row of skirts, all knee length, straight cut, in a variety of posh fabrics.

She fingers through the rack. "Don't you have something shorter? The hemlines are shorter this year." I glance at her plump legs. She has on a pair of shiny, blue short-shorts. As she swivels to peer at some blouses, I spot a grapevine of varicose veins.

A box of mini-skirts came in a week ago. Ulla hadn't noticed the length on the original order. When the package arrived, she pulled one skirt out and told me to label them for return. With any luck, the courier hasn't picked them up yet.

"Give me a minute. I think we have what you're looking for." I scoot into the storeroom. The box is still there. I fumble through the garments, do a mental calculation from European to Canadian, and pull out two skirts, a size 42 and 44.

The door opens and a breeze whips through the shop. Ulla whirls in just as the customer steps out of the change room wearing a size 42 mini-skirt cinched around her hips. The woman's legs look even more round with more bulging purple veins, but she stands in front of the mirror and says, "I love it. It's just what I wanted."

I peep over at my employer. She's come to a halt. Her face is bone white and blood-drained, her red lips a warning flag. She fires me a dirty look and then glances at the entrance with a pained expression.

I turn to the customer. "I'm so glad you're happy. When a lady loves her clothes, it brings out all her natural beauty." The woman beams and what I said becomes the truth. Her smile has transformed her.

Ulla is not capable of noticing such things. With her back turned on us, she's leaning on a rack of party dresses with one hand pressed to the side of her head.

As soon as the lady pays and leaves, Ulla walks to the wicker armchair near the dressing room and slumps into it. "Thanks be to God that someone did not come in, like Mrs Bellow, or Mayor Todd." She scowls at me, straightens her shoulders and picks a strand of copper hair off her black sweater.

"No harm done." I flip my palms up. "No one came in. The client is pleased, and you made a sale too." I force a smile, walk to the rack of skirts, and fuss with the hangers.

"I told you to send those skirts back. We do not handle such clothes." Ulla rises from the chair like a praying mantis. "How many times do we need to have this talk? We sell classics. Our customers leave here well-dressed, not fitted up as buffoons.

Have I not taught you a thing?"

"But the skirt made her happy." I'd love to add, 'She's not a miserable snob like you,' but I keep that comment to myself.

"*Ja,* happy, foolish looking, same as a clown." Her flaming hair prickles high on her head. "I have a reputation. I do not dress my customers for the circus." An ill-timed vision of a fake red nose on her hollow-cheeked face springs to mind. I choke back a laugh.

Not one person walks in for the next two hours. I stand guard behind the counter and write up an order for the fall collection of suits. Ulla buries her head in a magazine in the armchair by the change room, as far away from me as she can get.

Later, she visits her friend, Mary, in the shoe store next door and returns in a better mood. At closing time, I gather up my things to go home. "By the way, I need tomorrow afternoon off."

"What for?"

"I'd rather not say." Ulla would never understand my interest in tarot cards.

"Don't say. I will ask your mother then."

Oh, how I regret the day I ever agreed to work for my mother's best friend.

"Please don't tell her."

"Why not?"

"It's a medical concern. You know how she worries." I won't see the doctor about my vitiligo, but if I need evidence to back up my story, I'll simply turn around and lift my blouse.

"What's wrong?"

"Probably nothing. I'll be in tomorrow morning, but I have to leave at noon." I did try for an after-work appointment, but it seems Madam Lavinia works only Tuesday and Wednesday from 1PM to 4. It must be nice.

"What am I to tell your mother?"

"Don't worry her, okay?"

"I planned to take Cicero to have his nails clipped tomorrow at two. If he tears up my sofa, I'll have you to blame."

I leave and tramp home. What a bitch. For Christ's sake, I haven't asked for a day off in four years. I never call in sick. I put up with her pettiness and nagging. And it's not as if the tightwad pays me an outstanding salary. I get minimum wage and run the business for her. If I had any other skills I'd quit, but this is the only job I've ever had. I can sing and dance, but that's limited to shower-stall singing and dances in my living room. I have no talent, and I'm petrified of the stage.

When I open the door to my apartment, I'm still peeved. There's mail. When I pick it up, I notice a package from Ireland, but it's not Erin's handwriting on the outside, and my heart does a flip.

The next morning, I phone and leave a message to cancel my appointment with the psychic. I'm destroyed by the news of Erin and can't imagine stepping outside the apartment. I've been awake most of the night. My stomach is raw, and my swollen eyes have narrowed to slits. The contents of the envelope from Ireland lay scattered across my hardwood floor. I zero in on the clutter. Prone on the couch, in my red striped pyjamas, I'm a flattened penny on the railroad track of the past.

I cannot look back on my childhood without seeing Erin. I met her in Grade 2, when her family moved onto our street. The first day we played she said, 'I think I love you, Hally.' She was an only child like me, and for the next six years it conjoined us, our time together always spent at her place. Even at eight, I never took it for granted—the light, bright atmosphere of Erin's home. Erin and her parents were alive and funny, and they made me feel alive and funny too. Mr Thomas was handsome beyond belief, and in my early teens, I had an enormous crush on him. He loved to tease 'his girls.' Laughter and music filled their house—the antithesis of my place.

To be fair, Mother worked from home as a bookkeeper. The year I started school, she took over the bookkeeping for Dad's business. Within a few years, she'd signed on half the small businesses in Marpole. She worked long hours and needed quiet. So, when Erin arrived on the scene, it elated Mother. It got me out of her hair, and it suited her that we always headed to Erin's house after school. Mother never encouraged kids to visit our house.

My home life wasn't terrible though. No one abused me. My parents fed and clothed me. Dad adored me, but he was a quiet man and Mother called the shots. I never saw Dad grab Mother and spin her into a dance on the living room rug like Mr Thomas did, but a lot of kids might say the same. Since there was never any music on in our house, that was impossible, anyway.

So, Erin and I played at hers and it pleased everyone, in particular Mrs Thomas, who was super fussy about Erin's diet due to the Crohn's. She liked to keep tabs on every morsel of food that ended up in her mouth.

I should treasure my cheerful memories of Erin and her family, but the big final remembrance spoils it all.

At fourteen, I was a dewy-eyed innocent. The school term had just ended, and the promise of summer stretched before us. But then Erin announced that she and her family were off to Ontario for an entire month. Mr Thomas had lost his job. Mrs Thomas worked as a waitress and had booked extra weeks off. 'It's a good time to go,' Erin said. She hadn't been sick or hospitalised for months. She'd even put on a little weight. Erin was skinny and wasp-like, with insect-thin limbs, enormous green eyes and white-blonde hair. She and I couldn't have been more opposite. But that summer she looked healthier than I'd ever seen her.

What would I do for a month without her? The thought devastated me.

One day Erin asked her mom, "Can Hally come on holiday with us?"

"I don't see why not, but we'll have to check with your dad."

What a relief.

I knew Mother wouldn't object, and Dad always went along with everything she said, but I decided not to ask right away. Even though I knew Mr Thomas liked me, and I was positive he'd say yes, I'd wait until he agreed.

Summer in the Lake District sounded exotic and seemed

worldly. I was hyped about the trip and barely slept that night. Erin said her uncle's cottage was beside a lake. I saw us swimming, sunbathing, having barbecues outside, with music blaring from Erin's ghetto blaster. I had never been to Ontario. From the time we left Holland when I was a baby, I'd not been farther than Vancouver Island.

Also, it was a chance to be around Erin's dad, Julian. Not that I ever called him Julian. He was always Mr Thomas on the rare occasion I untied my tongue and spoke in his presence. I was wholly under his spell. When he teased me, I felt special. Don't get me wrong, he did nothing inappropriate. I didn't even wish for that. I wanted only to be near him and worship him.

In my eyes, Erin's family were perfect in every way, happy in every way, and back then, I believed that my birth parents would have created a home just like theirs, if someone had not forced them to give me up. I imagined this often in my youth—romantic fantasies of my natural parents and what catastrophic and unavoidable circumstances had separated us.

So, I ran over to Erin's place the next morning, expecting them to be goofing around as usual and busy making plans for the trip. When I knocked, no one answered. I opened the door and heard muffled sobs from the upstairs bedrooms, so I tiptoed up the stairs.

Erin was crossed-legged on her bed, rocking and crying, hugging her skinny arms with her bony hands. She looked up at me and wailed.

"Dad left us." She blubbered and shook. "He took up with some whore at work. That's why they fired him."

I stumbled toward her, stunned, and sat at the end of the bed.

"He didn't even tell us in person. He left a fucking note," Erin muttered between sobs. "I bet he's even taken her to Uncle's for the summer."

"What a coward." I couldn't think of anything else to say. So, I scooched over next to her and put my arms around her and hugged her for the longest time. It seemed like hours before her wracking sobs shushed.

That day I understood that happy families don't exist. During your lifetime, you may run over the odd bump of happiness, but eventually and without fail, the road leads to an abyss of despair. People are selfish, and someone's stupid, selfish acts will ruin things, and it always ends in tears. This revelation has helped me again and again, in my dealings with Mother and Ulla, and with every other person who's tried to pin me down with a pack of rosy prospects.

Erin never recovered emotionally or physically. Two weeks later, she landed in the hospital again. This time she had to have surgery, and they removed part of her large intestine. She came home with a colostomy bag, bedridden for the summer. In September Erin's mom decided they were moving back to Ireland, and they disappeared before my head was off the pillow. Despite knowing Erin had no choice, her absence felt like betrayal.

After Erin left, I never made another close friend. She and I wrote, but we didn't make plans to get together, or even talk on the phone, and I certainly did not share all my secrets. Over the years, I have often wondered why I kept up with the correspondence. I've come to realise that the letters were a sort of make-do friendship that filled a void in my dreary life.

But this news has split me apart. Erin's gone for good now, and we'll never hug or laugh again.

Friday Nights

Dear Erin,

It was good of your mom to write and return my letters. She respects your privacy and didn't unseal them, like my mother would have done. I suspect she didn't even read the open ones you'd saved. Your mom is one of the sweetest women on earth. Losing you must have devastated her, and if I had the right words, I'd send off a card.

Yesterday, I pored over all the letters and matched what I wrote with your replies. I soaked an entire box of tissues. As I read the paragraph where you talked about never having a lover, I cried. When you mentioned how bleak the prospects were for someone with a colostomy bag, I sobbed until my eyes almost exploded. It's too late for you now, and I'm such a silly bitch. I cried so hard, realising that I too could die a virgin. And the sad and horrible truth is, there's no physical reason for my situation.

So, I've decided to do something about it. As you know, online dating doesn't appeal to me. Wasn't it your mom who used to say, "Don't buy a tomato without squeezing the fruit?"

A potential lover will never magically appear in my apartment either, will he? So I plan to go out on the town every Friday night until I meet someone who'll solve my dilemma. I'll go alone and only once a week, but I will not stop until it's done.

Oh, Erin—I love you and miss you so much.

Hally

I fold the letter, stuff it in an envelope, and scribble the date on the outside. Then I walk to the closet. I grab the shoebox off the top shelf, haul it down, and cram the new entry into the end where I've marked "New" with a black felt pen. I'll need to find a bigger box because this one is already bursting its seams.

On Friday night, I push open the wooden door of Club Combo and step into the swarming barroom. A candle flickers on each table, and I catch a whiff of burning wax. The music hasn't started. Glasses clink amidst voices and laughter. Varicoloured pot lights illuminate the stage and the wallpaper glisters. I flip one edge of my scarf back, a warmth blooming in my belly.

The bartender nods at a free table across the room. I crane my neck and peer into the crowd as if meeting someone.

My high-heels click on the empty dance floor, and I glance at my reflection in the mirrored wall, pleased with the image. No one from my place of business has seen this outfit. The skinny pants accent my waist and make me seem taller. I've always wanted to be tall. Five-foot-five is so average. The cape-like scarf and red bodice top look impressive, if I do say so myself. I'm not the suited, conservative shop assistant who set out to work this morning. If a snobby patron of *Der Schwarze Koffer Fashions* looked up from the crowd right now, she'd never recognise me. But I peer around at the customers and realise that's unlikely. Most of Club Combo's clientele seem on the low end of middle-class and the high end of middle-age. I did well to discover this place. I feel young amidst this gang and enjoy an adolescent tingle.

It's been years since I've been in a nightclub. In my early twenties, I joined a few old classmates on occasion. They frequented the meat-market clubs, and after finding my way home alone at 4am several times, I quit going. This place is different. Maybe I'll hook up tonight. My crusade is for a freewheeling guy, someone open to an evening of fun. Serious intentions are not on the table.

So, it's 'don't take me home to meet your Mom, but take me home to bed.' I will not blurt this out, not that I've ever learned to blurt, but I need to get laid. Not on the first date, of course. This is the eleventh commandment, according to Mother. But it's a shame, because first dates are all I've ever had.

I check out the men at the bar. A man in his forties or fifties would be perfect—past the settling-down phase, or tried it and returned to reality.

A familiar man peers up from a two-day beard and panic

strikes. Was he one of my failed first dates? No, he couldn't be. He wouldn't grin like that. As I hurry to claim the empty spot hemmed in between the stage and back door, relief surges through me. After I sit, a server appears and I order a ginger ale.

Minutes later the waiter returns, tray held high, and a ginger ale lands in front of me. "You'll enjoy the band tonight," he says. "They call themselves *Bloodfire.* They're gypsies." He's garnished the drink with a piece of lime pierced through with a tiny umbrella. I pay him and tip fifty cents.

Four men advance to the stage. A rotund man hoists a squeezebox accordion that looks like a toy instrument pasted to his belly. A white-bearded gentleman with a curled-up moustache raises a violin to his chin. He's the only band member who's hatless. These are swarthy guys, with skin darker than mine, wearing long white shirts under vibrant-coloured vests. They dazzle in the red and yellow pot lights. One, with a playful expression, heads to a microphone gripping a flute. This could be fun.

When the last performer jumps on stage, I quiver. He's sensational, with a fedora cocked over his eye like a 1950s detective. He tips an upright bass out of its stand and I force myself to look away, terrified he'll see me gawking. I sip the ginger ale and sneak a sideways peek. This man is perfect in every way, chin-length hair, chiselled features, and tall.

With a whoop, the musicians begin. The first song is wild and exotic. I've heard this sort of Latin music before, but only on the radio. My feet twitch.

Four people take to the floor, but I wait. Dancing without a partner gives the wrong impression. Or does it?

As soon as six couples are dancing, I drape my scarf on the chair, step onto the dance floor, nudge into the throng, and jostle toward the stage. Soon, the music takes over and pulses through my core. Delirium sets in. I tip my head back and close my eyes. The notes lift my feet. My arms snake up. This is a musical storm as potent as a hurricane. Making love must feel like this, a leaving of your body, the whorls of sensation. I've read about it, thought about it, dreamed about it, practised on my own, but never braved the real thing.

The band plays a long line-up of tunes, and I dance, dance, dance.

When the music stops too soon, the clamour from the audience resumes.

I side-step an Asian couple, turning my back to the stage. I sense the charismatic musician poised for the coming tune. I spin around. His glance pricks me with excitement. The clatter in the club subsides. Then, it's as if the single beam of a pot light suspends us. The crowd disappears. With his eyes fixed on my face, he fingers the frets of his bass, and the strum vibrates my ribcage.

Someone taps my shoulder. The beam dissolves, and a new dance begins. This is an actual man wearing Birkenstocks and jeans frayed at the cuff. He's chosen me, with the air of a hero having rescued me from the shameful act of dancing alone.

He leads me away from the stage into a shadowy corner,

spewing a brume of whiskey and cigarette smoke. Then he grins, exposing mottled teeth.

If I run off, I know I'll never solve my predicament, so I stay. He grinds up tight and I resist the urge to back away.

It's painful to watch this man dance. His movements are awkward and unwieldy. I try to imagine him in a decent apartment overflowing with tasteful furniture, nice paintings, and bookcases. But I'm tortured by this mental image, where a large ghetto blaster sits perched on a makeshift shelf and stacks of empties line the hallway beside noxious pizza boxes. Then, in my vision, he grapples me toward a vinyl sofa with yellow foam poking through the cracks. I stop dancing, frozen with dread. I must make a get-a-way. I'm not that desperate, at least not yet.

I point to the washroom. As I'm trying to escape, he grabs my arm and hangs on.

"I have to go," I say. He chortles and tries to pull me back. I point again. "Really, I have to pee."

He lets go, and I flee to the toilet.

When I pass the stage, the tantalising musician pushes his hat to the back of his head, his dark eyebrows furrowed.

Huddled cowardly in the bathroom cubicle, I listen to women come and go. The music stops, and I'm relieved it hasn't gone on without me.

I plant my butt on the edge of the toilet seat. My legs feel numb. My head feels numb. On my first night out, I'm a failure at this already. The smell of old piss wafts up like poison gas.

Why have I wasted so much time? It's not only Friday nights, but Saturday nights, Sunday nights, and evenings during the week, one monotonous night bleeding into the next. The result? Here I am, cowering in a public toilet, and speeding toward old age with a reckless lack of *savoir faire*. My head drops into my hands.

The intermission goes on forever, but it's getting late and time to get home. Besides, I've indulged in enough self pity for one evening.

Someone knocks. The pointy tips of a pair of black stilettos appear under the door. "Anybody in there?"

"I'll just be a minute." I fake a bit of choking.

"Need any help?" It's a kindly voice. "A guy outside asked me to check on you. I assume it's you. There's no one else in here."

"I'll be okay. Shouldn't have had that shooter."

"Oh, sister, I hear yah. I'll tell him."

"Tell him he can go. I have a ride home."

I decide to wait five more minutes. The Birkenstocks guy will have his hooks into someone else by then. Then I'll slip through the crowd and get out.

When I push the bathroom door open a crack and peep out, it looks safe, so I slink into the main galley. With relief, I see the backside of my dancing partner at the bar. A drunk woman near the rear of the room squeals. When he glances that way I dash across the dance floor.

I snatch up my scarf and head for the exit.

Outside, I scurry down the alley toward my car.

A man looms up, and I gasp. Then my eyes adjust to the light and I recognise the hat. It's the musician.

"You leave now?" He has a sweet-sounding voice.

Startled, I run headfirst into a garbage bin on the corner. A bag of trash tumbles down and lands by my feet. At least it's dark enough that he can't see me blush.

He takes my arm and leads me around the trash. "The music, is not what you like?"

"No, I mean, yes, I loved it."

He squints at my face. "Come back inside. I think you run from a hoodlum. I will keep some eyes on him."

"Why would you do that?"

"You are like a sister." He swishes one hand, brushing my chin. "You are beautiful, like me. *Eres preciosa*."

There's nothing wrong with this guy's ego, but he is indeed beautiful. I can't place the accent—South American, Spanish? All I can see clearly in the dark alley is a white shirt under his vest. Then he smiles, a bright, even-toothed smile. It's just my luck to remind him of his sister.

As I head to the car, he strolls along beside me.

"I have to leave now." I stare straight ahead. To look at this man and breathe at the same time is impossible.

He doffs his hat and bows. "Please, you come tomorrow? We play again here. Also the weekend next."

"I'll try. I'm not sure about tomorrow."

He opens the car door for me. "Leandro is my name. Yours?"

"Halca."

I get in and fumble with the seatbelt. He stands next to the car watching, and I fumble for an agonizing minute before I hear the click of engagement. I start the car and drive off. At the intersection, I stop and glance back. He's still watching.

Leandro, is it? The name has a certain feral strength. I begin to trill out one of the Latin tunes played earlier, making up lyrics. As my car slips into traffic on Commercial Drive, I stop singing and chuckle. It's been years, I realise, since I've sung anywhere except in the shower.

I roll down the window and sing louder. I belt out the song with made-up lyrics and words that sound Spanish.

"Fajita, frittata, two tortillas, tapa, tapa, tapa, toco time...

A new-age hippie guy on the corner shoots me a bewildered look. I duck into the steering wheel and laugh out loud.

On Saturday afternoon, I should tackle that stack of bills on top of the fridge, but I'm out for a drive instead. With no destination in mind, my old Ford Focus rumbles off toward Commercial Drive.

I stumbled upon this 'quote of the day' on the internet. I know nothing of Greek philosophy, but the words of Heraclitus made sense, so I printed the quote and taped it to the dashboard.

To do the same thing over and over again, is not only boredom:

it is to be controlled by, rather than to control what you do.

As if it has taken control, my car pulls up to a parking spot near my favourite Italian coffee shop. It's right across the street from Club Combo.

Settled in a window seat, with a latte and a dog-eared copy of Linda Goodman's Sun Signs, I peek across the road. Club Combo has a large picture window facing the café, and I spot last night's band on stage. I suspected they'd be here. Musicians often practise at the club in the afternoon.

The band members wear the same white shirts and vests as the previous evening, minus the hats, but I have no trouble making out Leandro. Upright, beside his double bass, his head nods in time to music I can't hear. The white-bearded man, centre stage, makes a few wild gestures. They all stop what they're doing. A pantomime of flying hands follows. It looks passionate and charming—some musical debate. Then they return to their instruments. A delivery van rolls up, parks in front of the window, and blocks my view. "Shite." I stick my head back in my book.

I've flipped through an entire chapter and realise that I haven't absorbed a single sentence. And where did these people come from? An hour ago, most of the tables were empty. The coffee shop is buzzing now.

I scan the characters in the café. An old Italian man in a black suit reaches under the table to squeeze his wife's leg. The wizened woman shifts her body away from him and eyeballs the pastry counter. Three teenagers sprawl in their seats. One of them tosses up and catches a hack-y-sack over and over. The espresso machine purrs and a fresh waft of coffee pervades the room.

The delivery van blocking my view has disappeared, but the

street is teeming with cars, so I can only catch an occasional glimpse of the musicians. It's time to leave, anyway. The owner just frowned at me and glanced at the wall clock. I tuck the book into my purse and head out.

Under the outside awning, I stop and study Club Combo. The men are no longer at their instruments. But what if he's in the shadows watching me? He might think I've been spying on him. But that's a crazy thought. Without the make-up and costume, how would he know it's me? It's like being Batgirl—by day I wander incognito around the clubs I frequent at night. I chuckle and stroll down the street.

There's a shop window at the end of the block displaying tarot cards, incense, and statues of Buddha. A rack of belly dancing paraphernalia catches my attention.

I hear someone call out.

"Little sister." I remember that voice. It's him. Goosebumps tingle up my arms. How did he recognise me?

Without his hat he no longer resembles a 1950s detective, but as he gets close, I suffer the same shortness of breath as I did last night. The jovial band member walking beside him lands a playful punch on his arm and hurries past.

Leandro stops in my path. "Is lucky to see you again today. Your house, is near to here?" He hooks a strand of dark hair behind one ear. His hair is cut blunt like Robin Hood's.

"Yes, not too far." My voice sounds shrill. "I come for coffee on Saturdays."

"May I buy you café?" He moves closer and places one hand on my elbow. There's that sizzle in my gut again. He smells like incense.

"Oh, no, but thank you."

"Awe." He pouts, as if I've scolded him, but then he laughs.

"I'd love to, but I'm late for an appointment."

"Later then, you come to the club, *Si*?" He touches my fingers, and I tremble.

"I'm sorry, I'm busy tonight." This is a lie, but I'm sticking to my rule—only one night of dancing. The rest of the week, I'll try to be good. Plus, I am not sure if I can trust myself near this guy when a single touch has reduced me to a puddle.

"Will you meet with me tomorrow?" He's pleading, like a boy who wants a turn at bat, and he presses my hand between both of his.

"I don't know." I shoot him a weak smile and take back my hand, even though I'd wish he'd hold onto it for eternity.

He grins with all those beautiful white teeth and punches the air with gusto. "English Bay beach, near the bathhouse. Five o'clock, is good?"

This man does not allow for rejection.

"I am a nice guy, promise." He flips his palms up and winks.

I can't help it. I smile. "Okay, yes." I hurry down the street to my car. How very easy that yes came out.

On the way home I hum, "Sweet Dreams Are Made of This," over and over. It's impossible to get that tune out of my head.

Back in my apartment, I sit down with pen and paper.

Dear Erin,

I told you I'd do it. I went to a nightclub, all alone. Yes, you heard me right, alone. I even danced by myself. It was interesting. No, I didn't lose my virginity, but I met this guy and then I saw him again today, by chance. I've agreed to meet him tomorrow at the beach. He's a musician in the band—Spanish, I think, and amazing, but maybe a little too handsome. He reminds me of your dad.

I've not dated for three years. Do I even remember how to behave on a date? Do I really want to go? I didn't give him my number or address or anything, so I don't have to. I've got until tomorrow to decide. I'll keep you posted.

Your loving friend,

Hally

PART TWO

Cante Jondo

On Sunday afternoon, the West End is aflutter with the usual rare birds. I'm perched on a bench at the corner of Denman and Comox, bird watching, trying to smother a flurry of anxiety before meeting Leandro. I nearly bailed and stayed home. Then I reminded myself, it's only a date.

So, I'm here killing time a block away from where we're supposed to meet. I squint at a wall clock inside Drake's Dry Cleaning. It's a three-minute walk to the bathhouses. 'Don't arrive early,' is the advice from the "Ask Susan" column. I'll heed that warning—mustn't appear desperate. 'Don't be late either'—more advice from Susan. 'He could be a guy who gives up easily.'

An old woman approaches, with a hunchback the size of a sea turtle. She shuffles along, stooped, with her eyes fixed to the sidewalk. With the speed of an eroding mountain, she lowers her angled torso onto the bench. The poor old dear. If my back humped over that way, I'd hide out in my apartment.

Hiding suddenly strikes me as an excellent idea. I should go home and forget this silliness. Then I remind myself once more that it's just a date. There's a minimal chance this musician will be the one to plunder my virginity, and that may be for the best. He's too good-looking, and I don't need the heartache.

If Leandro is true to his name, he'll be a Leo—self-confident and passionate, unless he's a timid Lion Man. What if he isn't a Leo? I am only guessing. At first I thought Aquarius—he was so disciplined and determined at band practice. It's hard to tell by looks alone, but Holy hr-aka, he could be a Virgo. If he is, Linda Goodman says, any hint of romance too early is a mistake. What if he's an unreliable Sagittarius and shows up hours late, or not at all? Guys routinely pull that stunt. Wasn't the word *machismo* coined to describe Latin men?

Does his Zodiac sign even matter? I'm not certain of my own sign, so compatibility factors are hypothetical. And who cares, anyway? Still, sometimes I wish Mother had never shared the notation on my adoption certificate, June 15, approximate date of birth. It's the word approximate that troubles me, because I could be a Cancer, not Gemini.

I'll need to avoid any mention of astrology tonight. It may only be a date, but I wouldn't want to come off as a flake. Besides, it's a mystery why I even pay attention to horoscopes, but they are fun.

An androgynous street kid with a lime-green Mohawk sails past and into the arms of an offbeat waif who's waiting at the end of the block. As they embrace, I squirm with discomfort. Everyone except me has a lover.

At five minutes to five I step out toward English Bay, but stop at my reflection in a shop window and swivel to inspect my backside. These jeans fit just right, but should I have worn a skirt?

A thick-set bald man passes me. He twists around and winks. "You're gorgeous, honey." His skin-tight jogger shorts and water-bottle jiggle as he speed-walks up the sidewalk, leaving a wake of spicy aftershave.

I head toward the beach and instantly spot Leandro's fedora. He stands in front of the bathhouses lit by a beam of sunshine pouring out from a single slit in the overcast sky. When he sees me, he waves. A guitar case is slung over one shoulder, and a wicker basket dangles on his arm.

The slit in the sky closes. A dark shadow falls across English Bay, and a sudden burst of rain spurts down. Damn—my hair will turn into a Brillo pad.

As Leandro approaches, an umbrella springs open in his hand. "You are here. My heart laughs." His voice has the thrum of a bass drum.

"Thanks. You're a life saver." I peer up. "Do you always carry an umbrella?"

"No, but Eldora, she predicts the weather."

"Who's Eldora—your sister?"

"Not my sister, is the wife of Adan, the leader of our band." Leandro's tone softens. "Eldora is my *tia,* my aunt, but is mother to us all." He adjusts the umbrella to cover me better, and then he holds one finger up to his lips, smiles, and whispers. "She is a *chanelar* and predicts many mysterious things."

As quickly as the rain began, it stops. The sun re-ignites the beach and steam rises. Leandro shakes the umbrella, collapses it and hooks it on his forearm. With the fedora, guitar, and basket, he's the image of an eccentric vintage gent.

"A guitar?" I point to his case. "You play the double bass, don't you?"

"*Si,* I do. I play many instruments. Is like that with our people. We are born holding the musical instrument, and for me guitar is first."

"What's in there?" I'm no dating pro, but this must be rare—a guy who brings a picnic basket.

"Ah, a surprise." He winks.

We head out along the seawall toward Stanley Park. He's at least six inches taller than me, but our pace matches.

I study his gait—confident heel-to-toe footsteps in creased, but shiny, boots. I wonder how many places those boots have travelled, and suddenly it hits me. What do I know of this man? I have no background on him, his home, or his family. Good thing we're in a crowd.

"Does your sister live here?"

"My sister?" He seems puzzled. "I have no sister." We fall out of sync.

"But you told me I look like your sister."

"Ah, I say that because you are a sister." He touches my forearm. "Your skin—see? The same colour as mine, not black, not white. You are of the blood."

"Of the blood?"

"*Si*, you must realise... you are *Romany*." He cocks his head. "No?"

"I don't know my nationality. I was adopted."

He looks puzzled. "You know nothing of your mamá and papá?"

"That's right." I peer out over the Bay. It's lovely, what he's saying, but I suspect he's simply trying to make me feel better. "What do you mean by *Romany*? Are you from Romania?"

"No, we are *Romany*, travelling people. Here, they say Gypsies. In Europe, belief is we come from Egypt, so Gypsy, Egyptian, you see? At home, in Spain, *Gitáno* is the name they call our race." He continues with a sour expression. "But these are all words invented long ago by ignorant gadjè."

"What's a *gadjè*?"

"Is all others, not of the blood." He picks up my hand, and the callouses on his fingertips graze my skin. I can't be sure about his blood, but my blood is surging. I withdraw my hand.

We reach a small inlet at the north end of the main beach

where an aboriginal man sits carving a piece of soapstone. He gestures to his collection of miniature statues lined up beside the path.

Just past the inlet, we turn off the seawall and walk down a few steps fashioned from crude rocks. Leandro leads me into a cosy clearing, hidden from the walking path by a thick clump of bushes. A circle of stones harbours the soggy, acrid remnants of a recent fire. A sandy nook behind us, enclosed by greenery, seems an excellent place for a lover's tryst. Sex outdoors would be perfect, but I take a deep breath and push that notion aside. I'm getting ahead of myself.

Leandro shrugs the guitar case off his shoulder and squats to open the basket. A moment later he has a red-and-gold-striped blanket spread out on a log.

"You like *tapas*?" He motions for me to sit, and then he takes a seat on the log across from me.

"I don't know."

"*Mira esto*." He points to a platter heaped with cheese, bread, slices of sausage and stuffed peppers. A pang of hunger reminds me I've not eaten today. Leandro places the open basket near my feet. "You may serve the food."

"You want me to do it?" This confuses me, but I guess it must be a cultural thing, like a visitor pouring tea, an honour.

"Yes, you serve, please. Is important. With her touch, a woman, she adds happiness to the meal."

This idea of bringing happiness to our lunch oddly appeals to me, so I find two plates, portion out the lunch, and sample the cheese. "This is delicious."

"Is *Manchego,* sheep's cheese. Eldora orders it special from a delicatessen on Commercial Drive." He sets his dish on the log and beams at me, watching me eat.

Now I'm self-conscious that my mouth is full, and he hasn't taken a bite. "I should wait for you. Sorry."

"No need to say sorry. Is sexy to watch a woman enjoy food." He passes me a wine bottle from the basket.

I balance the plate on my lap, locate earthenware goblets, fumble to unscrew the lid, pour two glasses, spilling only a few drops, and give one to him. The privilege of serving must also extend to wine pouring. This should annoy me, but Leandro grins, and he's so obviously pleased with my awkward delivery of the feast that I smile.

He raises the cup. "*Sastimos*. I drink your eyes."

"The wine, the food—you thought of everything."

"Do not clap for me. My idea, but Eldora prepares us the meal." He gazes at me over the rim of his goblet.

"She went to too much trouble. I mean, it's great, but we could've found a café."

"We prefer not, the public eating place. Is like that with us. We only go if no other choice. A *Romany* woman should cook the food."

"Why is that?"

"Food prepared by *gadjè* might be..." He squints. I try to say *mahrime* in English... I think is... unclean or spoiled.

"Spoiled?"

"Yes, a *Romany* woman brings happiness to food, and she is also *whuzo*. To us, means pure. She knows when to wash. She will mix special herbs and say a spell too."

"A spell?"

"Yes, to protect the person who eats."

The spell business is over the top, even for me, but it is sweet he thinks I'm pure. I watch him lean forward, legs fanned out, feet planted in the sand. My gaze strays below his waist. It's a good thing he can't read my impure thoughts.

Then a few less pleasant thoughts invade my head. When I was naughty as a kid, Mother used to threaten me with the Gypsies. She'd snarl, 'I'll give you to them. You will sleep on the ground, beg on the streets, eat garbage. They are rogues and thieves.' I flinch, remembering her rants. Then I relax. I may not know Leandro yet, but I can tell he's no rogue or thief.

"What makes you so sure I'm *Romany*?" I scrutinise him above the waist. Dad claims that dishonesty shows on a person's face. Leandro's face is not only God like in perfection, but honest too.

He strokes my fingers. "Our skin colour, but is not all. Is the eyes, black with fire—is your shape." He traces a curve through the air with his free hand. "As true as the body of my guitar, you are *Romany*. One *Roma* can always tell another. We feel it here." He pats his heart.

This is an amusing speculation, but me, a Gypsy? It is, no doubt, his standard pickup line. I'm taking this guy too seriously.

Leandro eats now. As I watch him wield his fork, a vision blasts through my brain—of his fingers trailing over my naked breasts, up my leg, inside my thigh, his fingers touching my lips. Maybe he is the one. As he picks at his meal, I feast on his hands, the ragged short-cropped nails with flawless half-moons. I can't look away.

When his plate and mine are clean, I repack them and pour more wine, but his fingers never leave my sight. Then he reaches for his instrument case and plucks out a twelve-string acoustic guitar.

After the first few notes, I realise he's a master. This is not a rollicking tune, but a penetrating, mournful, musical tale that conveys love, potency, infinity, wholeness, and ancient pain. I've wept over a sad movie in the past, but a song has never brought tears to my eyes.

When it ends, he asks, "Do you love the song?"

"It's incredible." I dab a teardrop on my cheek.

"Is the guitar part of *cante jondo,* means 'deep song.' It has words too, but Eldora sings this song best."

"It doesn't need words." I close my eyes when I say this, the song still with me, flowing under my skin.

"You must hear Eldora sing. Do you sing?"

"Only in the shower," I tell him with a titter. The truth is, Mother never encouraged singing. But once a fourth-grade teacher said I had an excellent voice.

"I see the way you look. The notes melt the *kham* of your soul." He studies my face and points to the orange orb hovering on the horizon. "*Kham* is our word for sun and deep song, she is old as *kham's* first fire. No one knows when the deep song came to us, because we have no ancient books. But we have the *cante jondo* from the seed of time."

Gravel footsteps sound from behind on the rock path. Two young women appear and march toward us. One woman hikes up her Capri pants, parks herself on the log beside me, and addresses Leandro. "Can you play more?" Leaning forward, she runs a hand through her boy-short hair and sits at attention as if taking a seat in a concert hall. Leandro grins and begins a song.

Within thirty minutes seven more people have gathered on the small plot of sand, five of them young women. A rotund man arrives with his own chair, a cooler, and offers cans of Molsons to everyone. He sits, props his beer on a sunburned belly as big as a beach ball, and ogles the cleavage of a redhead who's cross-legged on the sand. A teenage boy throws a skinny arm around his eyebrow-pierced sweetie as they settle themselves in the sandy nook. Leandro begins another song. One part of me wants them all to leave, but I need him to keep playing. In a way I've never experienced, this music feels as if it belongs to me.

The listeners sit rapt. Even the Molson-pusher, engrossed in the music, has torn his eyes off of the redhead's cleavage, and he's tapping his sandal in the sand.

After performing for an hour or more, Leandro puts the guitar away amidst protest.

As he walks me home, I wonder if tonight will be the night. It's a first date, but to hell with that rule. Black chestnut branches hang in a near-dark sky, and a cool, fresh breeze ruffles my blouse. Leandro's hand brushes my arm as we stroll up the street and sweet agony floods my belly.

At the apartment door, he leans in and kisses me once on each cheek, making me dizzy with his spicy, incense scent. My legs turn to pudding. I'm ready at last, and positive he's the one. "Would you like..."

He interrupts. "Sorry, is time for me to go." With a palm on each of my shoulders, he pushes me to arm's length and looks into my face with a serious expression. "Is something I promise to do for Eldora and Adan tonight."

I could sink into the sidewalk. "Yes, I see." Thank God I didn't make a complete ass of myself. "Okay, thanks, I had fun."

Well, what did I expect? That he'd rush upstairs, lie with me, quit the band and spend the rest of his days lolling on my bed amidst my dirty underwear? It's probably for the best. Even a brave Lion Man would flee at the sight of my apartment. Besides, I've not thought this through properly. What if he did come up and I did lose my virginity? The sex would be awkward, because I'm a beginner. Then what happens next, is a question I don't have an answer for, because I'm not interested in marriage or any long term romance. My views on that won't change. Happy relationships may exist, but I've never seen one.

"You will meet them?" His voice gives me a start.

"Who?"

"Eldora and Adan. Eldora can teach the song to you."

My words burble out before I can swallow them. "I'd love to."

Then I experience a stomach-drop of unease. He wants to introduce me to his people, but why? Do they have to approve me before he'll sleep with me? But looking up at him, I realise none of this matters. He is so damn beautiful.

"Thursday afternoon? At start of week we practise. But Thursday, Friday afternoons, we rest."

"I work until five. But I'm off Friday afternoon." This is a lie, but I'll get it off. I'll just have to invent a reasonable excuse. Plus, it won't hurt Ulla to take care of her shop for one afternoon.

"I'll come for you at two o'clock." He points at the buzzer panel. "What number do I punch?"

"777."

De veras! He laughs, takes my hand and squeezes. "The Chariot times three."

My fingers quiver under his. "What's that?"

"The number seven in Tarot cards. Luck and success times three."

How ironic—first spells on our picnic lunch, now tarot cards, and I was worried to mention astrology?

"I want to learn more about Tarot cards."

"Then Eldora will draw the cards for you." He kisses my cheeks once more. My legs go wobbly again. He turns and strides away.

A few minutes later, up in my apartment, a rare urge to de-clutter commandeers me. All my dirty clothes, including a sweater I'd lost hope of finding, get crammed into the laundry hamper. I straighten the jumble of shoes in the closet, take four months of newspapers and magazines to the re-cycle bin, wash the fur-moulded dishes in the sink, and organise my bills to be paid sometime this week. I almost throw out the brown envelope from Holland by mistake. I must write Mr Vanderburg, detective of genealogy, and tell him I can no longer afford his services. He'll never find my birth parents. Besides, Leandro's told me I'm a Gypsy. I laugh out loud. What more do I need to know? And who knows? It could be true.

When I fire up the vacuum cleaner at 11:30, the guy in the suite below pounds on the ceiling.

Shortly past midnight, I stand in the middle of my apartment and appraise my efforts. The place is so tidy I don't recognise it. I stay put there for a while, taking in the utter spick and span. Even Mother would be proud.

Before going to bed, I scribble a few lines to Erin.

Dear Erin,

Well, I didn't chicken out. I've been on a date tonight, yes, a proper date. The guy's name is Leandro and, as I mentioned, he plays in the band from Friday night. Yes, I'm still a virgin. We didn't do much—just sat on logs at the Beach. He played his guitar, and a group congregated. Then he walked me home. He's asked me out again, and I said I'd go. I'm not sure if he'll be the one to take my virginity, but I'm considering him for the job. His band never stays in one place too long, so that's perfect. It'll be a straight-forward transaction—no mess and no stress.

I'll keep you posted.

Love

Hally

Lautari

The next morning I'm at the computer with a stack of mail, primed to pay bills. My neat streak knows no bounds. I take care of the hydro and internet first. Then I make a minimum payment on my Mastercard. The final envelope is the brown one from Holland. Mr Vanderburg can bloody well wait for his money. My chequing account shows a balance of $93.62 with payday over a week away. Still, I slice the letter open.

Good News, Vanderburg writes. *I have made progress concerning your parentage. Someone will contact you in the next two weeks. This party requested I say no more, and I must abide by their request. My fee, I also waive. If you wish to speak with me after the meeting, I am at your service.*

Sincerely yours,

H. Vanderburg

After reading this over three times, I still don't get it. He's the only one who should contact me. And what's with the mystery, and why waive his fee? Plus, I did not give him the okay to share my details with anyone else, whether or not he's charging me. His job was to find information on my birth parents and pass it on. I should sue the idiot, but he's over there and it's probably not worth the grief. But I want to strangle him. Who is this 'someone' and how will they contact me? Has he left me open to a scam? Now I'll have to monitor my phone calls and email for dodgy characters. What if he's in on it? I took the messaging on his website at face value. What if Vanderburg's a con man after my money? Then I lean back in my office chair and relax. If it's cash he's after, I get the last laugh. You can't squeeze water out of a rock. I crumple the letter and toss it in the wastebasket.

Leandro drum-taps his fingers on the steering wheel. We are en route to where he lives, riding in an old van he calls *La Gran Puta*. He waves to the space behind us crammed with amplifiers, instrument cases, microphone stands, and cords. "This is how we move the equipment."

I shift to find a spot on the seat with no springs poking through. The vehicle is a junker, but dangling from the sun visor, a shiny gold toy trumpet lends a festive mood. It's a brilliant summer day, the sky a sheet of sequinned glitter.

Since reading the letter from Vanderburg, I needed to clear my head, and this outing is a welcome distraction, even if what I suspect is true. I'm being brought in for inspection.

Sitting next to Leandro, I find it hard to concentrate. I'm as bad as a besotted schoolgirl and it's embarrassing. So, I'm clammed up, trying to focus my energy on the scenery. If Mother taught me anything, it's how to keep things impersonal.

"They cancelled Club Combo on the weekend. For two weeks,

we have no job now." He grins. "A little summer holiday for us. The sun, she shines, and *la vida es buená.*" He rolls the window down and leans his head out. The wind catches his hair and he tips his face into it.

"How far is it, to your place?" I ask when he ducks back in. We've passed through Stanley Park and up onto Lion's Gate Bridge.

"Is just over there." He points to the shoreline across the inlet.

Minutes later, he takes an exit off Marine Drive. We cruise along a winding dirt road under the bridge where the terrain is quiet and rustic, a few houses cached in the trees at odd intervals. It's as if we've materialised onto a rural country lane in another century.

"I've never been here." I've lived thirty-two years in Vancouver. Leandro, who's been here for a nano-second, has once again shown me a brand-new place. Actually, I don't know how long he's been here.

"How long have you been in Canada?"

"We move here six years ago, from Andalusia in Spain." His expression turns serious for a moment and he grips the steering wheel. Then he runs his fingers through his hair and slaps the dashboard again and points. "We are here." We pass a totem pole and a sign that announces the campground. "Is Native Indian land," he says solemnly with his voice hushed. I sense he's proud to bring me here. "We stay in their campground all summer. We love to be near the water. Also, in August, we play at the Potlatch, so the chief, he charges a smaller rent for the space." The van tumbles over potholes and sets off a jangle of metal behind us.

"How long will you stay in Vancouver?"

"We stop here today and who knows where tomorrow? Our home is the *autobús*." He flicks the dangling toy trumpet and smiles. "The world, she is our family. In Spain they call us *Lautari*. This is the word for *Roma,* who travel and play music. We are lucky. Where work is, we go." He reaches over and squeezes my hand. "This is a good place in summer. When the wind is warm, many gigs turn up."

I wiggle my fingers out from under his, but this doesn't seem to bother him. He doesn't miss a beat, and slaps the dashboard, humming like the carefree drifter he is. But right here, right now, his presence unsettles me, and it's crazy how the tone of our skin matches. My hand is still burning where he touched it. What if I fall for him, really fall for him?

The road straightens as we near the waterway, and I gaze out at the ocean, calm and ripple free today. Before long, a two-storey wooden house rolls into view. A hand-painted sign over the door explains it's the campground office. In the back yard there's a heap of twisted auto parts, but a shiny blue Dodge Ram sits out front. I wonder how safe this part of town is. I know what Mother would say. 'See that junk, and the fancy truck. Must be drug dealers.'

"This year we arrive as soon as they open to get the best site." Leandro points to an old Greyhound bus surrounded by shade trees that seclude it from the rest of the campground. We putter by a few trailers, a motorhome, and several tents, but I see no one.

The van bumps over campsite ground and stops near the Greyhound. One side is canopied, and it reminds me of a kiosk at Greek Day, with pots and baskets hang from ropes strung under its canvas ceiling. Below this, two wooden picnic tables sit end to end on a room-sized carpet patterned with yellow stars and blue moons. It's like a page from an astrology book. A mismatched assortment of folding chairs circle a metal cauldron brimming with chunks of charred log. We get out of the van.

A man I remember from Club Combo steps down from the bus. He's the musician with snowy hair, and he looks casual today in sweat pants and a knee-length orangish shirt. "You are Halca," he says. "My name is Adan." He pumps my hand and then leans over and kisses it. "Leandro told us of your beauty. He did not stretch out the truth." At this he chuckles, and the tips of his white moustache quiver. "Now I understand the recent fire in his shoe."

I glance at Leandro. Blood has rushed to my face, but he winks and shoots me a confident smile. Then he hunches his shoulders, flips his hands palm-up, and laughs. "Is *bonito,* she is. Would I lie?" Then he takes my elbow and leads me to a folding chair with a thick Persian tapestry draped over it. "Please, sit here." He smooths a wrinkle out of the heavy cloth, ushers me to sit, and then turns to Adan. "Where are the others?"

"Scoop came to take them fishing." Adan points through the trees to an ancient looking wharf at the shoreline. "He promises crab for our dinner tomorrow night. Ah, here is Eldora now, with coffee."

A woman appears in the bus's doorway. She's carrying a wooden tray, and on it, a blue ceramic decanter with four miniature cups. In a flowing red tunic and purple skirt, she's even more colourful than the rug. As she walks toward us, I see she's not a young woman, but the creases around her eyes are laugh lines, and only a few silver streaks weave through a waist-length, dark braid.

"Come, meet Halca." Adan touches the small of his wife's back.

"You do not look like a Halca." She stops two yards away to scrutinise me.

I cross my arms and glance at my feet. But I shouldn't let her intimidate me, so I straighten and match her gaze straight on.

"I think I will name you Milagros." She sets the tray on a picnic table. "It means miracle, and this is the miracle, that Leandro brings a *chica* to meet us."

She hates me. I know it.

"*Si*." Adan chuckles. "We worried about Leandro when we played that gay bar."

Eldora opens her arms wide, walks to Leandro for a hug. "Not our Leandro, never. Is simple. Too few *Roma live* here and he has no taste for the *gadjè* girls, eh?" She puts her hands on either side of his face and kisses his forehead. Releasing him, she turns her attention back to me. "So, tell us about you."

"There's not much to tell." What do they expect me to say? I doubt they'd be interested in my job. Who would be? And I've just met these people, so I'd rather not bring up my iffy ancestry.

So, I blurt out the first thing that pops in my head. "If you don't like Halca, my dad calls me Hally."

"*Si*, Hally, is better. I will call you that." Eldora leans over and kisses me on both cheeks. "Your voice sounds American, *mucho*. You were born here, in Vancouver, Hally?"

Maybe she does like me. "No, I was born in Holland, but my parents moved here when I was a baby."

"So, your mamá and papá, they are *Lautari*?" She nods. "Must be, to travel so far from home. Strange we haven't crossed our paths."

"Oh, no, they're not musicians. My father owned a concrete business. My mother used to be an accountant. They're both retired now."

"I don't know any *Roma* who are concrete keepers or accountants." Eldora cocks her head to one side.

"No, my parents aren't *Roma*. They're Hollanders. They adopted me in Holland." I'd rather not discuss this, but this woman has drilling eyes. If left alone with her, I fear my entire life story might spurt out—and bore her into an early grave. Would she still like me then?

"Someone from Holland adopts a *Roma*? Is no wonder they left the country."

"I don't understand." She has me baffled now.

Eldora pours coffee. "The Dutch, they detest the *Roma*. Liars and thieves, they call us." She passes me a small cup. "Cream? Sugar?"

"No, black is fine."

"And we only lie and thieve part of the time," Adan says and snickers. His violin is out of the case and he's buffing it with a soft yellow cloth.

"Europeans," Leandro says with a scowl. "See why we come here?"

"Your authentic mamá, she no longer lives?" Eldora eyeballs me as she passes coffee to the men, then perches on the picnic table bench with her cup.

"I'm not sure," I tell her. "I was abandoned at birth."

Eldora slaps Adan on the shoulder. "Who would leave behind a baby girl? A *Roma* would not." She leans forward and examines me again. "It may be you are Greek?"

I'm not sure what to say. Leandro steps behind me, rests one hand on my shoulder, and gives it a squeeze.

Adan shakes his head. "No, No, my love. Look at her. You have eyes. She is *chachipeñi Romi.*" He squints at me. "Genuine—no confusion." He waves his hand to indicate the topic's closed and then twiddles the tip of his moustache. "And the story of your mamá's life, who knows? Bad things happen to our people all the time—things we cannot control."

I think this means I've passed inspection, but it's bizarre they've decided I'm Romany. When Leandro said the same thing, I assumed it was just a pickup line. But I suppose it does no harm to let them believe it, and it might even help in my efforts to get laid. Deep down, though, they must know as I do, my skin tone doesn't make me one of them.

I've always realised my ancestors could have come from a

hundred different countries, or dozens of diverse cultures. Holland is not all white-skinned natives, and I'm told that's where I was born. That's all I'm told, but I guess it makes me a Hollander. But with no memory of the country, I don't identify with it. I've been in Canada for over thirty years, and it's not home either. I'm an alien inside out. I can't imagine belonging to a race of people like Adan, Eldora, and Leandro do.

A motorboat glides into the dock, and its engine roars and then sputters to a stop. A ponytailed man jumps out and ties the boat. Minutes later, three men stomp up the path to the campsite. I recognise the horn player and the accordion player from Club Combo. The ponytailed man is a husky Indigenous guy. A cage teeming with crab dangles from his enormous arm.

Leandro introduces me to Felipo, Mendez, and Scoop. Felipo, the laughing uncle, pulls me up out of the chair with childlike enthusiasm. He kisses my cheeks, then releases me to Mendez before he bounds off. A smothering hug from the rotund accordion player follows. His shirt is damp, and he smells of seaweed and cigar smoke. "Pretty girl," he says as he lets me go.

All this hugging and kissing is foreign to me, but oddly okay.

Scoop holds up the crab cage for inspection. "See, a good catch. I'll take them back to the water now."

"Is he letting them go?" I ask.

"No," Leandro says. "The water keeps them alive. His wife, Janine, returns from the North tomorrow, and then we celebrate. You will come?"

Before I have the chance to answer, Felipo reappears with his horn in one hand and Leandro's guitar in the other. He hands Leandro his guitar. Mendez opens a compartment under the bus and pulls out his accordion case.

A few minutes later they're playing. It's upbeat, playful music. Felipo sings a verse, then Adan. Their voices leap, land and leap again. I cannot take my eyes off Leandro with his serious, focused expression. I imagine him gazing at my naked body, the way he's looking at the guitar—instead of strumming, his fingers trailing along the side of my neck and downward. He glances over at me. A pleasure-pain, that I cannot ignore, scutters through my groin.

When the tune stops, he beams, his forehead beaded with perspiration. "Ah, Hally, remember? I promised you *cante jondo*." He beckons Eldora and the musicians play again—the same haunting music from our night on the beach. When Eldora sings, I realise Leandro was right. She sings it best. Her tone is eerie, and in an inexplicable way, the song dismantles me. Two children poke their faces out of the bushes, solemn and wide-eyed.

When they finish, I'm almost too numb to speak, but I have to ask her, "What do the words mean?"

Eldora closes her eyes for a moment. "Is hard to make into English. It tells about the home here. That my fingertips start the fire here." She clasps her hands over her heart. "We come from nowhere, but is all here inside us, everything we want or need—all our pride and all our joy."

Later, as Leandro drives me home, Eldora's words echo in my

head. I ponder the fact that nowhere is where I come from, at least nowhere I can name. But it should be enough. I have fire. I have a heart. I've just never learned the pride and joy part, but maybe I could.

Leandro pulls up to the curb in front of my apartment building. "Tomorrow afternoon, can I come for you again? Two o'clock?" He plays with a lock of my hair. "You can show me your city and then later, Joe's party?"

I fight back a grin. "I'd like that." He wants to see me again, and I'm thrilled, but sitting beside him in this vehicle is dangerous. What if I lose control and try to drag him upstairs? I sense he'll reject me again, and it's clear, even though I don't know why, that if our future includes sex, he will have to initiate it. Also, I'm not positive I could go through with it right now. Something in that song has cracked open my breast plate.

I lean over, plant a light kiss on his cheek and hop out.

Upstairs, before turning in for the night, I grab a pen and paper.

Dear Erin

But I sit and click the pen over and over. I can't describe the evening I've just had, and I certainly haven't processed it yet. Maybe tomorrow, I'll have a better handle on Leandro and why the sight of him turns me into a blathering, lovesick idiot.

Spirit in Stanley Park

Here at my desk, pen in hand, I listen to the coffee machine burp and sputter. The fresh aroma clears my head. I've slept on it and have a better perspective on Leandro and his group now. Yesterday, the romantic notion of a gypsy lifestyle put me under a spell. They fool themselves with it too—the freedom of the traveller's life, the intense bond they share, and the belief they're endowed with certain gifts as a birthright. Gypsies may be fabulous musicians, but just like everyone, they struggle along, presenting their phoney, carefree facades to the world. They might think I'm one of them, but they're fooling themselves about that too.

Dear Erin,

I met with the musician again. His name is Leandro, and he is Spanish. He's also a gypsy living in a caravan parked under the Lion's Gate Bridge. I went there with him yesterday, and he introduced me to the band members and their matriarch, Eldora. They are an odd bunch. Remember how my mother used to rail on about the gypsies? She'd be apoplectic if she knew I was seeing one. Anyway, it seems too much trouble just for sex, but what do I know of dating rituals?

Leandro's returning this afternoon. I'll show him around my hood, and then we're off to his place for a party tonight. My virginity issue won't be fixed today, but at least I have something different to do. I'll fill you in on the details later.

Love always,

Hally

'A handful of patience is worth a bushel of brains,' is a pet phrase of Mother's. At 2PM, this mumbo jumbo echoes in my head as I rush downstairs to meet Leandro.

His van isn't out front yet. I grab a copy of *The Courier* from the lobby and wait under the awning outside. After flipping through a few pages, I toss the paper on a low cement wall and check the time on my phone. He's five minutes late. Has he stood me up?

A fine mist of rain blears my view of the neighbourhood. I lean my umbrella against the side of the building, hoping I won't need to use it. It's a chequered hand-me-down from Mother. Two of the ribs are bent and it makes me feel derelict.

Up the sidewalk, I spy a woman in a red, hooded raincoat and rubber boots. She's checking out each doorway against a piece of paper she's holding. Fewer people than normal are out today. A tall man with a moustache walks his twin corgis. Across the street, an old lady trundles along with grocery bags slung on her walker.

The lady in red looks familiar. When she reaches the apartment complex next door, I recognise her.

"Eldora?" She's the last person I expected to see.

"Ah, Hally, our little *Roma*. I find you." She opens her arms, tumbles toward me and gathers me into an enthusiastic, but bony embrace.

I step back, smoothing the front of my cardigan, damp from Eldora's raincoat.

"Sorry, I made you wet." Eldora unbuttons her coat and fans her face with one hand. "Is raining hard when I left. Then the bus, so packed."

A disturbing idea worms into my head. Did Leandro send her to dump me? She takes care of everything for him, his picnic lunches, his umbrellas—does she break up for him too? Could he be such a coward? No, there must be a logical explanation. She's come to Kits for a specific reason. Maybe he told her to meet us here.

"Is Leandro on his way?"

"No, is not coming. He asks me to come and tell to you. They have a surprise gig in Cache Creek, so they cancel the party tonight."

My stomach muscles tense. I don't mind missing a party, but I was looking forward to showing Leandro the city. Still, he sent Eldora to let me know, and that's something. "He should have called me."

"Oh, he forgets to ask your number." She tut-tuts and shakes her head. "Leandro neglects practical things, like taking the phone number of a new friend."

"Ah, I didn't think to give it to him either." This is a lie. Now I remember it did cross my mind, but he didn't ask, and Mother told me a long time ago, 'Only desperate girls volunteer their phone number.'

"Is he away for long?"

"For two weeks, we suspect. After that, they are back again here." Eldora's sculpted cheekbones are scarcely visible under her hood.

I sigh. Now my de-flowering will take two more weeks at least. I strive for mother's 'handful of patience.'

I point to the top floor of my building. "Would you like to come up?"

"Will you walk with me instead? I take a long walk every day, and is nice to have company." She squints at my umbrella and boots, nodding with approval.

"Yes, sure." A long walk doesn't appeal to me, but it seems rude to say no. She knows I was meeting Leandro and have no other plans.

"Let's go to Stanley Park. Is a spirit there I want to visit." She looks out toward the ocean.

"A spirit? What sort of spirit?" Tarot cards are one thing, but faeries in trees?

"You'll see." Eldora flashes me an impish grin and takes my arm.

We hop on the ten-seat ferry to English Bay. It's raining on the other side, and we set out towards Stanley Park. Eldora starts out at a good clip, hunched beneath her raincoat. Under cover of the hand-me-down, crippled umbrella, I struggle to keep up—a derelict orphan in the backwash of this seasoned hiker.

We pass the bathhouses where Leandro met me that day and then a jetty of stones where we had the beach picnic. As we hike, Eldora chatters away. She tells me how the *Romany* people are born to love nature. We walk and she talks. I'm at ease in her company, as if we're lifelong friends.

"We enjoy a special bond with the First Nations peoples of Canada," she says. "Is because their ancestors travel, same as we do. And like us, they celebrate the trees, and the sky, and the sea, and all of this." She smiles big and throws her arms wide.

Her enthusiasm is catchy. Even the wet weather can't blur this fabulous seascape. The North Shore Mountains, snow-capped year round, loom behind the ocean, melting into the horizon. It fills me with a sense of awe. As a girl, when Erin was still here, I spent entire days outdoors enjoying nature. I'm not sure why that changed.

"Almost there," Eldora picks up her pace.

We arrive at a set of steep steps, climb them, and stride along a service road past the Tea House Restaurant. Then she leads me into a dense cluster of bushes. Snug in this thicket, a boulder rests on a deck of flagstone squares.

She ushers me to step close. "Is a memorial to Pauline Johnson. I discovered it my first month here in Vancouver." Eldora points to a face carved in the stone. "One hundred years ago, is put here. In this place I sense a spirit, so strong."

It may be madness, but I feel it too—the air vibrating with an unearthly presence. I close my eyes, tip my head back and let it fill me. Then, still in awe, I peer at the carvings again.

"Pauline Johnson was a First Nations writer, wasn't she?"

"*Si*, Janine gifts me her book, *Flint and Feather*. She wrote poems about Stanley Park. She held this place in her heart, and I love the verses. Makes me remember García Lorca, our famous *Romany* poet."

So, they have poets as well as musicians.

"Pauline Johnson's papa was native, but her mama was English." She traces one finger over the sculpted cheek of the poet's likeness.

I wonder about my natural mother and father. Were they both of the same race? Do I look like them? Do I have my mother's nose, my father's eyes? Are my birth parents even alive? If I searched for them, what would I find—a headstone, by a service road, in the middle of nowhere?

Eldora's attention remains fixed on the sculpture. "They permitted no other person a grave in this park but allowed her ashes buried here."

A chickadee flies in and lights on a nearby bush. When a car rumbles past, the bird flits away.

Eldora takes my elbow and steers me out of the thicket. "Come, I remember another place that belongs to Pauline Johnson."

I follow Eldora across the road onto a different path. I've never explored the inside passages of Stanley Park. A snippet of worry curls up. "Do you know how to get back?"

"*Si*, I visit here all the time."

The rain has stopped, and sunlight leaks through dense

greenery. Even though the trail goes on and on, I sense we're on route back to the city.

We reach an intersection.

The stump of a dead-standing tree marks the entrance to Cathedral Trail. It's forty feet tall, at least ten feet in diameter, and I've never seen such a tree—apartment size at its base.

Eldora gestures for me to follow. "Is the other place I spoke of."

Farther along the path, more enormous trees arch overhead. I stop and gaze skyward. "I get why they call this Cathedral Trail." Flickers of brilliance spatter through an archway of branches and leaves, like light through stained glass windows.

The forest is rife with gentle sounds—a chirp, a twitter, the scurry of a thin squirrel skidding down a tree trunk. He lopes across the path. Lineage is of no concern to this lucky creature. He only cares that his agile body can leap beyond the length of his tail.

"Pauline Johnson gave them the name Cathedral Trees." Eldora says. "They are hundreds and hundreds of years in age." She winks. "Even older than me."

We move past the cloister and enter an altered landscape where the late afternoon sun is blinding. The whir of a single-prop plane overhead blots out the soft noises of the copse.

The trees here are war-torn, flattened, a scene from a science fiction movie where the world's in ruins. A giant cedar rests on its side next to the trail. Its root pan is thirty feet high, exposing an underbelly of boney roots, and I smell the dead dirt clogging its white veins. A dozen other trees lie upended too, propped like enormous coins balanced on edge. I remember the big storm that passed through two years ago.

This is what can happen, I realise. Even these old-growth cedars, here for centuries, weren't free from danger. Still, it feels safe here, as if the trees have whispered, 'It's okay, because all things living and lifeless occupy the universe in harmony.'

Eldora reaches to touch the naked root of an upturned tree. "Janine says, when the storm happens, the elements do battle, and the wind won this fight." She steps in a slow circle. "Seems to me that the trees were old and tired and decided to lie down. The wind, she helped them. But, is possible I look at it this way because we *Roma* hate war."

"Is war against your religion?"

"We believe in God." Eldora smiles. "But not like the Catholic believes. We sense his presence, but never pretend to see him. His power is here in the woods, and this we understand."

When Cathedral Trail ends, we turn onto another path that circles a pond overgrown with reeds. The Vancouver skyline is visible now and only a short distance away.

"Pauline Johnson named this place too, Lost Lagoon." She stops near a building called Nature House and leans over the fence, gazing at the water. "I love to stop here and imagine her, so many years past, paddling her canoe."

Pauline Johnson is a historical figure, so I can bring up a hazy vision of what Eldora sees. I wish I could do the same for my own measly life story.

It's quit raining, and I glance at my damaged umbrella. I hate it. There's a plastic garbage bin beside the Nature House. I throw the horrible thing into it, and I'm instantly flooded with relief. I'd rather end up soaked than carry it one more moment.

Then I turn and stare at my reflection in the window of the Nature House—the dark, unruly hair, my skinny shadow. "It's strange. I'm the complete opposite of the woman who raised me. We don't look alike. She and I have a different view of the world. I've never felt I belong to her, and I know she's not told me everything about my birth."

I've blurted this out loud, but Eldora takes it in her stride. "Have you asked your mother straight?"

"She always changes the subject. It's the secrecy that bothers me." The questions create a scuffle in the pit of my gut. Were my natural parents criminals, or mentally ill? Was I the aftermath of a rape. Do I even want to know? I tell myself the earth and sky should be enough, and now, in this moment, I'm almost convinced.

She touches my arm and says, "Ask her again. All you dream, it will start or end soon."

Leandro claims Eldora is a clairvoyant. Maybe it is time to demand answers from Mother.

We follow the path back into the city. When we part at the bus stop, Eldora kisses my cheeks, European style, one, two, three.

Leak Windows

I've decided. No matter how terrifying the mystery of my origin is, I need the truth. The detective is a con artist, so who can I go to? Only Lieke—the one who fed me, clothed me, and harassed me my whole life.

My trusty Ford Focus shoots under the ornate Millennium Gate of Chinatown. After steering into an empty parking spot on Pender Street, I sit for a few minutes clenching the steering wheel.

Each Sunday afternoon, at precisely 1:00 PM, Mother visits the Dr Sun Yat-Sen Classical Chinese Garden, where she stays until 3:00 PM on the nose. The Gardens bring out Lieke's gentle side, and it's the best place to approach her. I won't let her change the topic this time.

It's as if hiring the detective in Holland has created pandemonium. Now, a band of gypsies think they own me, and a mysterious stranger claims knowledge of my origin. Soon my vitiligo will be impossible to cover, and every glance in the mirror reminds me of my iffy gene pool.

I jump out and push the car door shut. A dingy quilt of cloud hovers overhead.

A billboard on a store across the street announces in large white letters, 'Everything is Going to be Alright.'

The girl at the ticket booth takes my ten-dollar bill.

Passing through the elaborate wooden archway to the main courtyard is like stepping into a strange universe. The *feng-shui* harmony of bamboo replaces the bluster of Chinatown, with pine and ginkgo trees pushing up between pebbled paving tiles. A fountain babbles over a miniature mountain range of limestone rocks, water-sculpted into beastly shapes. Below this display, lily pads drift in a pond. It's peaceful, without a soul in sight.

Mother used to bring me with her on Sundays. The last time, I was twelve, and I can still see her. She's parked on a bench around the corner at the end of a passageway which overlooks another pool of water. This is where I'll find her, sitting upright, knees together and pointing toward the pavilion across the pond, hands folded in her lap, staring at floating carp.

When I step into the corridor, I'm surprised at how accurate my memory is. She's in that exact position, face composed, but her eyebrows spike up when she sees me.

"I need to talk to you." I wish my voice wouldn't squeak.

"Shh... Can it wait? The Koi are eating." Mother lifts one side of her sweater to reveal a bag of thawed-out peas. "They are hungry all the time now." The bag rustles as she digs in for a handful of peas. "It is because they take no food in winter."

"Please, can we talk?" I move in closer and whisper. "You're not supposed to feed them."

"But look, they recognise me." The fish hover near the surface of the murky water like giant goldfish. Each scaly skin is spattered with a kaleidoscope of colour—Jackson-Pollack-designed fish. Lieke tosses a few peas into the pool. "Did you know, Koi can outlive a human? One female Koi once lived to be two hundred and twenty-six. See the Sanke there." She points to a large white fish, airbrushed with a black and red design. "He could be a hundred years old. A comparable fish is worth a thousand dollars."

This attention to detail tells me Mother's in an agreeable mood.

"Sit." Lieke taps the bench beside her. "But stay quiet. Watch them. Listen to the water trickle."

I do what I'm told. For five minutes that feels like two hours, I hear only the sound of my breath and peas plopping into the jade water. A hint of fishy pond scum tints the air.

Then I touch her on the shoulder. "I hired someone to look for my birth parents. He calls himself a detective of genealogy." I struggle for a tone of compassion. "I need answers. I need to know who I am."

Mother's face fossilises, as it always does when I bring up the past. "You know who you are."

"I'm not sure I do." I search her face for any signs of softening but detect no movement, not a single muscle twitch.

Lieke reaches into her bag for more peas. "What has he told you?"

"That the orphanage flooded, and its records were destroyed.

That he could find no reports of a newborn abandoned at that train station. That I owe him money." I smile and pat her arm, hoping to lighten the mood. Mother doesn't need to know he's waived his fee.

"You should not have wasted your money." She continues to stare stoney-faced at the Koi. "How can he tell you if I can't?"

I reach out and pat her white knuckles. "Tell me anything. Please, Mother. What happened? How did you find me? How did it work back then? How did you hear about the orphanage? Did you choose me from a room full of babies?"

Mother pinches the bridge of her nose. "Why do you need to know?"

"Because I'm curious. We are not from the same people." I squeeze her cold, stiff, pale fingers. "Where did my grandfather come from? What language did he speak?"

"Like I said before—I cannot tell you." She makes a fist under my hand. "You were left on a doorstep. The nuns at the orphanage took you in and told us nothing more."

These are the exact words dad used when I tried to squeeze the story out of him, as if they've rehearsed the same lines.

She crumples the empty pea bag. "It was good luck to have a chance for a newly born. We had just passed the screening." She nudges my hand off hers. "To get approval to adopt was a complicated business. They asked many questions." With a humph, she gazes out across the pond again. "Where you were born or who gave birth to you, we had no details." Shifting her knees away from me, she peers at the open rafters. "Our neighbours called us crazy. They warned of hereditary illness. They said, 'What if she turns out to be crippled, or insane?'" She shakes one hand out as if trying to flick pea juice off her fingers. "They almost had me convinced, but not your father."

"What did he think?" When I asked Dad, he'd said, 'Go talk to your mother,' as if they'd agreed on the story and he wasn't trusted to say it right.

"He was certain you would be fine, healthy. I thought he wanted a son, but when he saw you, he decided. He does not often insist." She looks up into the branches of a bamboo tree, leaves rippling in a faint breeze. "It was the least I could do." Then she lowers her voice even further. "I could not bear a child." Her shoulders slump, but only for a second. She straightens and stares brusquely at me. "Are you happy now?"

"So, there's nothing else?" My determination is draining, as it has before, but I'm still not convinced she's telling the whole story. "Come on, Mother. There must be more."

"Because you were an abandoned baby, there was an investigation." She glances at her watch and then springs to her feet. It's as if staying past 3:00 PM would hex her day. "Your father worried they might find the birth mother, cancel the adoption, and take you away, so we made plans to emigrate."

She's speaking as if she's told this story a thousand times, but I've never heard so much.

"It was difficult to get work in Holland, even for a skilled craftsman. But that's not why we left. What your father truly wanted was to leave Europe so we could keep you."

I stand. "What about you? Did you want to come to Canada? Did you want to keep me?" I'm quivering inside, and not sure I want the answer.

"It did not matter what I thought." She turns and marches halfway down the corridor. "See these windows. They are called Leak windows." She runs her hand over the elaborate latticework of white inside a square opening in the wall. Then she moves sideways. "Stand to the side and you cannot see through, but then shift to the front." She steps to face the window. "Now, see the picture it makes. The landscape leaks into view." Her expression is the one she reserves for her spotless kitchen after the Saturday cleaning. "And each window is different, each design and each picture." Next, she does something that rocks me to the core. She lays one arm across my shoulder, just for an instant, and says, "We have made a good life here, *Ja*?"

"The man from Holland says he's found some facts."

"About your birth?" Her body stiffens.

"Yes, but he hasn't given me any details."

"He's lying." Her tone's gone cold again.

"He said I'd be contacted—that someone is coming here to see me, but I'm not happy that he's shared my contact information."

"You are right to be careful. This man plays you for a fool. He's a trickster. Stay away from him." She shrinks back from me with an anxious expression. I expected her to be upset, but why be scared?

Then Mother paces ahead, eyes fixed on the herringbone walkway. "No mention of this to your father, okay?" She stops in front of another Leak window, but she's jittery now.

I guess Mother is trying to protect Dad's feelings. He'd be heartbroken to discover I hired that detective. She might feel betrayed too, but it's difficult to tell with Lieke. She's no emotional babbler.

Later, at home, I sit at my desk, basking in afternoon sun that's flooding my apartment. It's amazing Mother dropped her guard with me. Not for long, but it's a first. I felt close to her for an instant. We had a genuine mother/daughter moment—plus I learned a few new things.

Not once has she mentioned an investigation, or that Dad's main reason for emigrating was to ensure they could keep me. And I assumed either she or dad were barren, but I've never heard her admit responsibility. I still suspect she's keeping information to herself, but maybe there's a good reason. She might be looking out for me, the same way she's protecting Dad from my deceit. And thank God I can count on her not to tell, because Dad's been good to me, and I've betrayed him.

I pick up my pen.

Dear Erin,

Remember I told you I hired a detective to search for my birth parents? He's turned out to be a fraud, so I guess it's a dead end. I was only after medical history, anyway. Maybe there are things we're better off not knowing.

Let's say you found out your family had a history of heart disease. Just realising that fact might bring on a heart attack—so ignorance is truly bliss. I read once about a lady who was sure she had cancer. She was at the doctor's office non stop for years, and they could find nothing wrong. Then, after decades of stressing about it, she developed stomach cancer. She'd talked herself into it.

The other issue—my virginity. That's on hold too. The musician is playing out of town for two weeks. So my life is back to its normal, humdrum, monotonous pace. Right now, I think that's best.

Drearily yours,

Hally

Poor Erin. She could trace her roots back hundreds of years—Irish all the way. She knew both her parents, even if her dad was an asshole. But what good did that do her? Her life wasn't any happier than mine and she died a virgin at thirty-three. Hell, I can't help thinking, if I perished in a car crash tomorrow, it'd be the same for me—a wasted life with no significant human connection.

Part Three

The Setup

When Ulla phoned and asked me over to her apartment this morning, I prickled with dread. I assume she hasn't summoned me to celebrate my stellar job performance. Maybe she plans to fire me—I can only hope. I neglected to return those short skirts when she insisted and sold two more last week, but she wasn't in the shop at the time, so how could she know? I've hidden the skirt box in the back corner of the storeroom—a place Ulla never goes.

It's been two years since I've been to her place. It's my day off too, and I'd rather be anywhere else, so I'm paused outside her condo door. I finger the Hermes vintage scarf at my collar. It was a Thrift Store find, but it's pretentious, so I take it off and stuff it in my purse. Why do I need to impress Ulla? I ring the buzzer.

She ushers me inside and then darts off to the kitchen.

This apartment reminds me of the Queen's palace in Narnia, a fortress of ice and hoar frost. I sit on a white leather sofa, survey the spacious room, and wonder how often Ulla has the gleaming, floor-to-ceiling windows cleaned. The room is a repository for carefully placed, colourless metal and glass end tables. Near the French doors, in a wicker basket, Ulla's dog Cicero is curled up, snoring. I hope it stays sleeping, but the creature snorts and comes alive. He bounds across the milk-coloured carpet and leaps into my lap.

Cicero has a non-stop dripping, piggy snout and a wide, wet tongue that goes straight for the face. I seize him under the front legs and hold him at arm's length. "Ew—no you don't."

"Cicero, bad dog—get off Halca." At the sound of Ulla's voice the wretched thing barks, gyrates like a whirling dervish, and claws my arm. I drop the yelping beast on the floor and it lets out a high-pitched yipe.

"Ouch, that hurts." As I clench my stinging wrist, a streak of blood springs up on my forearm.

Ulla sets a tea tray on the sideboard. "You are a naughty boy, Cicero," she says with a doting tone.

He jumps at her shins, tail wagging.

"Let me see your arm." She steps forward and leans over to

inspect the damage. "Ah, it is nothing—just a scratch." A minute later, she slides open the patio door, bends, and scoots the mutt outside with a gentle pat.

The doorbell rings, and Ulla strides toward the entrance, red hair blazing against the white, white of her living room. Then she disappears into the front hallway.

I'm rubbing blood off my arm when Mother steps into the room, followed by Ulla. They stand side-by-side in black skirts and pale turtle-neck sweaters—a twosome of complicity.

"Mother, what are you doing here?"

A disturbing memory surfaces, of being ambushed by Mother and Ulla one day after graduation, the night they decided my future. My incarceration began after that. I went to work at Ulla's shop and I've been there ever since—for fifteen long, tedious years. I'll never forget Mother's expression that evening, her cool pose of triumph as she announced the scheme.

The two women advance, but I'm ready for them this time. They will not bully me. I am not the same person I was at seventeen.

"Come, Lieke, sit beside Halca." Ulla pats Mother's shoulder. "Wish I could wear that shade of cream. It matches your hair exact." Then her eyes narrow. "You did not buy that sweater from me."

"*Nee*, this old thing? I've had it for twenty years. You have seen it."

"*Ja*, I remember now. You wore it when Halca passed from primary to high school." Then Ulla glances sideways at me. "Your mother, she saves her best clothes for the important occasions, eh?"

I feel queasy. "What's important today?"

"You will see. Ulla has wonderful news." A slip-smile appears on Mother's face. I close my eyes and pinch the skin above my nose. What Mother considers 'good news' never jives with my thinking. I glance up at Ulla as she navigates across the room with the tea tray.

"Let's drink tea first," Ulla says.

How I itch to escape. These ladies love to draw things out. They huddle in rabid attention to each other and launch into the pros and cons of hormone therapy for menopause. Both women are past menopause, but Ulla is on the pro side. Why suffer, when there's a pill that works? Mother is on the con. She is, for the most part, opposed to pills of any sort. Next, they're on to euthanasia, but I've missed how they made the leap.

Mother says, "In that state, put me out of my misery. You would do that for me, Halca, *Ja*?"

This makes me wish I had a barbiturate cocktail on hand. "Can we discuss something more cheerful?"

"Okay, the news—the business sold," Ulla says. She springs up, disappears into her den, and arrives back with a stack of papers, dumping it on the coffee table in front of me. "I will spend the winter in Heidelberg, with my cousin. *Ja*, no more headaches."

"Congratulations, I guess." I squint at the paperwork. A form on Langara College letterhead has me curious what this sale has to do with the school. I also wonder what my prospects are. "Will the new owner run the shop herself or keep me on?"

"Now, that is what we must discuss." Ulla looks over at Mother. "Should I explain, Lieke, or will you?"

"*Ja,* you explain," Mother says.

"She has a couple conditions of sale."

"What's that got to do with me?"

"You are a condition of sale."

"A condition of sale?"

"*Jawohl,* the new owner requests you manage the store. She also asks that you take night courses in business administration, to gain the proper knowledge."

"Who is this new owner?" I look from Ulla to Mother and back to Ulla again. Mother's teeth flash one of those I'm-so-clever grins and it becomes as clear as Ulla's gleaming windows. I shudder. "You didn't?" A knot of anxiety plugs my throat.

"*Ja,* I have bought the store. It is a solid investment and your father agrees. We have been to the bank and the lawyer and closed the paperwork. It secures your job and future. Ulla can retire. It is what they call a win-win, *Ja*?"

"You've signed the papers?" These two have me pushed to the precipice. "Did you consider asking me first, since I'm a condition of sale?"

"It is such an excellent solution for everyone." Ulla leans over and pats my shoulder. "You'll still be there, and it puts my mind at rest about the business."

I stand. "No, I won't be there. You can't make me run the store, and I will never study business administration. I told you that,

Mother." My eyeballs feel like they might burst.

"You need to think, and we understand." Cicero is outside scratching on the glass, and Ulla gets up to let him in.

"I don't need to think. This is not what I want. You bought the store, Mother, you run it." I snatch my purse, and then at the door, I turn back and shriek at them. "I quit." The dog growls, scratches across the hardwood floor, and clamps onto my pant leg. Angry tears erupt as I shake him off. I try to slam the door on my way out, but the mechanised closer kills the momentum, and it shuts with barely a sound.

Before driving off, I lean on the hood of my rickety Ford Focus and try, without success, to calm my quaking limbs. So I climb into the car and just sit there for a while, gazing out onto the deserted street. A finger of panic pokes my gut, and I pound the steering wheel. What have I done? Then I start the car and head home. Once I'm on the road, I realise my jitters are mixed with something else too—excitement. It feels like I could fly.

At home there's a message on the answering machine from Eldora. "Tomorrow night, the men return. Is a good excuse for the tarot card reading. Come early—be here when they arrive. Can you make it?"

I curl up on my sofa and push the entire afternoon out of my mind. *The Princess Bride* is playing on tv and I watch it for the umpteenth time.

By bedtime I'm blissful and content, and best of all, free. I fall asleep reeling with seductive images. Leandro is strumming his guitar on the beach under an azure sky. A red and orange tarot card, The Lovers, floats on a golden breeze.

Tarot Cards

My delight of yesterday was short-lived. This morning I can only think about my depleted bank account. I open the fridge to see a couple of limp carrots, a half litre of milk, two hard-boiled eggs, and three pieces of mouldy bread. My stomach growls. How does an empty refrigerator create such hunger? I fill the kettle for tea.

Why didn't I consider my catastrophic finances before quitting my job? There may have been room for negotiation—especially the college courses. Mother surely wouldn't force me to study something I'd despise.

But I can't undo it now. I'd rather slit my wrists than beg for my job back. Plus, those two women are both responsible for how dirt-poor I am—Ulla for the stingy salary and Mother for making home so unbearable that I moved out early, with no training for a decent career. If I've made life difficult for them, it serves them right.

I'll be fine—I can sell the car and look for a job.

The kettle whistles. I fix the tea and sit at my desk.

Dear Erin,

Yesterday I quit my job at Der Schwarze Koffer. Ulla sold the shop, and it's time for a change. I'm not sure what I'll do yet, but it won't involve selling clothes.

In the meantime, Eldora, the matriarch of that gypsy band, has invited me over for a tarot card reading this afternoon. I realise how mumbo jumbo this sounds, but it might be interesting. Plus, Leandro the musician returns today, and I plan to be there when he arrives home. I'll let you know how the cards fall.

Love always,

Hally

I go to the closet, take down the shoebox that holds our correspondence and slip the latest entry in. I really must find a bigger box soon. One corner is beginning to split open.

As my car bumps up the dirt road, I wonder what possessed me to come to this deserted, creepy campground. Grey clouds hover above the tree line, and there's not a soul in sight. I don't see the shiny Dodge Ram parked in front of the office. Even the motley jumble of pots and pans, strung under the canopy beside the bus, are quiet and lifeless today.

Is this an omen? As Mother would point out, I barely know these people. I can practically hear her. 'Why drive to this awful place to meet complete strangers? Why can't you act normal?' I let off the gas and turn the wheel, intending to leave. Whenever Mother worms into my skull, I'm not the greatest company.

Then Eldora appears in the bus window and waves.

I abort the getaway, pull into an empty camp spot, and get out of the car. Since I have no job, I may as well kill some time. I struggle for optimism, telling myself that Mother is only in my head now, not in my face.

I wonder if Eldora's tarot cards can predict how I'll pay next month's rent.

The bus is a dark blue, weather-worn Greyhound spattered with rusty holes around the wheel wells, something I didn't notice on my first visit. On the side panel, someone's painted a gypsy caravan with musical instruments bursting out the back of it. This is fresh bright paint, and the riotous colours lift my mood.

I knock, and the door echoes with the timbre of solid wood.

"Come in." Eldora's voice sings out.

Then I step into the lair of a clairvoyant. Everything—the cushions, curtains, cupboards and carpets are multi-coloured and luxuriant. A stained glass lamp illuminates the room, an inviting contrast to the dreary outdoors.

Eldora sits at a booth-style table, a deck of cards fanned out in front of her. They're twice the size of normal playing cards. "Ah, Hally. Is nice you come. A surprise for Leandro today."

So, it will be a surprise. Why did I assume he invited me?

She scoops the cards up, then stands, strides forward, and draws me into an incense-infused embrace. "He'll be so happy to see you."

"What time do you expect them back?" I ask.

"This afternoon, later." Eldora wears a kaleidoscopic blouse with long winged sleeves. She smoothes a strand of hair behind one ear. Her hair is down today, sable strands flowing in an unbroken line to her waist. God, she's exotic. I'd die to look half that good in my sixties. I pat my ball of messy curls. It's impossible to be exotic with frizzy hair. And what was I thinking? A cotton V-neck top? It looks as if Mother dressed me this morning.

She points to the table. "I was heating up the cards. Come, have a seat. Is nice to have you here. Days are quiet with the men away."

I point at the cards. "Have you been reading the tarot for long?"

"*Por siempre*. My mother's sister in England taught me. Many years ago. The year my blood first flows."

"Aren't you from Spain?"

"*Si*, I was born in the province of *Málaga*, near the Mediterranean, but *Mamá* was *Romany*, from England, and *Papá* was *Gitano*. Is the name they use for our people in Spain. I grew up *Gitana*, but only a few of us use the tarot. Those with the gift, usually stick to traditional ways."

"What's traditional? Palm reading?" I had my palm read once, years ago. The woman pointed out my broken lifeline, and I inspect my hand now, tracing the line with a fingernail. She said the break was significant and predicted a mid-life, near-death event. I hope mid-life doesn't begin at thirty-three.

"Oh, no." Eldora laughs. "Palm reading is for the *gadjè* only, to make money. Many *Gitana*s do it. Is no magic in it, but to earn cash, the sisters, they tell silly women what they want to hear."

Thank God I didn't blurt out my story.

Eldora leans across the table and places her fingers over my hands. "But for us with the gift, you never, never use for money. Will spoil the magic."

I lean forward. "And you have this gift?" It sounds screwy, but I'm fascinated.

"*Si,* passed to me by the sister of my *mamá*."

"So what is traditional in Spain?"

"You know, snip a pig's ear or bat's wing to put under the pillow. Or, sometimes they place in a tiny bag around their necks." She tugs on a thong circling her neck and pulls up a wrinkled leather pouch.

"You're kidding me."

"No, is true, but not to worry. This little purse has no pig's ear or bat wing, only a luck charm." She laughs and tucks the pouch back inside her top. "But the snippings, they are nothing but a tool to help the *hechizo,* no different from tarot cards." Eldora rubs one dainty fist above her left breast. "The ancient words live in your heart. Not even necessary to say out loud, but you need the gift. Only a few of us are blessed—is rare."

"Do you study to learn it?"

"No, you are born with the skill, from your *mamá,* or her *madre,* or your *tia*. But to use correct, a woman in your family must guide you. Is why they send me to England to live with Mamá's sister." Eldora chuckles. "It makes my *tía* queasy to snip body parts from animals, so is the tarot she learns instead, and then teaches to me. Tarot cards call up the ancient magic and works with our talent. Should I show you?"

"Yes, please." Ancient magic—I can't resist.

She bows her head, mutters a few words I don't understand, picks up the deck and shuffles.

"We call this the Celtic Cross. I will ask what the next road on your future brings. Something about your love life, eh?" She dashes off a naughty smile that makes me reflect on every wanton thought I've ever had.

Then she slides the cards toward me. "Now, you must cut."

I hesitate. The psychic world fascinates me, but it scares me too. So I brace myself, reach, and pick off a sliver of cards.

"Now, I draw the first card, the Significator." Eldora selects a card and flips it face up. A glimmer ripples the length of her hair. "Is the Queen of Cups and because you are dreamy, I pick it for you."

I've never thought of myself as dreamy, and I'm not even sure what she means by that.

She gathers the cards, shuffles, and then splays them face down in a semi-circle.

"Choose nine cards. You must do this part. The *magia*, it comes from you. I am here only to puzzle up what it means."

I pick out nine, one at a time. Is it my imagination, or are they hot? Cardboard can't heat up from shuffling, can it?

She begins the reading. As she flips cards over, her expression alternates between delight and seriousness. After one of them she says, "Hum, The Lovers." It depicts a naked man and woman standing under a tall winged figure.

Given my virginal state, any reference to lovers must be positive, but I detect a trace of concern in Eldora's tone.

"Is about love, but hesitation too."

That makes sense. She's nailed it. I'm prone to hesitation but tired of it too. Besides, it's not hesitation anymore. Desperation is a better word. My face flares with embarrassment remembering how I threw myself at Leandro.

"Look, the VIII of Wands." She tips her head and looks at it quizzically. "The wrong side faces up. If the card comes up right side to me, it shows arrows of love and a happy end. But in this position, tells of a family quarrel. Could be nothing to do with love."

The lamp flickers as she says this, and an eerie sensation grips me. This is getting creepy. I didn't mention the fight with Mother, or the shop fiasco, or quitting my job. My stomach roils. Lieke's never-ending presence is meddling with my tarot reading, and now she's intruded on my love life too.

"That's strange," I tell her. "I fought with my mother last night, and my boss. I quit my job."

"Good for you." Eldora shoots me a thumbs-up. "I mean not the fight, but your job. You don't enjoy the work, *Si*? *Un momento* and life passes us by. Must fill our days with *felicidad*." She studies my face so intently I squirm.

I hope she's finished now. This has gone on too long, and I don't want to know what's coming next.

An engine roars outside, a welcome distraction. "Are they home?" I crane to look out the window.

"No, is not the band. Is Scoop. His truck, it sounds like a tortured bull."

She continues with the reading. "You will meet a relative—unknown for many years. This person suffers from a broken heart, because of something stolen." Her forehead wrinkles. "I wish I could see more. Is hard to say if she's a man or woman." Then Eldora closes her eyes, rests her elbows on the table, and presses her fingers to her temples. I watch her concentrate for two or three minutes.

Finally, she opens her eyes, shakes her head, and flips another card. If she zeroed in on something, she isn't saying. Then, tapping her finger on the flipped card, she beams and tells me to expect wealth and excellent fortune, and to expect it soon. That's more like it. I entertain an optimistic notion. What if detective Vanderburg's mysterious stranger arrives with news that I'm the long-lost child of a wealthy, powerful family? I know it's ridiculous, but what if he's legit and I get some actual information?

This has my head whirling, so I'm relieved when Eldora flips the last card.

"This shows the result. Is the spirit message, combining all the power of your cards." She turns it over. "Another Queen and Queen of Wands too. Oh, Hally. Now I am sure you are *Romany*. So many Wands." She lets out a noisy puff of air and leans forward with an intent expression. "What I tell you today is true. We associate fire with the wands. Is a fierce fire that burns free, same as the flame in our people." She throws her arms wide open. "AAAaaa. Change comes for you—explosions of change."

I'm not confident I could survive explosions of change. This is beginning to sound wacky. Tarot is just a game. It defies all reason to rely on prophecies spawned by a random flipping of cards.

I pick up the Queen of Wands and inspect it. Goosebumps flare up on my arms. "Doesn't this black cat symbolise bad luck?"

"No, no, the black cat is lucky. See how he sits ahead of the throne. He guards his queen. No, everything points to amazing fortune for you, but some challenges first."

Before I can ask her, what challenges, there's a rap on the door.

"Eldora, are you in?" I don't recognise the voice. It's not Leandro—maybe Adan?

Scoop ducks into the bus, a giant in a lumberjack shirt. "Adan just phoned. He asked me to give you a message. They won't make it back today. He didn't want you to worry. He said to tell you nothing is wrong and he'll fill you in tomorrow."

A stone of disappointment settles in my gut, and I stand. "I should leave now." This announcement is abrupt, I realise, and even rude, but Eldora seems to understand.

"*Latcho Drom,* dreamy one." She smiles and hugs me again before I go.

On the drive home, I rehash the tarot reading. I'd love to believe it, the mystery relative, the wealth and good fortune.

In my suite, I see someone's pushed an envelope through my mail slot. The message inside is short and to the point:

Meet me at the beach by the Maritime Museum on Thursday at two o'clock. This is concerning information obtained from Henrik Vanderburg of Amsterdam.

Putrika.

I clutch the slip of paper with shaky hands, then flip it, searching for clues—a telephone number or an address, but the other side is blank.

Before the tarot reading, I would have trashed the note, because God only knows who Mr Vanderburg has given my name to. But now I wonder if it might be legitimate. The detective waived his fee, so someone must have paid him. Whoever wrote this might have information on my birth parents.

I examine the envelope for a postmark, but there's no mark or stamp, so the mailman didn't deliver it. This troubles me. How did this Putrika get into the building? My uneasiness spikes. No one in our apartment complex ever lets a stranger in.

Thrill and Thwart

The next morning, my door buzzer lets out a piercing caterwaul at 10 AM. I gawk at the box on the wall and pick up the receiver.

"*Hola,* Hally. Can I take you for coffee?" It's Leandro's voice.

I scan the room. The apartment is still shipshape from my cleaning spree, but then I glimpse myself in the mirror. Yikes! My hair is sticking out like a raven-haired Einstein. My eyes are slits embedded in puffy sacks and I'm wearing the rattiest pair of pyjamas. I ask him to wait downstairs and leap into action.

A splash of icy water on my face relieves the swelling around my eyes. The hairdo is more problematic, and only a complete soaking will tame it, so I grab a blue knit slouch hat, tug it on, and step out of the apartment. Halfway along the hall, it registers that I'm still wearing pyjamas. Whoa, get it together, Halca. I scurry back to suit up in jeans and a blue top to match the headgear.

At the bottom landing, I spot Leandro through the glass doors, leaning against a tree. My stomach lurches, my legs go rigid, and I brace myself against the wall. Here's me, little Orphan Annie, rushing to meet this guy who could be on the cover of GQ magazine. I want to flee back upstairs.

He turns, notices me, and smiles. The panic attack curls up and melts into the stairwell. I open the door and step outside.

"Your hat is, how do you say, groovy?" He chuckles.

I cringe. What was I thinking—wearing this kooky new-age hippy headgear?

When I get close, he tugs the slouchy end of the hat and with one finger grazes a dark mole above my upper lip. I've always hated that dot, but now it tingles like a genuine beauty mark.

He drapes his arm across my shoulder and leads me down the street. The weight of his arm makes me shiver with excitement, but at the same time, warms me. I've never felt safer in my life. We stop at a cafe where he buys coffee, and then we stroll toward Kits Beach. At the waterfront, we veer west along the seawall.

"Did you miss me?" Leandro bunts his hip against mine and sends a jolt to my private parts.

"Maybe, a little." I have missed him more than expected, and my girly bits are damp.

He points ahead on the path. "I remember a spot there." A few minutes later we veer off to a patch of sand. There are at least thirty sailboats adrift in the bay and several cargo ships anchored to the horizon. The breeze slides ribbons across my face.

"Sit beside me." Leandro taps a log and reaches for my hand. "You have been well since last we met?"

"Mostly, but I'm stressed out. I've quit my job." Caged under his fingers, my fist does a hummingbird flutter.

"*Si,* Eldora mentioned." There's a smile in his voice. "Is good news. Now, I will see you more."

"I'll find another job." I'd rather not talk about anything employment related. Sitting here next to Leandro, tickled by an ocean breeze, even my sorry financial state can't spoil the moment.

"You should enjoy the time to yourself."

"You're right. But sadly, that won't pay the rent."

He digs in his jean's pocket and pulls out a roll of money. "You need how much?"

I gasp. "No, I'm not asking you for money."

He pries my fingers open and presses the entire bundle into my palm. "Please, you keep it. We won a good wage for Cache Creek."

Why would he hand over a wad of cash to a near-stranger? "Honestly, I'm fine." I drop the cash in his lap. "Tell me about your trip." Leandro returns the money to his pocket.

Then he recounts the gig in Cache Creek, how most of the audience danced and clapped, even if it was a country music crowd and the band did not know a single song requested.

"No one can resist the Romany music," he says.

Perched beside Leandro, with his perfect white teeth, a hand pressed over mine—even the air seems to titter. The ache in my groin mushrooms.

We sit in silence for a while, then he leads me back onto the path. This is it. In ten minutes we'll be at my place. He'll come up. I imagine unbuttoning that shirt, kissing his neck, running my fingers up his bare chest. I have no hesitation and no second thoughts. Still, a few questions niggle. Will it hurt? I've read it can be painful. What if I cry? What if I'm a terrible lover? What if I really suck at it?

So, when we reach my apartment building, I hesitate before asking, "Want to come up?"

"*Si*, I would love to see your home."

Leandro follows me up the stairs, and inside my suite, he peers around and smiles with approval. "*Fantástico*."

Thank God I spruced the place up. My apartment is not swanky, but today it's tidy.

He points to the dresser. "Is nice—with a *cómoda* in the room centre."

"Yes, I prefer it there. It's my only decent piece of furniture."

Leandro's looking at the bed now, and I'm glad I made it this morning. I hope it seems inviting.

He glances at the wall clock. "Soon, I must leave. We start a new gig tonight. Is equipment to move today and then we rehearse."

"That's good. You're getting lots of work." I set a cup in the sink and swipe a scatter of crumbs on the counter. I don't want him to go. This moment feels so right. I've waited and waited. Any doubts I once had have vanished, and I now know he's the one.

Then as if I willed him to do it, he steps close to me and pulls me close. At last, I think and slip my hands up under his shirt. He smells like nutmeg, and his skin is the softest leather. I nuzzle his neck. We share a long hypnotic kiss that's almost a dance, and my mind flees my body. So, when he pushes me to arm's length, I'm stunned.

"Eldora informs you have never made love with a man."

An ice cube of confusion slithers down my spine. Why mention Eldora, and why would she say that? I didn't tell her.

"Where did she get that idea?" My face burns.

"Eldora, she just knows." He smiles. "Don't be sad. Is a good thing. Many *Romany* women wait, and now I have told my body not to hurry." He pats the zipper of his jeans. "Is plenty of time."

"But I want to hurry." Oh my God, I cannot believe this. He can't back out now. He started it. I throw my arms around him again.

Laughing, he lifts me up by the waist and twirls me. "Patience, little one. I must go soon." He sets me down and pats my cheek. "I imagine we are to mean more to each other than, how do you say, a quick roll in the hay?"

I wish he didn't have such sexy eyes.

He kisses my forehead. "Tomorrow night you will come to the Bar Knave? Is where the band plays next. Do you know where it is?"

I nod and force a smile. "Yes, I've been there. It's a nice club." Bar Knave is far from my thoughts, but I need to hide my shame. It's risen from my belly and settled in a wellhead deep behind my eye sockets.

How could I throw myself at him after vowing to never do it again? He must think I'm a slut. I gape at my hands, fingers clawed, hanging near my knees.

Leandro suggests we meet at seven o'clock tomorrow after rehearsal and before they begin their first set. Then he's gone.

This must never happen again. I need a different man—someone who doesn't make me lose my grip. I collapse on the sofa, bury my head in my arms and try in vain to hold off the tears.

When I've soaked the pillow and the heaving stops, I strip my clothes off and throw them onto the floor. In the bureau mirror I notice the white blotches near my shoulder blade are whiter than yesterday. Naked, I trudge to the bathroom, turn the shower on hot, step in, and reach for the brush.

It's a beige brush, similar to the one Mother used on me, firm enough to redden the skin, with barbs not quite sharp enough to draw blood. I soap the bristles and scrub, starting at my neck like she always did. I can almost hear her mantra as I scour, 'Dirty girl, look at this neck. Shh, not a peep out of you.' She added this last bit because of the time Dad stepped in and said, 'What in heaven's name are you doing, Lieke?' Mother lifted my six-year-old arm and pointed to a dark patch on my elbow. 'See how dirty she is. What does she do to get this way?' Dad said, 'Stop that. It's her skin colour. You'll tear off her skin.' Dad's reasoning made no lasting impression though, and weekly, until the age of ten, the beige brush came out. Finally, one day I smuggled that brush outside and dropped it in a dumpster. After that, I bathed myself.

Six months ago, when I spotted the first white blotch on my back, I bought this brush, realising that Mother had been right all along. I am a dirty girl.

When I come out of the shower clean and red-raw, I notice a pile of money sitting next to my computer. Why would Leandro do that? What does he want from me? Obviously not sex.

I pick the money up and count. There's fifteen hundred dollars in bright crisp fifty-dollar bills. Holy crap, that must be every penny he earned in Cache Creek. I cannot believe he's done this. He's not rich. Why would he toss this amount of money at me? It's just plain weird. I'll return the cash tomorrow night, and then that's it, and I'll never see him again. I pop the money in my purse and sit to my desk.

Dear Erin,

Well, I know how to pick them! The musician, Leandro—it's not going to work. I've seen him again and my virginity is still intact. He's dragging his feet, and I just want to get it done. At thirty-three, I've no time to piss around. It shouldn't be so tough to get laid, but maybe he's just the wrong guy. On Friday, I'll start the nightclub circuit again. Surely I'll find someone willing soon. I'm also on the lookout for a new job. Wish me luck.

Love forever,

Hally

Jobs can't be terribly hard to find, and I remind myself how lucky I am. Millions of people are in worse shape than I am. I've never gone hungry. Somehow I'll pay my rent before the first of the month. I own a car I don't really need. Getting rid of it will save me a pile on insurance, too. I snatch a black marker and sheet of paper from the desk drawer and write, "**For Sale**" in bold letters and then add my phone number.

Back upstairs, after posting the sign on my car, the telephone is ringing. Could it be someone for the car already? If so, that was quick. I snatch up the receiver.

"Hi Hally." It's Dad's voice.

"Hi back, is something wrong?" I can't remember the last time he called me.

"Mother told me what happened at Ulla's."

"What did she say, Dad, that I'm a selfish ungrateful daughter?"

"No, your mother would never say that."

"Really?" I know she would, and so does Dad, but he plays the dutiful Dutch boy, always trying to plug that hole in the dike.

He puts on a cheerful tone. "I will take you for breakfast tomorrow morning. Mother meets with Ulla, so she won't even notice I'm out."

After we hang up, I realise I haven't thought about the note slipped under my door all day. I grab it off the top of the fridge and read the message again. On second reading, it divulges no new insight, so I toss the paper on the table. But, I owe it to myself to check it out. If I don't go and meet this Putrika tomorrow afternoon, I'll always wonder about it. Dad doesn't have to know, because chances are slim that Putrika will offer up any real answers.

I'm exhausted beyond sleeping or even thinking, so I turn on the television and flick through every station until I find the channel with old re-runs of *Friends*. I can't concentrate on the tv, though. Dad's sneaking out to see me, so this means Mother must be furious. Will he and I have to meet on the sly from now on? Man, I've made a mess of things, and I'm guessing he'll try to patch it up—ask me to say 'sorry.'

Feeding Seagulls

A brouhaha of seagulls and people throng the market square at Granville Island. I squint into the bright morning sun, searching for Dad. He's easy to pick out, slouched against a wooden post, dressed in a blue-and-white striped shirt, baggy cotton pants, and deck shoes. When he called, I assumed he wanted to discuss the business with Mother, but I notice he's holding a brown paper bag and I'm touched. We haven't spent time feeding the seagulls in years.

He sees me and points to the entrance, paper bag in hand. We meet at the door and hug. Inside the cavernous marketplace, the kiosks overflow with teas from around the world, scarves, necklaces, knick-knacks, health foods, and local wine. An aroma of fresh-baked cinnamon buns permeates the air. We head left to the pastry shop that's been there forever.

"Let's get in line." He leads me to the end of the queue. There's only six or seven people ahead of us.

When I was a kid, Dad and I spent many hours lined up at this booth for pie. The wait was always worth it. I appraise the desserts in the glass display case and salivate. The chocolate cream is a serious temptation, a towering whirl of whipped white over velvety filling. As we near the cash register, the shopkeeper nods.

Dad points to a four-inch high mound of pastry. "A piece of apple pie."

This is what he always orders. I suspect the expression 'American as apple pie' has something to do with this. How he still struggles to fit into this culture.

"Chocolate cream for me."

The man serves up enormous pieces, and we carry the plates to a window table. The pie is a morsel of melting heaven on my tongue.

Dad digs in. "*Wonderbaar.*" He winks, but with a faint frown, and I recognise that look. He's going to bring up the altercation with Mother.

He glances at the rafters. "Your mother says you have quit your job at the dress shop."

"It's time to try something else."

"I told Mother, when she and Ulla brewed up this plan they should ask you first, but you know your mother." He lifts a heaping fork of crust-covered apples. "When she takes hold of an idea, she sees no reason."

"I can't work for her. You understand, don't you? Christ! I'm thirty-three years old." I tap my fork on the edge of the plate.

"What will you do?"

"I don't know—start a new career?"

"Then do work that makes you happy, Hally. Happiness is more important than money. You have no child, no husband to worry over yet." Dad gazes at his pie wistfully.

I always thought my dad enjoyed his work, but what if he hated the construction business? Did he sacrifice a different life for me? Still, he must have wanted me, because no one adopts without wanting a kid. I was no accident.

"Dad, I'm curious. You never mention life in Holland, before we moved here. I'm curious about where I came from." I try to keep my voice light and conversational.

He adjusts the band on his wristwatch. "What do you want to know?"

"I was found abandoned in a train station and you got me from the nuns. That's all you've ever said." It's the short story he and Mother have pitched for years. "There has to be more. Didn't the nuns give you any information?" I squash the pie with my fork.

"I don't remember if they did." Apple pie is no longer the focus of his attention. "You should ask Mother." He twists his paper napkin.

He can't still worry someone might whisk me away from them, as Mother said.

"She needs help in the store right now. Could you consider?"

I drop the fork. I won't even dignify that with an answer—asking me to go on bended knees to Mother. Plus, he's evaded my question.

"Tell me about when I was little."

"You were a *mooi* baby, dark eyes, *sprankelende ogen*."

"Was I underweight, chubby? When you adopted me, did I

appear well cared for? How was I dressed?"

Dad strokes his chin. "I only recall the earrings. Your mother couldn't wait to get home and take them out. She was angry over that. It upset her someone would pierce the ears of a tiny baby."

"Earrings? Mother has never mentioned earrings." I finger my earlobe. "Do you still have them?"

"No, I never saw them again." He rubs his eyes. "I remember they were gold with a red stone. Maybe she gave them away." He fingers his cheek. "But, I should not have brought them up. Please don't ask Mother about them. It upsets her to talk of the past."

"Why is that, Dad?"

He tosses the twisted napkin over a chunk of uneaten pie, shifts sideways in his seat, gazes out the window, and obviously has nothing more to say. Dad seems dejected now, and this was not my intention. I'll stop the interrogation. But I will confront Mother over the earrings, if she and I ever speak again.

Outside, a tuxedoed man, wearing a top hat and playing a mandolin, has drawn an audience. When the market door swings open, his jaunty song lifts my spirits. He's singing, "I'm Henry the eighth, I am, Henry the eighth, I am, I am."

"Come on, let's go listen." I summon up a cheerful smile.

Minutes later, we're outside amidst the crowd. By the second song, Dad is tapping his foot to the music. He ruffles my hair. I'm mesmerised by the mandolin's plunk, the singer's *falsetto* and the salty ocean breeze. A child toddles to centre stage in front of the performer and begins an adorable penguin dance. The audience howls and the teeny fellow, enraptured by the music and the attention, dances on. I get how the little guy feels—the same way I do on the dance floor. Ah ha, that may be my problem. My emotional development didn't get past the age of three.

After the musician finishes, I go and drop a dollar into his mandolin case. It's full of fives and tens and toonies, and I do a quick mental calculation. He's earned over a hundred dollars, and it's not even noon. It's a shame I don't play an instrument. I'll bet this guy isn't worried about paying his rent.

As Dad and I stroll away, he hands me the brown paper bag.

"Yes, let's feed the birds now." I reach into the bag, and the contents rustle. "This isn't bread crumbs." The sack is full of cash, tens, and twenties. "What's this, Dad?"

"With no job, you will need money." He waves a hand as if to say, it's nothing. "But I wish you would think it over again, helping in the shop."

I hold the bag up. "Did you rob a bank?" Mother never lets him have much cash.

He winks. "I save pocket money for a rainy day."

"It's not raining." I stare up at the ultramarine sky and then at my dad's face, amazed at his generosity.

Dad puts a hand on each of my shoulders and tweaks my chin. "Best to not tell your mother. It will be our secret."

I shoot him a conspirator's grin, happy that some things remain the same. It's always been him and me against her.

"Ulla did not pay much. I am aware. Mother also realises you have no money and hopes it will force you to reconsider. She does not understand that if you change your mind, it has to be your choice."

I nod, speechless, but I want to tell him, 'I'd starve rather than work for her.'

"I told her to hunt for someone to run the shop, but she has not started. She is certain you'll return."

"Oh, Dad, I love you. I'll pay back every penny. I promise." I give him a hug. "I can't give in to her. You get that, right?"

"You don't have to pay it back, just agree to stop and consider."

I nod, but with the knowledge I will never return to selling clothes. And there's that other business pinging me with guilt. I've decided to go for it. In a few hours I'm off to meet the mysterious Putrika, hoping to gather details of my birth father. How would Dad react if he knew? He'd think, and rightly so, that I've betrayed him.

On the walk home, after we've said goodbye, my thoughts return to the detective's letter and the note from Putrika. It's not too late to change my mind. As soon as I'm back at the apartment, I resolve to rip up that message and forget the whole business.

Once inside, though, I read the note again. What sort of name is that? I glance at the clock. It's noon. I'm supposed to be at the Maritime Museum at two. I sit at the computer, bring up Google and type in Putrika.

The first hit is a baby-naming site. The name is Sanskrit and means puppet, doll, or small statue. I know little about Eastern culture, but I know that Sanskrit is an East India language.

Another site tells me Putrika is the Hindu title for an only daughter, and when a man has no son, he passes the privileges and responsibilities of a son to his oldest daughter. This is the only time a Hindu girl keeps her father's lineage after marriage —a mixed blessing, according to the website. Hindu men rarely marry a *Putrika* because the woman never fully belongs to them. So this Putrika must be a woman, an Indian woman, and an only daughter.

I get up, go to the mirror and run one finger down my tawny cheek. Yes, it makes sense. I could be Indian.

It's forty-five minutes before the meeting. My radio alarm clock is digital, but it's ticking in my head. If I'm determined to avoid this meeting, I'll need a distraction. I grab my latest book, *Water for Elephants,* and sink into the sofa. It's a wonderful read, but I can't concentrate. Like Rosie the elephant, it's not clear what anyone expects of me. The words blur across the page.

Leandro is convinced I'm *Roma*. Eldora says the *Romany* people originated in India, so it is possible I could be Gypsy, not Indian. This is a relief, because at least I've met some gypsies. I don't know any East Indians. I attended school with some Indo-Canadians, but none of them were friends. Come to think of it, I had no real chums of any culture during my early years, except Erin. I was a skinny bookworm with a mother who struck terror into the heart of every child who ventured near her.

Thirty minutes left. The digital clock shoots darts into my eyes. "What a twit I am." I thump my forehead with the heel of my hand. Why did I hire that detective in the first place, and why should I even care about my roots? People are just people—a truth in every culture and every far-flung corner of the earth that breeds humans.

I stand and pace the length of the studio flat, and remind myself this Putrika may have nothing to do with my natural parents. She didn't allege to be my mother, or sister, or aunt. She only claims to have information.

It's quarter to two. Fifteen minutes to go. It'll take me at least ten minutes to make it to the Maritime Museum. If I don't go, will I ever get another chance? Will I regret it for the rest of my life? I stare stock-still at the clock. Why not go and just have a look—no commitment? Putrika doesn't even have to know I'm there.

Putrika

Milky wisps of cirrus slither across the sky above the Maritime Museum. I read once that clouds like this predict a storm, but the only storm brewing right now is the twister in my stomach. Why am I so anxious? I'm only going to look.

Near the entrance to the museum, a totem pole sits in the middle of the walkway, and it strikes a wrong note here, in front of this A-frame with its glass-paned roof. West of the building, a steep cement stairway descends to the seaside. I stop, lean over a railing, and scrutinise the rendezvous site.

On the beach below, a man wearing a dark suit looks out to sea with hands clasped behind his back. Like the totem pole, he seems misplaced. Close to him, there's a shopping cart heaped with curious junk, half-capsized in the sand. Next to the cart, an old fellow, with a scruffy beard and a handsaw, stands cutting a piece of driftwood. A woman sits sideways on a nearby log, watching his efforts, her full skirt fanned out. I see only her backside. She's wearing a bright yellow kerchief and a thick braid of grey hair trails down her spine. I suppose she must be with the sawyer. It's funny though, to see a vagrant with a wife.

Either I'm early, or Putrika is late. Halfway down the steep stairway, I spy a girl sitting on a blanket facing the water. Could this be her?

Once my sandals hit sand, I venture closer. She has pale skin and pixie-cut fair hair. This girl doesn't resemble me, but what did I expect—that I would easily identify my contact as a long-lost mother or sister? A grain of grit has lodged between my sandal's sole and the pad of my foot. I stop, slip the shoe off and bang it on my thigh.

I'm less than four feet from the girl, sizing her up. She must sense my stare and turns. "Can I help you?" Her pale eyebrows arch up as steep as the museum's roof.

"No, sorry." I swing around and walk away.

The old man's saw screeches. Sailboats bob on English Bay.

A male voice sounds. "Miss."

I swivel to see the dark-suited man. The lady, I guessed as belonging to the woodcutter, stands next to him. Never have I seen such an unlikely pair. He has fat lips, a round face, slicked-back hair, a slight frame, and resembles a child dressed up in his daddy's clothes. The woman is a page ripped right out of National Geographic. She's decked out in a multi-layered red and blue sarong over an ankle-length, crinkly skirt. On her head, she wears a yellow kerchief, tied bandana style. Her onyx eyes are embedded in an eiderdown of wrinkled skin.

"My name is Roberto. You received a note to join us here." His accent is similar to Leandro's. There's no point trying to play dumb. Somehow he knows it's me.

The elderly woman steps close, inspecting me. She grips his arm with brown fingers bedecked in silver rings. Gasping, she speaks a streak in a language I don't recognise, waving her hands excitedly. I think I hear my name. The man pats her bangled wrist as if to reassure her, responding in the same dialect.

"Is she Putrika?" I ask.

"Yes, please allow me to introduce." He gestures to her. "Putrika does not speak English, so I am to translate for her."

She's staring at me as if through a telescope.

"Is this concerning my birth parents?" My question sounds faint and flat, the complete opposite of the spark that ignites in my throat. I ought to flee the scene, but I stay to hear what she knows or thinks she knows. I couldn't run if I tried. Some connection with this woman has me rooted to the spot.

Roberto speaks to her, and she replies with a flap of jabber and another flurry of fingers. "She says, in time she will inform you."

Questions explode in my head, but all I manage to squeak out is, "Did she write the note?"

"No, I wrote it for her."

"How did you get into my building to deliver it?"

"I did not go in. I rang the buzzer, but no answer. A man in the lobby offered to deliver it."

The woman wags her head like a bobblehead doll. Then she flashes me a gold-tooth smile, transforming her face. Despite my doubts, I grin back.

"Why did you ask to meet here?"

"This place is near where you live. Is not too crowded. Putrika detests crowds and prefers the out of doors."

"What did she say? I thought I heard her mention my name, but it sounded like Hally, not Halca. Only my dad calls me Hally."

"No, she said Kali. She said, 'It is Kali.' Putrika says you look just as your mother did."

A tremor whips through me. "She knows who my mother is?" How can this woman assume she knows my life story with a single look? Plus, she's not asked me a single question, and that's bizarre. She's old, but her eyes are bright, not rheumy with age. Still, I wonder how keen her eyesight is. She claims to know my natural mother, but is she dead or alive? Why isn't she here? Ah, but maybe she is.

"Is my mother here, in Vancouver?" Oh God, has she been here all along?

Roberto repeats the question in their strange tongue. She shakes her head and blurts out a stream of impassioned dialogue tagged with more theatrical hand gestures. When she's finished, he turns his attention back to me. "No, she is not here. She also says your mother is unaware of this meeting. Putrika asks me to tell you, your *mamá* searched for years to find you but had to stop, because too many times, ruined hopes stabbed her in the heart." Roberto taps his knuckles on the lapel of his jacket. "But Putrika could not give up. She always believed she would find you. Then a month ago, a nephew told her of your Mr Vanderburg. *Comprende?* You were stolen from your parents in 1979 at two months of age."

I squinch. This story is insane.

"Then, she's wrong. I can't be this Kali she's looking for." Why would Henrik Vanderburg send these people to me? My excitement fizzles, but I'm relieved too. I take the first deep, even breath I've had in hours.

But I owe them an explanation. "It's true. I was born in 1979, and the details of my history are sketchy, but I do know this. No one stole me. Someone abandoned me at a train station in Roosendaal en Nispen, in the Netherlands." This whole affair feels like a waste of time. Putrika doesn't speak English, and the alleged mother probably doesn't either. Henrik could have told them anything, or the facts didn't translate well. "I'm sorry. Mr Vanderburg gave her some misinformation."

He translates this, and she becomes agitated and lets out another torrent of words. I only catch, "No, no."

Roberto speaks again. "She says there is no mix-up. She has located you after all these years, and now she will rush home to tell your mother. Then, when your mother digests the news, you will meet."

I search the woman's face. She seems convinced her story is true. Could it be? My breathing goes erratic again. I have no idea who abandoned me at that train station. What if, after taking me, a baby thief changed his or her mind and dumped me off?

"Where is home? Holland?"

"They live in Buenos Aires."

"Buenos Aires? That's in South America, isn't it?" One things for sure—I'm not from South America.

"Yes, far from here, in Argentina."

"Well, I can't go there." Geography was never my strong suit, so I'm not sure where Argentina is, but one thing is certain. I'm broke and cannot afford a trip to Vancouver Island, let alone South America. Pressing the side of my neck, I will my pulse to slow. "I don't have the money to travel." If they're conning me, the charade's over.

Another conversation fires up between Roberto and Putrika. "If money is the only problem, do not worry," he says. "She will pay for the transportation, but first she must speak to your mother and prepare her."

"Why does she need to do that? If she's sure who my mother is, and money's no issue, then why wait?"

"She says you will understand later."

As if to cement the deal, Putrika steps forward and draws me into a hug. She smells of sweet pipe tobacco, the kind Dad used to smoke. Surprisingly, I hug her back. She lets go first. Then she takes my hand with both of hers, pumps it furiously several times and pats it. Her hands feel warm, and her gold teeth flash in the afternoon sun.

"We will contact you." The man takes her elbow and leads her away.

They've only taken a few steps when Putrika turns and scuttles back. This time she grabs my hands and squeezes with a force I can't believe.

She pauses and looks into my eyes as if she's found a trajectory into my brain. Then her face crumples. She turns again and shuffles off. The translator touches her back as if to steady her, and they tramp up the sandy beach together. Again she stops and I wonder if she'll return for one more hug and handshake. Instead she pulls out a small pipe, stuffs it, strikes a match to light it, and waves.

I watch the pair walk away with a scary sensation I've side-stepped the vortex of a storm, but there's a dust devil or two lurking on the horizon.

Dear Erin,

I have just had the oddest experience. Remember the detective of genealogy I told you I hired? He wrote claiming he's found out something on my birth parents. As you know, I have no interest beyond my medical history, so it pissed me off when he forwarded my contact information on to a third party. This third party requested a meeting. I had decided to pass, but curiosity got the better of me. So, I've just met the weirdest old lady and her absurd translator. She's from South America, and doesn't speak a word of English. The encounter was like a scene from a B movie. The woman claimed to know my birth mother, but held back the details. It's got to be a scam, and I won't let them take me for a fool. As Mother always says, 'If it sounds too strange to be true, it is too strange to be true.'

It's best to put the meeting out of my mind and avoid further contact. I've more important things to stress over anyway—like finding a guy to solve the virginity issue.

Love forever,

Hally

Part Four

Bar Knave

Bar Knave is a newer place on Granville Street, with sleek black windows and a metal-railed entrance. It's not my kind of hangout. At nine-thirty, the band will go on stage. Leandro asked me to meet him at seven, but when I park the car, I'm already two hours late. My head's still twisted from meeting Putrika, but this can't wait. I cannot keep Leandro's cash.

It seems impossible it's only been one day since the musicians returned from Cache Creek, one day since I last saw Leandro, one day since I shamefully threw myself at him. This'll be a quick visit. I'll return his money and move on.

I lock the car and proceed to the entrance. In a ticket booth, inside the door, a bald guy sits bent over a newspaper.

"Fifteen dollar cover." He speaks first and then glances up at me. In his black shirt and white bow tie, he embodies the arrogance of the place.

"I'm not staying."

Resting his chin on his hand, he inspects me with slitted eyes.

"I'm friends with the band."

He blinks twice and resumes reading. "Okay."

Side-stepping around the corner, I peek into the room.

I've only been here once before, but it's just how I remember it, complete with pretentious new-age clientele. The glass tables are agleam, many still empty. A bartender stands at ease behind the club's signature onyx countertop that's lit from below and glows blue. I catch a whiff of scent—a blend of floral and lime. Electroacoustic music plays in the background, and I wonder how the audience will take to Leandro's band. On my one-and-only earlier visit to this club, a DJ played a weird mix of rap and African hip-hop.

I spot Mendez first. He's near the stage, balancing one haunch on a stool. Adan's white-whiskered face flickers ghostly in the platform footlights as he twiddles with an amplifier knob, ear bent to the speaker. At a nearby table, Felipo lifts a pint of beer. Then he laughs, his eye on something across the room.

I follow his gaze to see Leandro leaning against a column, chatting with three nubile young women. With his fedora and

Moorish profile he fits right in here, a handsome coyote who's paused to sniff the air.

A slinky blonde reaches up and pats his hand. She's decked out in a pumpkin tank top that barely covers her bulbous breasts. Implants, no doubt. Beside her, a girl with an icy platinum updo, fingers her studded dog collar. The third, a brunette, fusses with a fuchsia, mini-length ballerina skirt.

I'm not dressed for this place. Mother's endless tirade comes to mind, 'If you insist on that long hairstyle, wear it up. Try to look sophisticated.'

Maybe she has a point. My hair is wild in all directions. This colourful scarf, swishy skirt, and sandals are not the uniform here. Unlike Leandro, I don't blend in. There's no coyote in me. I'm more like an African hedgehog in a snowstorm.

Leandro hasn't noticed me. He pulls out a chair and sits with them. I can't hear a word, but he's waving his hands, enjoying an enthusiastic chat with these tarts. How could he? I refuse to go over there. But I need to return his money, so I have to stay. I head toward Felipo and Mendez.

Felipo stands, hugs me and with a burble of laughter says, "Our *Roma* orphan."

"*Hola,* Hally." Mendez tucks one fist under his third chin and surveys the scene across the room. Squeals erupt from the table of girls. He grins and points. "Our Leandro is *muy guapo,* is he not? The young women they nose around him, like children to a *clavel* blossom."

Adan jumps off the stage. "Ah, but mature women with

excellent taste, they love me best." He beams and strokes his well-groomed white beard.

It strikes me they're used to this attention. It's a game to them.

"Where's Eldora?" I take a seat across from Mendez. "Didn't she come tonight?"

"She has throat pain and stays home to rest." Adan ruffles my hair, reminding me of how un-chic it is.

He winks. "Of course, when Eldora enters a room, the other women disappear. She has *Romany* beauty as you do too. A *gadjè chica,* beside you or beside her—no contest." Then he jumps back on stage, grabs the microphone and taps it twice. It makes a hollow pop and then he whispers, "Leandro, you are wanted."

Leandro glances over, grins at me, and shoots to his feet. The girls eyeball him as he strides across the floor. He pulls me up from the chair and kisses both cheeks. "Ah, Hally, *encantadora*. At last, you come." Then he drapes an arm over my shoulders and leads me to a quiet spot beside the stage.

All thoughts of leaving flee my head. I want to stay in the crook of his arm for eternity. He touches my cheek, looks into my eyes, and takes my hand. A zing skitters up my arm.

I step back and draw a deep belly breath. "Adan told me Eldora isn't here because she's sick."

"Yes, some nights she stays home. To sit and watch, it makes her sad." His expression turns sombre, but he speaks with a warm tone. "At home in Spain, at the *Zambra,* she was the *artistá famosa*. Since we come here, she performs not so often, but misses it. This is her curse—the music, it seizes her soul. Is like that with us." He lets go of my hand and presses his palm to his chest. "But too, is the throat malady. Adan asks her to use her voice not so much."

"Doesn't she worry about Adan on his own? He claims all the beautiful women love him."

"*Si*, they do. They adore his *sabiduría*—they sense how wise he is and see he has the joy of youth in old age." He shoots Adan a devoted smile.

This respect for Adan moves me. "He's not that old, is he?"

"His seventieth year has passed."

"Wow, I would never have dreamed he was that age. Do the women who flirt with him, ever tempt him to stray? They must be hard to resist."

Leandro's eyes flash and a strand of dark hair falls across his cheek. "Adan? Never—is not our way. For *Roma people*, love between a man and wife is different from the *gadjè*. Our love is loyal to the maximum. A *Romany* woman comes to her husband *lacha y trupos*, a virgin, and with him she stays for life."

"Always?"

"Yes, always, for us who keep with traditional ways." Leandro pats his chest.

So, that's why he doesn't think it's odd I'm a virgin. This soothes me, but when he moves sideways and his shirt opens, I yearn with every cell in my body to remedy that situation.

As we stand listening to rap music droning from the speaker overhead, I pour out the story of hiring the detective, the rendezvous with Putrika and her suggestion I go to Buenos

Aires to meet my natural mother. I tell him only what she said, not my take on it. I'm not sure yet how I feel.

Leandro squeezes my hand when I've finished. "This woman, you do not believe her?"

"She took one look at me and claimed to know everything about me. She didn't even ask questions. It was eerie." My head throbs.

"I see you once and know you are *Romany*. The old woman, is *Romany* too?"

"I didn't ask. She could be."

"So, will you go?"

"No, I can't afford it, and I told her. Then she promised to pay for my travel or bring her here—the woman she claims is my birth mother. I expect it's a scam."

Leandro frowns. "Visiting Buenos Aires is not a good idea. I have been there."

"I've heard it's an amazing city."

"*Si,* but can be dangerous too, and you're right. This smells a little like the fish." He has a puzzled expression. Several minutes slip by in silence, and then he claps his hands. "But, if you want this trip, I will pay."

"No, I can't take your money." I reach in my purse and pass him the cash he left in my room. "I have to return this, too."

Leandro makes a fist and frowns at the bills. "Why do you give it back?"

"My dad gave me enough for rent, so I'm okay now." I pry open his fingers and force him to take it. "And there's another reason I can't go to Buenos Aires. I have no passport." But as these words leave my mouth, I see myself walking into the passport office.

He tucks the money into his pant's pocket.

"I should go home." I touch his arm.

"You will not stay?" Leandro slants his head to one side with an exaggerated grimace.

"It's been a long day, and I'm exhausted." My mind skips past everything that's happened in the past few days—Dad on Granville Island, then Putrika, and now this nightclub. What I need is peace and quiet.

"Is early. Please." He takes off his hat and plants it over his heart. "*For poco tiempo*? Adan too, because if you go, it makes him sad."

I didn't enjoy Club Knave the last time I was here. But Leandro seems so keen to have me, and instinct urges me to stay.

I nod. "Okay." At least I know the music will be great.

During our conversation, the room has erupted with patrons. The ticket booth guy strides onto the dance floor. He stands, monitoring the action, hands behind his back, flexing his beefy biceps, his white bow tie glowing under the fluorescent lights.

I check on the flirty girls. A group of college kids now occupy their seats. I experience a moment of relief, but then glance to the band's table and see they've joined Felipo. Obviously flirting, he howls with laughter. On stage, Mendez balances an accordion on his ball-shaped belly, and Adan is tightening the bow of his fiddle. Tune-up chords resound over the voices and laughter.

"Come. The music starts soon." Leandro takes my elbow,

zigzags me through the tables, and parks me next to Felipo.

"You've come back." The busty blonde peers up at Leandro, batting her mascara-laden eyelashes.

"Yes, and now we play." Leandro tugs on Felipo's arm, leading him to the stage. Felipo walks backward, ogling the girl's breasts.

Cornered at the same table with these bimbos, who haven't even acknowledged my existence, I wish I'd stayed firm on my decision to leave. But it could be worse. I'm not truly with them. All I see is the backs of their heads bobbing atop bare shoulders.

A fiery gypsy tune erupts. Tired as I am, it's a tonic, and my muscles quiver. But I will not dance alone and give these hussies a chance to ridicule me.

A skinny kid with wire-rimmed glasses approaches our table and asks the busty chick to dance. She dismisses him with a snotty expression and a head shake. He shrinks to a pretzel.

Minutes later, the three girls sashay onto the already crowded dance floor. They push through to the front and gyrate, facing the musicians, not an ounce of rhythm between them. The song has a rapid beat but the blonde swirls her hips like a belly dancer, stargazing at Leandro. Between tunes, she leans against the stage and crooks her finger. When he squats and laughs at something she says, bile rises in my throat. I burst from my chair. This tart will not occupy one more second of his attention.

The snubbed pretzel boy is sitting two tables away. I march over and pull him out of his seat.

I can instantly tell this young guy knows how to dance. He spins, dips, and twirls me under light but confident gestures as we whirl toward the stage.

When we're beside the girls, I turn to face Leandro. He's watching me, and only me. Adan launches a violin solo. Leandro does a quasi tap-dance next to his upright bass. He winks and blows me a kiss. The blonde notices, goes rigid, and impales me with a look of disdain.

I stay up dancing with my young guy until the first set ends. When the music stops and our faces are slick with sweat, I kiss him, *Romany* style, once on each cheek. He grins as if he's pulled off a double backflip on his skateboard. We return to our seats.

"Like a *flamenco* star you dance," Leandro says when he joins me.

While I was on the dance floor, the girls collected their stuff and decamped.

"I have to leave." I slump in the chair. The day, the dancing, I'm exhausted.

Leandro doesn't argue this time. After farewell hugs from Adan, Mendez, and Felipo, he walks me to my car, promises to call tomorrow, and kisses me until my spine dissolves into the pavement. That kiss cements it, and I realise that whatever he wants, I'll never be able to say no to this man.

Duende

Dearest dear, dear, Erin,

My mindset has flipped 180 degrees since I last wrote. I've seen Leandro, the gypsy musician, again and changed my mind once more. He is absolutely the one I want to take my virginity, regardless of how long it takes. If you could only meet him, you'd understand.

I have also rethought the episode with the weird lady at the Maritime Museum. Her name is Putrika, and there's every sign that, like Leandro, she's a gypsy. She's not given me many details, other than she knows who my birth mother is, but has promised more information soon. Still, it's likely a scam, and if so I'll accept that, but I do want facts. Yes, you were right all along. I am dying to learn about my natural parents. It might be a disaster, but I need to know.

On the work front, nothing has changed. I'm still unemployed. I've applied for EI, and because the business sold and Ulla laid me off, I qualify. I'll have money coming in again soon, so I can relax and look for an interesting job. I may even have a proper career one day.

Oh, and I almost forgot. Putrika says my birth mother lives in Argentina, and I might need to go there to meet her. So today, I'm heading downtown to pick up a passport application.

Love you and miss you,

Hally

Outside my apartment, I pat the hood of my car, warmed by the sun. "We may not have to part company after all, old friend." On my Record of Employment, which arrived two days ago, Ulla declared me as *'laid off.'* This was kinder than I expected after shouting, "I quit" that day. Maybe retirement has softened her. But I bet Mother doesn't know. If it were up to her, it would've read, *'left without notice'* and they'd reject my application for sure. So, the stars seem aligned for officialdom, and I'm off to the passport office. After meeting with Putrika, I printed the form, filled it in, and then obtained the required signatories. Now I just need to file the application.

I'm thirty-three years old and have never travelled. After graduation I considered going to Europe, but went to work in Ulla's store instead. Hell, I've never been farther than Abbotsford, but in a couple of months, there'll be nowhere I can't go. A passport will open my world.

I climb in and drive off. Traffic is light and I sail over the Burrard Bridge, squinting into the sunshine. The sky is the same level blue as the ocean. Downtown, I find a parking spot, and start out on foot. I stop at a closet-size shop advertising "Five Minute Passport Photos." It takes ten minutes, not five, but straight from there, I head to Sinclair Centre.

A friendly security officer, posted by the elevator, assures me that they process passports within six to eight weeks. It seems a long time, but I have no immediate plans. When I think about a trip to Buenos Aires, my heart beats like a bongo drum. Leandro insists it's dangerous, so he'll just have to go with me.

There's a long wait upstairs at the Passport office, but I'm given a number, grab a seat, and pick up a copy of *Travel Digest*. There's an article on South American hot spots. Buenos Aires is second on the list after Rio de Janeiro. The piece suggests that if you want to really experience Argentina's local colour, you must brush up on your Spanish.

I spring from the chair when my number pops up on the digital readout. A woman behind the wicket takes the application form and checks my ID.

Once outside again, I mull over the Spanish issue. After twenty minutes with Putrika, I had a colossal headache from fixating on her foreign speech. What if nobody in Buenos Aires speaks English?

It's clear what needs doing. I jump in the car and head for Chapters at Broadway and Granville. On the second floor, I find two Spanish courses on CD. One promises to guide me through basic conversational phrases and the other proclaims I can "Learn Spanish in Song."

On the way home, I daydream about Leandro. He's next to me in bed. I hug the pillow while singing a song to him in Spanish. He smiles, touches my cheek, ever so lightly, and gathers me into his arms.

A light's blinking on the answering machine when I step into my suite. I push play. It's Leandro's voice. "Guess what? No work tomorrow. Bar Knave has paid a bonus and Eldora plans a celebration. At five o'clock I will come for you."

Yes, yes, yes! I'd wave streamers if I had them.

I settle to the computer with a bag of chips and "Conversational Spanish." The first exercise reminds me I have no facility for learning languages. It's all gibberish. I eject the disc and try "Learn Spanish in Song."

The lyrics appear, someone sings the line and then the translation comes up. This is more like it. By seven that evening, I'm cross-legged on the bed, singing full-throated.

En la tienda

En la esquina

Se vende mucho.

(In the store... on the corner... much is sold)

Es verdad

No es muy barato

Es verdad...

(It's true... it's not very cheap... it's true)

The next afternoon Leandro picks me up, and we drive to the campground party. As the truck rumbles through Stanley Park, I study him. His hair is askew. He's slouched forward, one hand on the steering wheel, left arm crooked out the window, carefree and confident, a man at ease in his skin.

"So, you don't play tonight. Is the job at Bar Knave finished?"

"They have asked for us again next month. We have no gigs booked until then." Leandro grins and tucks a strand of his hair behind one ear. "This means I will have time together with you."

It doesn't seem to bother him, not knowing when he'll work again.

"You'll be okay without wages for that long?" A week ago, my joblessness had triggered a spurt of acid in my throat and a non-stop echo of Mother's rants on financial insecurity. I'm so relieved to have EI money coming in soon.

"Was a good bonus from Bar Knave. Now we make a *fiesta*. For tomorrow, we worry not so much." He takes his eyes off the road long enough to toss me a delighted grin.

I wish I could live more in the moment like he does.

I gaze at the pointed peaks of the North Shore Mountains resting golden-black against a blue-blue sky and hum a simple tune from the "Learn Spanish in Song" CD.

Last night, the lyrics played over and over in my brain as I fell asleep, but this morning my throat was sore. I searched the internet and discovered it's important to warm up your vocal cords before singing. After writing out the steps, I did breathing exercises and then tongue trills and scales, shoulders low, chest relaxed with one hand on my diaphragm. What a difference it made when I practised an actual song. Anything seems possible today, even learning a new language. *Es verdad.* My skull still vibrates with the sound. *Es verdad,* it's the truth.

Leandro slaps his knee in time to some internal music. "Tonight will be a party *bueno,* because Eldora's *tío* from England is here."

"Is that her uncle?"

"*Si,* the brother of her *tia,* her aunt." He gives me one thumb up. "You pick up a little Spanish."

"Not much, but I want to learn."

"His name is Vandlo. Athalia, his daughter, and her husband arrive with him. She was only a *niña* when last I saw her. Now, she is married."

We drive over the bridge and then turn under it. As we near the campsite, I clasp my hands in my lap, an attempt to stop them trembling. Then I scold myself for being too skittish, because there's nothing to worry about. Eldora and Adan invited me back so they must approve of me. What's the worse that could happen? They'll chatter on and on in Spanish or *Romany* and ignore me. I'm getting used to that. With any luck, I'll soon be picking up words here and there.

We roll through the campground entrance. "The visitors, are they musicians too?"

"No, Vandlo has business with horses, at the race track, I think." He winks at me. "Athalia's husband helps him. I know you will like them. They are *Romany*."

"Are they from Spain too?"

"No, from England, but of the blood. For us, Spanish or English, it matters not. We are one people."

He brakes to a stop just inside the gate of the campground. "We park here when it's busy." The site is full of RVs and tents tonight.

As we stride toward the bus, an elixir of wood smoke and barbecued meat drifts our way. Felipo is crouched by the fire pit, turning a haunch of pork on a metal grate. Beside him, Mendez sits wedged into a wooden arm chair.

The gypsy camp has the atmosphere of a street market this afternoon. Pots and pans under the awning chink festively in the slight breeze. A long table, draped with an electric blue cloth, hosts bowls of salads and plates of tapas. Janine and Scoop are arranging platters of food.

Eldora's zodiac rug is out on the grass where three people sit cross-legged in the sun. An older man, with a Frank Sinatra face, wears his pelt of black hair slicked into a ponytail. Beside him, a guy with ginger hair and milky skin sits next to a dark-skinned, dark-haired girl. I get up on tiptoes and whisper in Leandro's ear. "The redhead, he doesn't look *Romany*."

"No, he is Irish. Is the reason they come here." Leandro ruffles my hair and plants a light peck on my cheek. I'm confused by his answer, but pleased with the kiss.

Before I can question further, Eldora steps down from the bus, followed by Adan. They pause for a moment and then glide toward us. Eldora faces her husband and points to the back of the Greyhound. "Time to get the wine." Adan is wearing a holly-red tunic tonight. A gold chain on his wrist sparks off sunlight as he hurries to fetch the wine.

Eldora's full length dress trails in the grass. "Hally, come and meet my *tío*. All the way from England he comes."

Taking my elbow, she leads me to them.

Eldora's uncle springs off the carpet and extends both hands. *"Sastipe. Katar aves?"*

He holds onto my fingers and shakes and shakes, grinning,

with mischief in his smile. Eldora said he came from England. I'm not sure why he's speaking Spanish. Maybe it's because I'm with Leandro.

"I'm sorry, but I don't speak Spanish." I pray it won't be long before I do.

Eldora throws her head back and laughs. "Vandlo doesn't either, Hally. He spoke to you in *Romany*, and asks where you're from."

Vandlo peers at me. "Is it true that you don't know our language?" His Cockney accent surprises me. "It's a shame that. Too many of our young'uns don't these days."

Leandro comes up behind me, places a hand on each of my shoulders, and whispers into my ear. "Now, *comprendes*, this proves it beyond any argument. Vandlo sees it, so was I not right? When you're of the blood, we can tell." He gives me a squeeze. "Hally has just discovered she is *Roma*."

The man's forehead wrinkles.

I explain. "I was born in Holland, but I've lived here most of my life."

"Well, blimey, that sorts it. There's not many of us, this side of the pond, to pass along our tongue."

Adan returns with the wine and before long, the early evening air rings with excited chatter. Felipo carves steaming slices of pork at one end of the table. Eldora dishes up salads and Janine doles out full plates. Each salad is a riot of colour—chickpeas, peppers, and carrot sticks bursting out of the bowls. The meat gives off a smoky, spicy aroma.

As we sit, circled around the fire, I nibble at my food listening to the banter, astonished that these people have welcomed me into their lives. The Irish guy, introduced as Ian, remains aside from the group, gazing morosely at a mound of potato salad on his plate. My heart goes out to him. He's awkward here, a foreigner, and I should feel the same, but I don't. I marvel at how relaxed I am.

"In a month, it'll be water under the bridge," Vandlo says. "Then, it's home we'll go, right sonny?" He reaches to wiggle his son-in-law's ear.

"Meanwhile, we're having a proper honeymoon." Athalia cuddles up to her young husband.

I lean into Leandro and whisper, "What does he mean, water under the bridge?"

"Ah, Athalia fell in love with a *gadjè*." Leandro slaps Ian on the back. "Sometimes, who we love, is no way to control, *si*?" He flashes Athalia one of his devastating grins. "I bet your *mamá* had a nice *Roma* boy picked out for you."

"Her *daj* is stubborn as a tree." Vandlo raps his temple with one fist. "But she'll miss us by now and forget all this nonsense once we're home."

Leandro turns to me. "Is not so ordinary for us to marry someone from outside. Only a few years ago, Athalia would be banished from our people forever. Today we are more tolerant."

He raises one eyebrow, soliciting agreement from the others, who nod.

"Of course, first there must be a show of anger, and the couple goes away. After a month or two the family forgive. Not like when the tables turn." His voice grates as he says this, and the calm expression dissolves. "If a white princess loves a *Roma,* the rich *gadjè,* they never forgive." His neck cords pulse.

I don't know what to say.

Eldora leans over and puts one arm around him. "Was a bad time for you."

Then she looks at me. "Long ago, at home in Spain, Leandro fell in love, but they were both *chicni,* very young. She was not of our blood and her father worked in the government. The *politicos* hate the *Roma.* For Leandro to stay in Andalusia becomes unhealthy."

"That's awful. What happened?"

"They forced her to marry an old man." Leandro's tone is harsh. "She would not go against the father's wishes."

No one says another word for several uncomfortable moments. This reminds me of how little I understand these people and their customs. So why is it I'm so drawn to them?

Leandro crosses his arms in front and stares straight ahead. "Is no matter now. Was many years ago."

Adan jumps up and scurries to the bus. Minutes later, gypsy music blasts from a pair of speakers, and a party mood takes over. Eldora's uncle leaps to his feet. He's a wiry man with shining ebony boots to match his pitch-black hair. He vaults across the grounds to the side of the office, returns with a sheet of plywood, and tips it over next to the rug. It falls with a thump in a cloud of dust. Then he hops onto it and begins a foot-flying dance, clapping his hands above his head, heels drumming the wood.

One by one, each man takes a turn. Even Mendez shows surprising agility. His beach-ball belly rolls and drops with every stomp. At the end of his performance, he hurdles into the air and lands with a smash. The plywood cracks. A star-shaped fissure fans out from the middle of the board and everyone laughs, Mendez the loudest.

When Leandro takes the impromptu stage, he sidesteps until he's in front of me. Then he gyrates in a way that makes me gasp. Hoots of hilarity follow. The music stops and his arms V up in a trapeze artist pose. Then he bends, reaches for my hands, and pulls me to my feet.

A new song begins. Leandro lifts me, twirls and sets me down. He claps, stamps, and leads me into the dance. I've tried *flamenco* before, but never like this. His arm is an extension of my arm. We're in perfect sync. When he dips me back, my hair grazes the floor and my hips float up to brush his. He spins me, and my body is on fire, ablaze in the whorl of this hypnotic music.

When the song finishes, I collapse against him. His shirt is sweat-drenched, and I fight an urge to lift it and stroke his bare, slick skin.

He takes my hand and we bow. Then standing side-by-side, Leandro announces, out of breath, "I'm in not such good shape for this." Whoops erupt.

Adan disappears into the bus. The tune changes and with it, everyone's mood again, from jubilance to seriousness. A woman's voice vibrates from the speakers. I've never heard such tone, a rich sea drone, an electrified fish of sound. I feel the song as much as hear it, flowing deep in the pit of my gut. Leandro closes his eyes.

I touch Eldora's arm. "Who is that singing?"

"Is Kopana, the queen *artistá* of our people. Is passionate, *Si*?"

I shiver. "It's astounding."

"What you experience, we call it *duende*." Eldora clutches her throat.

Leandro tilts his head to the music. "*Duende* is hard to explain. Is bigger than the heart of a song. The musical soul, the *alma musical*, rips out of the singer, and with all life's breath, Kopana gives us her song."

Eldora reaches out to squeeze my hand. "Do you know of Federico Garcia Lorca—our famous Spanish poet?"

"You've mentioned him before." I add that name to the list in my head. I'll read his poems one day, and in Spanish too.

Eldora closes her eyes. "He wrote, 'there are no maps nor disciplines to help us find the *duende*. We only know that he burns the blood like a poultice of broken glass'..."

No one speaks again until the singing stops.

When another song begins, a happier tune, Eldora turns and says, "Did I tell you the story, that one time I met Kopana?"

Leandro cups his chin in his hand and leans forward. "Hally has not heard it."

"Yes, years before we lost her, when she was a child and not so famous." Eldora gazes off. "Was in London after a performance.

I was a young girl living with my *tia*. Kopana was from *Málaga*. She asked me where was my home? I told her Andalusia. She said it was near to her home in the south of Spain, but she had many questions, 'Did I live in a cave? Did I perform at the *Zambra*?'"

"Is she dead?" The thought saddens me.

"No, we choose to believe, not dead. One day, poof, just like that, she vanishes."

"What happened?"

Leandro fingers his gold ring. "Some think a jealous *gadjè* killed her."

"I prefer the idea others say." Eldora leans forward. "That her money she keeps safe in her caravan. That she packs up her possessions and runs away to a quiet life." Eldora crosses her arms, as if shivering. "After a concert in Berlin she was to visit the Caves. It was her last performance before she disappeared. Do you remember, Leandro? You were only *un niño*."

"Yes, a little. I remember the *drabarni*, the fortune teller, who came down from the upper caves to warn of her trouble."

"She was young and beautiful, like you too, Hally." Eldora pats my cheek. "I need to show you something." Then she gets up and sprints to the bus. After she's inside, the music changes again. Moments later she arrives back, holding a CD in her hand. She holds it out. "Is a present for you."

I study the woman on the CD cover. She *faces* away from the camera, an exotic creature, draped in a spectacular costume of veils, red, yellow, and purple, with one slender arm arched over her head. What presence—it's a pose of radiance and fearlessness. Minutes ago, I ached to sing like her, and I would have sacrificed my heart for the chance. Now, I'd part with my soul to have her style.

"But, it's your CD." I hand it back.

"No, no, I insist, is a gift." Eldora slips it into my purse with a smile. I lean over and hug her, and it feels natural to do it. She is bony and warm and so full of life she vibrates. The embrace should seem foreign and awkward, but feels so incredibly right.

A slow Spanish ballad flows out of the speakers. A sliver of sun glows orange on the ocean. Hushed voices hum. A teenage boy comes over and whispers something to Adan. He follows the boy to the office. A few minutes later, Adan returns, grinning and rubbing his hands together.

"A new job. On Saturna Island for two weeks." He skips toward us, throwing off sparks of excitement. "The owner of Bar Knave, he gave our name. Is a pub gig at a fancy marina. They have a campground too."

Adan's enthusiasm cannot ease the stab to my chest at the news. Leandro will be gone for two entire weeks.

Adan tweaks Eldora's chin. "Ah, *Amorcito,* just yesterday you were longing for a trip."

Eldora claps her hands. "They will pay the ferry cost too, so we can take the bus?"

"Yes, and all the passengers." Adan pinches his white beard to a point. "Vandlo, you will come, too. Is a chance to explore the spectacular island. The day following tomorrow, we leave."

"I love the islands." Eldora puts her arms around her husband's waist and twists around to look at me. "Hally, you too must join."

"Yes, come with us, *Princesa*." Leandro takes my fingers and rubs them between his warm hands.

A moment of elation overwhelms me. Then I remember my appointment on Friday. "I can't. I have a meeting at the Employment Insurance office about finding a job."

"The job, it can wait, no?" Leandro looks crestfallen.

"They'll only pay me if I'm here, in Vancouver, actively looking for work. I have to prove it."

"Then, I will hire you to come with us. You are our new booking agent, is what we'll say."

"Yes, you must join the trip." Adan slaps his leg as if it's settled.

"I'll see." These musicians live so hand-to-mouth, and I'm no booking agent. I can't take their money. Plus, there's the cash Dad gave me, and I need to pay that debt as soon as possible. I give Leandro a hug. "I'll let you know tomorrow, *bien*?"

That Spanish word, it just slid out. I enjoy a twitch of delight.

Tunnel Noise

Leandro and the band left for Saturna Island five days ago. Before they went, I called the campground. I didn't make excuses, but simply asked Janine to relay the message. I couldn't go with them. It was a practical decision. I need a job. But this morning I should be poring over the classifieds. Instead, I'm on route to the pedestrian tunnel leading to Granville Island, because I can't stop thinking about acoustics.

I have devoted most of my week to vocal exercises and learning every song on the Kopana CD. It's been a challenge too. The CD has no printed lyrics, and she sings in Spanish, so I've had to memorise the sounds, not the words. I searched for Kopana on the Internet and couldn't find one English translation for any of her songs. But I've pulled it off now and can manage all fourteen numbers from the CD. It was easier than I expected too. Something about the music has burned those tunes into my brain.

As I near the underpass, puffy clouds blot out the sunshine. It's early enough that foot traffic is light, and late enough too I hope, that the vagrants who sleep in this tunnel will have moved on to bottle collecting and whatever else they do.

Inside, there's a new exhibit of graffiti. A month ago, street artists had these tunnel walls forested with blackish evergreen trees, painted over and over in various sizes. Every few months, the city creates a fresh canvas for the artists with bombs of grey spray paint. Today, the passage has a haunted house theme, flies trapped in spider webs, a dark castle perched on a hill and streams of ghostly, faceless, flying figures. I finger the image of a ghost.

Six or seven feet in, I stand erect, place one hand on my diaphragm, shoulders low, chest relaxed and try the first line of a Kopana song;

Vestida con mantos negros...

My voice sounds no different than in my apartment, so I explore a few spots deeper inside the tunnel. Twenty feet in, the acoustics are phenomenal, and the reverberation is wicked. This is the professional sound I'm looking for. I take a deep cleansing breath and sing full on:

Vestida con mantos negros

Piensa que el mundo es chiquito

Y el corazón es inmenso...

This passionate place in the song threatens to rip my throat apart. But it's amazing. I can hit the high and low notes just as well as Kopana. The tones strut, pause, sway and cavort like a dance. As I perform, the tunnel walls dissolve into thousands of moving, visual particles that soon fade off until only sound exists.

After I sing the last line, my surroundings refocus. A couple in jogging duds, a dark-complexioned man and a twenty-something girl stand watching me. My cheeks feel the heat of a blush.

The girl steps forward. "Wow, that was intense. Man, do you have pipes." She puts out a hand. Before I have the chance to react, she presses a loonie into my palm.

"Oh, no, no." I try to give it back. "I'm not busking."

"No, you're performing," the jogger guy says. "And, what a performance. I've sat in stuffy auditoriums after paying gobs to hear singers not half as good as you. Here." He reaches into his pocket, pulls out two five-dollar bills, and hands them to me.

The dark-skinned man speaks to me in Spanish and I have to say, *"No entiendo."* Hmm, I pulled that Spanish phrase off nicely. He also slips me two fives.

When they leave, I hurtle outside and drop to the grass in the sun, still clutching the crumpled bills. I stare at my shaking hand. They actually gave me money. They liked my singing. I imagine myself onstage at the Queen E. Theatre, in front of adoring fans, accepting a Grammy award, and throwing a kiss to Leandro who is gazing up from the front row. Hmm.

A couple of giggling girls skip by and interrupt my reverie. An old woman emerges from the underpass pushing a walker. Several Japanese tourists scuttle along the sidewalk, chattering. The acoustics were perfect, so I ache to go back inside the tunnel and do it again, but shyness strikes. There are too many people here now.

Besides, I never planned to busk. I'm not even sure it's legal. I read once that you need a licence to perform on city streets. But how would they catch you? I've seen a lot of buskers, but never any busking cops. Then a thought occurs that prompts a deep inner chuckle. If Mother knew about this, she'd be mortified. I get up and head home.

The employment opportunities section of the local paper lies open on my kitchen table like a Death Notice. Most of the jobs demand two to five years of experience and specific skills. One ad reads, *Retail Sales Manager for a fashion boutique*—no company name listed. I suspect it's Mother's ad. I pick up a pen, draw an inky box around it and then black it out with crosshatching.

How would Mother react to me busking? Besides her shame at my public display, I can imagine her standing there, hands clamped over her ears. She detests all things musical. I remember watching "The Sound of Music" on tv in the 90s, and how she ranted on and on about how dreadful it was. After that she vetoed musicals. Who could hate Julie Andrews? And when I was young, if I dared to trill out a few lines of a song, she'd cut in with, "Shush, quiet. What a noisy girl."

I circle two ads in red ink that don't ask for experience. One is for a Guest Services representative at a local spa and the other a Travel Sales Consultant in a downtown office. When I phone, both positions are filled. I scribble the company names and numbers. Hopefully, this will satisfy the EI folks.

The next day at noon I'm at the entrance to the Granville

Island underpass again. Today I am prepared. I've shooed away shyness and garbed out in my best gypsy effort, complete with a pair of hoop earrings and a spin-around skirt. I have my slouch cap in hand.

I stop at the acoustical zone, drop the cap, warm up with a few tongue trills, and then begin.

Streams of pedestrians flow by, not weekend busy, but steady. I belt out every Kopana song I know over and over. I sing and sing. Coins jingle into the knitted cap. A few bills flutter past my feet. After two or three hours I add dancing to the performance. With a snap of my fingers overhead, I twirl and the audience applauds. They love me. I've got this. I'm a true *flamenco artistá*.

On Thursday I bring in two hundred and three dollars in four hours.

On Friday morning, it doesn't seem important to show up for my EI appointment, so I return to the underpass again. In only five hours I make another two hundred dollars, all mine, all tax free.

It's Saturday afternoon, when the coins are dropping in time to a lively tune, that I hear a screech coming from the tunnel's entrance, "Halca." This interrupts the most extraordinary refrain of the set. Already, I think of them as 'sets.' I recognise Mother's voice, but don't look over that way, praying I'm wrong. I close my eyes and finish the verse. When I open them again, she's pushing through the spectators like a bully Koi after peas in the Chinese Garden pond.

Ah, Christ! I should run, but find myself rooted to the spot.

"What are you are doing?" Her voice is high pitched, squealing. She plants her hands on her hips. A man in cowboy boots steps forward to flip a bill into my hat. Mother swats his hand. "Go, get—put your money away. Find another clown show." A growl escapes her throat. Then she confronts the small audience, waving them to leave. "Off you go—all of you, go, go." The listeners back up and scurry off.

Mother turns on me. "Mrs Hammel told me she saw you. I did not believe her. Are you determined to disgrace me?" Spit flies out of her mouth. "Begging!" Her arm goes rigid and her hand jacks up to strike mode. I remember how hard she can slap and step back, slamming my shoulder against the cement wall. I wince in pain.

Mother's pale skin has flushed to vivid plum. Her blue eye is icy and the green one, an eerie shade in the dim light.

"This has nothing to do with you." I struggle to keep my voice calm, but a banshee has slipped into my throat. "I'm not begging. I'm performing."

"Nothing to do with me? My daughter, making a monkey of herself mooching for money." She's still poised to strike, but now her arm is shaking. "Performing—is this what you call it? Hat out, like a tramp, when you have a respectable job. It is everything to do with me. I'm humiliated. You are an ungrateful, wicked girl." Mother wheezes, a squealing, sucking sound and then slumps forward. She stands, eyes fixed on the ground, hands clutching her knees. Is she having a heart attack?

I step toward her. "Are you okay?"

"Godverdomme." Her curse echoes off the walls.

"Come on, let's get you outside." I stoop to pick up the money-filled hat and then lead her out, huffing and puffing. Several feet along a path, I find her a place to sit. Her face is drained of colour.

Nothing could have prepared me for this—Mother hunched on the park bench looking vulnerable and wasted. Her skin is ghostly white, and I've not noticed before how wrinkled she's getting.

"I'll walk you back to the car," I say after her breathing has returned to normal. I take her arm and help her stand. Through her thin jacket, I touch her sagging skin and flaccid muscles. A surge of pity overwhelms me.

"*Ja*, good." She resurrects to military bearing. Halfway up the path, she stops and stares at me from head to toe. "What are you wearing? A costume for the circus?" She glares with disgust at the hat of money, then grimaces. "And that makeup. Are you taking drugs? Maybe you've started selling your body too?"

"How can you be so awful?" I let go of her elbow and step away. My eyes are burning. She's a horrible, hateful old woman. How could I entertain a single sympathetic thought for her? I should have left her stranded in the tunnel, wheezing to death.

I turn and flee toward the seawall, running fast and far, past the fancy apartments, the fish dock, and the outdoor pool. I run until I'm gasping so hard, my adrenaline evaporates the tears attempting to smother me.

On Sunday, I don't sing once.

On Monday, I phone the EI office and ask to speak to the counsellor. "I'm sorry I missed the appointment. I was ill on Friday."

The woman interrupts. "You didn't need to phone, but thank you. The new owner of *Der Schwarze Koffer* Fashions called this morning and let me know you're going back to work at the dress shop, so I've put a stop on your claim. You are very lucky to get re-hired so soon."

I can't believe it. How many ways can Mother find to screw me?

After the counsellor hangs up, I press the receiver into its cradle. I bear down on that cradle and twist, imagining Mother's throat. The phone topples onto the carpet. "The meddling old bitch." I go to the closet and snatch my gypsy outfit. The city must have tons of places with great acoustics

Shoe Drawers

A week later, I park a block away from my parents' house to elude their gossipy next-door neighbour Mrs. Parker. Mother is at the shop and she can't know I'm here. I have two things to do. First, to return the cash Dad lent me. I've earned more money in the past ten days than in a month of working for Ulla. Second, I'll try to squeeze information out of him about my adoption. If I see Putrika again, I want to be armed with information.

Dad's in the garage with the door open as usual, like a photo shoot in *Popular Mechanics*. He's set his saw up on the concrete floor today, and pieces of wood lay strewn around his feet. The glass jars of nuts, bolts, and screws sit smothered in sawdust. Even the tools are coated. Intent on his project, he doesn't notice me. He's bent over what appears to be a drawer on his workbench, sanding, and humming "The Wreck of the Edmund Fitzgerald."

I've not seen Dad in the red leather shop apron since he took up inventing. He's like some quaint European woodworker out of the nineteenth century.

He turns and waves. "There you are. Just this minute, I thought of you." He tosses the piece of sandpaper on the table saw and lifts his creation. "Come, see what I made for Mother." He flashes me a prizewinner smile.

As I get close, the aromatic sawdust triggers a sneeze, but I sidle up to the workbench to get a better look. The drawer is only five inches deep, but at least three feet wide. "What are you building? An enormous dresser?"

"No, come, see." He puts one finger to his lips, tucks the framework under his arm and I follow him to the front door of the house. "But, you must not mention to your mother. I want a surprise for her birthday."

"Your secret is safe with me." My stomach jerks. I was trying to put Mother's birthday out of my mind. It's less than a week away. "You realise, Mother and I aren't speaking."

He shoots me a sad smile. "Yes, she told me. Give her time."

I'd love to explain that if I never hear her voice again, it'll suit me fine, but I don't want to spoil his mood. I've had more peace in the past two weeks than the past thirty years, so I've decided I'll have nothing to do with her in the future. Dad will get used to that in time.

Dad pulls a wooden wedge from the back pocket of his jeans, props open the door of the house and points at the bottom step. "Look, do you see something unusual?"

I squint. "No." The stairs gleam as usual, a polished, treacherous oak platform I once had to navigate in slippery woollen socks.

"Ah, but watch." His eyebrows shoot up. He drops to his hands and knees on the interior landing, on the beige mat with *Welkom* imprinted in black. With one finger raised, he says, "Your mother, she hates the piles of shoes by the door."

"Yes, I remember." Every afternoon when I came in from school, the first words Mother shrieked were, 'Pick up your shoes. Put them away.' There was hell to pay too if a crumb of dirt dropped off a shoe onto the immaculate oak stairs *en route* to the closet above.

Dad takes a putty knife out of his apron, wedges it between the vertical and horizontal joints of the step and the riser panel pops out.

I squat and peer into the gap above the tread of the stair. He's attached fresh strips of wood to each side.

He picks up the drawer and slides it into the step. "For shoes." It glides with ease as he pushes it in and out twice. "When the varnish is on, you will not notice it. I plan to add a very thin handle here." He runs one finger under the top lip. "This too, will be almost invisible."

"That's clever, Dad."

He beams up at me. "I made three. They will go here, here and here." He points to the bottom three stairs. "Fifteen pairs of shoes, five for each compartment. I kept this a secret. She has not even noticed the work." He chuckles, pops the original riser back into place, retrieves the putty knife and stands, holding his invention. "Do you want coffee?"

"No, I don't think so." I dig in my purse, pull out the brown paper bag and hand it to him.

"Will we feed the birds?" He winks and takes the bag.

"No, I'm paying you back. That's everything I owe you, plus interest."

"This money was a gift." He tries to return it.

I hide my hands behind me. "No, no, I have enough cash and I've paid the rent."

The bag crumples in his hand. The last time I saw him look so strained was in high school; when the stray cat he fed secretly in his workshop, the one he named Brinker, came down with distemper. "Don't worry, Dad. I can take care of myself. I won't starve."

"I know." He leads me back outside and into the garage.

The sawdust has settled. The Shop-Vac sits in its normal spot in the corner, plugged in and ready to go. He'll fire it up at least an hour before Mother gets home and suck up every speck of dust. Her zeal for spotlessness extends into his workshop.

He drops the bag back into my purse. "You keep this money for me. Your mother told me how you are earning wages. I suspect it is not steady. You may need to borrow again." He gives me a squeeze. I love his familiar soapy smell. "Is it safe, what you are doing?"

"I can imagine what she told you. She probably said I'm begging on street corners, but that's not true. I'm singing, and it's fabulous. There may even be a future in it." He studies my face and I see he's not convinced. "And yes, Dad, it is safe. There's always a crowd of people."

He places one hand on each of my shoulders. "I understand you don't want to continue at the dress shop. But why not work in a bank or office? You could find employment like that. Mathematics—in school you were good at figures."

"I'm still looking for a regular job." This isn't exactly honest and the words catch in my throat. But yesterday's paper is on my table at home. I just haven't opened it yet.

He nods, content with my lie.

"If mother hadn't phoned the Employment Insurance office and told them to stop my claim, I'd qualify for payments."

"What did she do?" He stares at me and cocks his head as if he hasn't heard me right. Then a vein on his temple pops up.

Another one joins it. Within moments his forehead swarms with a nest of pulsing purple veins.

Now I wish I hadn't mentioned it, but since I did, I may as well explain. "She told them I was returning to work at *Der Schwarze Koffer*. They stopped my claim."

His cheeks turn blood red. "She promised she would not interfere." His arms go rigid at his side.

I step back. I only remember seeing Dad angry once when I was eight years old. He came home early one day and found me confined to my room crying. Mother and Ulla had locked me in there and gone off shopping.

Now, in slow motion, he swivels to face the workbench. His face contorts in a maelstrom of rage as he hefts the drawer he was working on up over his head. It hovers there, mid-air, suspended for what feels like minutes. His arms are stiff, straight-up, and his body vibrating. His biceps twitch. A beam of sunshine ignites his pale hair. Motes of sawdust hang suspended in a grainy aura around him.

"*Kutwijf*," he curses in Dutch. I've never heard him use that word. The drawer flies out of his hands. It hits the cement with an ear-piercing explosion and bursts into pieces. Splinters torpedo into the driveway.

Then everything goes quiet, like a muted war documentary, where Dad as the main character has just opened fire on the room. But this is my dad. He's not violent. I take a step forward, reach out and touch his arm. We stand in the open garage both staring at the cloud of dust until his shoulders slump.

"It's okay, Dad. Really, I'm fine. I'm making money. I don't need EI."

He moves his head back and forth as if doing yoga stretches for his neck.

It's a shame Dad ruined one of his creations, but I'm glad he's angry at her. He puts up with far too much. "I'll skip her birthday dinner, though. I can't see us getting through a meal together." I know Mother will throw a tantrum when she realises I'm not coming and I pity him. "Besides, I have a date Saturday." This is a blatant lie. Leandro hasn't called, and the band isn't due back until Sunday.

"*Zo,* a boyfriend?" He looks worried again. I shouldn't lie to him.

"Yes, but we're just friends."

"When were you planning to bring him to meet me?" There's a hint of tease in his voice, but it's mixed with tension.

"He's only a friend." I step close, give him a peck on the cheek. "You'll be the first to know if things get serious. I wanted to talk to you about something else though."

Dad glances around the workshop. "Ah, look at this mess." Then he bends, picks up a couple pieces of shattered wood and gently sets them on his workbench. His appears calm now, except for a tic at his jawline.

He stops tidying up and rests one boot on the bottom rung of a stool. "*Ja,* what do you want to talk about?" I can tell he'd do anything to take back the last ten minutes, so it wouldn't be fair to fire questions at him right now.

"It's nothing." Besides, he's likely told me everything he knows of my adoption. And Mother was right. It will devastate him to find out I'm searching for my birth parents. Before I tell him, we need to sit down and talk. I have to let him know it's not personal, that he's been an awesome parent, and no matter what I discover he'll always be my dad. So, today is not a great time. I have to get home, change, and hurry to catch the after-work crowd at Yaletown. Yesterday, I brought in over a hundred dollars there in under three hours.

Dad looks over at the other two drawers stacked against the wall. "There is time to make another one." He sits on the stool, hands on his knees and leans forward. "You can talk now. I will not throw any more drawers."

"No, it's not important. I've got to run—later." I hug him quick and break away. It's sad. I know he won't confront Mother over the EI claim. How could he? He'd have to admit how he found out, how he's been talking to me behind her back.

As I head to the car a few drops of rain spatter my face. But, in the distance, streaks of sunshine reflect off the high-rise condos of Yaletown.

Dear Erin,

I've not written for a while, so there's catching up to do. I applied for a passport right after my last letter and should have it by next month. However, the mystery woman, Putrika has not reappeared, and maybe won't. I'm okay with that. Life ticks on.

I'm still unemployed and still a virgin. Leandro is off working on

Saturna Island, and he's due back in a couple of days. He hasn't bothered to call in two weeks, so chances are I'll never see him again. It wouldn't surprise me if he stays on the Island. That's what gypsies do, don't they? They move on.

One thing I've not told you about is the busking. Yes, you heard me right—busking, out on the street, just me and my hat full of money. It seems people enjoy my singing, so you were right all those years ago. Remember, you were my biggest fan back then? Don't even ask me what Mother's take is on my new vocation. You can imagine.

I've made good money in the last couple of weeks busking, but I know it can't last forever. Winter is coming, and with it the rain, so I need a regular job. Plus, yesterday a cop stopped me in Yaletown and asked to see my permit. Apparently, you need to get one from City Hall before you can legally sing on the streets. I haven't applied, and I'm not sure if I will now. I'm actually going for a job in a dress shop again. This place in Yaletown needs someone, so I've picked up an application form. The thought makes me want to slit my wrists, but sometimes we all have to do unpleasant things.

Love Always,

Hally

The Naam

Blue moonlight slices through the slats of my Venetian blinds. A woman bawling in a neighbouring apartment shatters the nighttime peacefulness. I stuff the pillow over my head to muffle the squall, but it's useless. She sobs and sobs. I realise that could be me, crying my eyes out over Leandro. As I think this, tears threaten. I never intended to miss him, but I've done nothing but wait for him and miss him since we met.

It started out so simple—my virginity issue. Now I'm a mess. He's back soon and might come around, but then what? He'll leave and keep leaving and leave again. That's what gypsies do. In a way, it's for the best that Leandro's been away. When he's gone, I'm not under his spell. He's an unhealthy obsession, and I must purge him from my mind. If he comes calling, I need to run and hide.

I kick off the covers and get up.

The blinds shriek as I open them and the room floods with moonshine. On the table, where I tossed it earlier, a dress shop application form sits in a luminous pool, white as a funeral shroud.

If it wasn't three AM, I'd escape into the tunnel and sing every song I know. Instead, I pull on my gypsy skirt, throw a jean jacket over the t-shirt I wore to bed and head outside. I gulp in the cool evening air and sprint along Maple Street on route to The Naam.

The Naam is a twenty-four-hour vegetarian restaurant left over from Kitsilano's psychedelic days, a place of solitude for night-owls. It's been months since my last serious bout of insomnia. My mouth waters, anticipating the double-fudge chocolate cake, so I pick up the pace. I run full out—four blocks straight uphill until I'm sweaty and gasping for breath, and then walk the final half-block.

As I near, the cafe windows ooze warm, yellow light. I open the wooden door and step inside. Only three patrons tonight—a half-asleep hippie chick with an enormous backpack, a relic with a fuzz of white hair, who might be an escapee from the old folk's home, and a thirty-something guy in track pants reading a hardcover book.

The room has a folksy setting with antique wooden tables. The air smells of herbal tea and incense, and the new-age music soothes with its lapping water and chiming bells. On a sandwich board near the entrance, I read the inspirational quote of the day; *The best way to make your dreams come true is to wake up.* How apt.

I choose a seat by the window. A woman in her fifties, wearing a bohemian kerchief, brings me a menu. She keeps one eye on me while wiping an adjacent table.

As I thumb through the hand-written menu, my stomach growls. "I'll have coffee and the double-fudge cake. Can you bring that first, please? And then the El Topo Dragon Bowl."

The waitress looks amused. "Good for you, sweetie—dessert first. Live life for the moment." She disappears into the kitchen.

I lean across to the next table and grab a copy of the free paper, *Music Around Town*. There's a piece on Lena Horne. She died two years ago at ninety-two. 'She had a great run, the old girl,' according to the writer. I remember her song, "Stormy Weather" but I've never tried to sing it. The article suggests that the CD, *Lena Horne, Fifty Greatest Masters* offers the best compilation of her work.

This singing fetish has me gobsmacked. A month ago, the only time I sang was in the shower. Now, it's all I think about. But I am aware my vocal chords will not generate a steady income. How many artists subsist on their art? Even Leandro's band goes through anxious, lean times. Living in the moment is fine, but it's more pleasant if you're not hungry.

The waitress returns with steaming coffee and cake immersed in a pool of glossy chocolate fudge. I dig in, and it's heavenly. When I've finished that, she brings out the Dragon Bowl. The serving is bigger than I remember. Heaped on top are slivered carrots, sprouts, and beets, but my tongue recalls the chipotle peppers and I go at the dish with caution.

When my bowl is empty, I glance at the paper again, but the words don't register. My blood is surging with double-fudge, and the tune "Stormy Weather" is running over and over in my head.

It's five AM when I arrive home, flick on a lamp, get a pen and sit to fill out the dress shop employment application form. But the pen trembles in my grip, and I cannot persuade the nib to touch the paper. To hell with it.

After staring at the form for a while, I begin to fold it. I pull the top corners of the form down and marry them, forming a V. My fingers remember how to do this, where the next fold goes, and the next, and I smooth the paper flat each time, running one thumb along each seam. When it's finished, I stride to the window, lean out and cast my paper airplane off. It catches the early morning breeze, airborne for a moment, then wobbles, shudders on the downturn, and crashes into the gutter.

Yes—the last time I felt this relieved was when Mother and Ulla took off for a month to Florida.

At nine AM I head to Centaur Music and buy Lena's Master Hits CD.

At home, it doesn't take long to discover I'm no Lena Horne. No matter how hard I try, I cannot sing Lena's high notes. My voice is deeper, huskier. Then I ask myself, does it matter? No, of course not. Every artist brings an individual style to their work. Before long, I'm belting out the Lena song, varying the intonation, giving the tune a flamenco twist.

By two o'clock in the afternoon I have "Stormy Weather" memorised and start on "The Man I Love." At four o'clock, I'm drained of energy and realise I've been up for over twelve hours. I switch off the CD player on the bedside table and sink into the pillows.

The intercom bleats and wakes me with a jolt. I leap from bed and glance at the clock. It's five PM. In a flash, I remember Leandro said he'd be home today. I glimpse myself in the mirror, baggy-eyed and hair askew. The buzzer sounds again, and I don't move toward it, but stand there, watching the intercom, humming "Stormy Weather," trying to blot out the sound. It rings ten more times before it stops.

I put the CD back on and learn "Old Devil Moon."

Kali

The intercom squawks and my arm hairs quiver. When I ignored the buzzer last night, I regretted it, because I do want to see Leandro again. I rush to the hallway and snatch the handset. "Hello."

"*Hola.* Halca Visser, is this you?" The voice sounds Spanish, but it's not Leandro. I recognise the slightly stilted speech. It's Roberto, Putrika's translator. "I bring a message for you."

"Wait there. I'll come out." I head downstairs.

It's late morning and faded, not dark, but sombre, as if nature has airbrushed the sky grey. Roberto has on the same black suit he wore to the beach when he translated for Putrika. His smarmy aura unsettles me.

The sky's grey tone creeps into me, as I guess what's in the letter. Putrika must have gone back to Argentina. He's come to tell me it was an unfortunate mistake, that I'm not the one, that they've found the real girl.

He passes me a lumpy package with an envelope taped to the top. "Putrika has returned to Buenos Aires."

I knew it.

"But she notifies your mother, who sent this by courier, asking me to deliver as soon as possible."

"Is the letter in Spanish? Do you need to translate?"

"I'm not sure. I have not opened it."

After pulling it off the package, I tear open the seal, pluck the handwritten pages out, scan the first few words, and tell him, "It's in English." My fingers are shaking.

"Awe, is upsetting for you." Roberto steps forward and hugs me.

I stiffen. It's as if a water snake has slithered over my shoulders. In fact, he smells of a pet shop and must sense my disgust, because he releases me before I push him off.

Then he presses a business card into my palm. "Here, if you need help, call me." He turns and strides away.

I sit on a nearby bench to read the letter.

Dearest Kali,

My mother, Putrika, came to you. Let me tell you why. For many years we search for a child stolen from us in 1977. Long ago, my hope flew away, but Mother is certain she will find a clue. She spots the scent many times over the years, but discovers only disappointment.

We have found this child, and it's you, Kali. That is your name, the name I give you at birth.

I cannot believe that after so many years we find you. But, my mother, your grandmother, Putrika, is drabarni, *and she perceives the truth.*

Mother suggested you come to Argentina. Please no, you must not fly. We will come to you, but sorry, not by airplane. This, I try to explain later. So, by land and sea we travel.

Our driver explained to us it will take many weeks. You have questions, and we will soon answer them, but for now I send a package. In it, find a present given by your papa on the date of your birth. I send it to prove what I say is true. Before you put it on, your grandmother asks you to touch your lips to the stone, for luck.

Love you,

Mother

My chest caves in and I rip open the package. There's a photograph and a pendant on a gold chain. The stone of the necklace glints blood red. I squint at the picture. It's a Polaroid, blurry, sepia tone, but I see a much younger Putrika, same braid, same colourful garb. She holds a newborn with bright eyes and a thatch of unruly dark hair. The baby is wearing earrings. Gooseflesh bubbles up my arms. Could this be a picture of me? Dad said I had earrings when they got me. I stare at the photo, while rocking backwards and forwards on the bench.

Then I reread the letter. I've heard the word *drabarni* before. Eldora said it's *Romany* for fortune teller. So Putrika must be a gypsy. But she's from Buenos Aires, and none of this makes sense. My parents adopted me in Holland, not South America.

I clutch the gold chain in one fist, finger the gem, and it throbs. When I kiss it, heat radiates from the stone. Then I fasten the necklace behind my neck. The pendant against my chest is as warm as the summer sun or Leandro's lips.

I glance at my apartment building, and it's as if I've conjured Leandro up from my thoughts. He's in front of the lilac bush watching me—a breathtaking portrait propped on a backdrop of bloom.

"Leandro?"

"Who was that man? What did he want with you?"

"He brought a letter, and a parcel. Why didn't you let me know you were there?"

"I love to watch you." He grins, strides toward me, and sits on the bench.

"The man—he was the translator." I remind him of the old woman who claims to know my birth family.

"You told me of the woman but not a man." His eyes flash mischief, and he tweaks my chin. "What other secrets do you keep?"

I have been hiding things—my skin condition and the singing. But the singing is a white lie. One day, when I'm better at it, I will sing for him.

I pass him the letter. Leandro scans it and then nods.

"She says your name is Kali. Nice name. Is like *Sara e Kali,* a patron saint to our people."

"Why didn't you phone me?" He needs to understand how upset I've been. "I thought you'd left for good."

"Never."

"What did you expect me to think?" A squeak escapes my throat.

"Oh, my *princesa*. I am sorry not to call. Is a big reason for this." He looks miserable. His arms circle me, and sadly, I know I'll forgive him anything.

"What do you mean?" I'm squashed against his shirt blubbering. I suck in the spicy smell of him. "Is it because you don't want me to expect too much? Is it because you care for me only like a sister?"

"No, no—I am crazy in love for you, not like a sister—never a sister. The first moment I see you, I realise." He strokes the back of my head. "Was wrong, not to call, but we receive news. Terrible news, that I need to tell in person."

"What news?"

He holds me at arm's length. "Eldora is sick. The doctor, he says is cancer, in her throat." His face crumples in pain.

"God, no. Are they sure? She's so healthy." I remember how she sprinted around the seawall the day we went to Stanley Park and how she sang at the campground. "Poor Eldora. How is she?"

"Still smiling, preparing food, teasing, but the kick in Adan's foot has died." Leandro's fingers clench. "She tells us not to worry. The *medico*, he wants to give radiation treatments..."

"Oh no. When?"

"... but, Eldora says no radiation, or the other thing, chemo."

I rest my hand over his. "Can I see her?"

"Yes, of course. She asks me to bring you to a party tomorrow. Our friend Rosario closes her cafe and we celebrate."

"A party?" Why celebrate in the wake of such awful news?

"Is a going-away party. Eldora seeks a healer in Andalusia."

"She and Adan will go back then?"

"Yes, we all go." He gazes up as if he's lost in the past. I should ask him when they plan to leave, but I don't. This is what I knew would happen. It's in his nature. He'll disappear and never come back.

"I must leave now."

My body caves in on itself. I attempt a calm expression, but obviously fail.

He pats my head and says, "Only for this afternoon. Adan needs me. But tonight, can we see each other? Let's go to the beach, okay?" He takes my hand and squeezes. "Eight o'clock?"

Part Five

On the Beach

Dear Erin,

I can't believe it, but I've heard from a woman claiming to be my birth mother. It doesn't make sense, because she lives in South America, but she's sent a letter and a necklace, which has a strange alchemy and heats up when I touch it or think about it. I know that sounds crazy and maybe it's all in my head, but she claims it was a gift from my father at birth. That's the only mention of a father, so now I'm super curious. She says the old lady, Putrika, is a fortune teller who's identified me as the child kidnapped from them in 1977. The story is iffy and suggests a scam, but I cannot, for the life of me, figure out what their angle might be. They've not asked for money, or personal information, so I have to trust there's something to it. Or it could be, they're just nutters. Apparently, she is coming to Vancouver, so I guess I'll find out more then.

On the romantic front, my gypsy musician is back from Saturna Island and I'm seeing him tonight. He and the band return to Spain soon, because his aunt is ill. Didn't I tell you he'd take off? The aunt, Eldora, is the matriarch of the group. She's like a mother to Leandro, so I can't bail out with her sick, even if it will break my heart when he leaves. But he's still in town for at least a week. Wish me luck, that I won't be a virgin for long. He's picking me up in a couple of hours, so maybe tonight is the night.

Love always

Hally

As I wait for Leandro, I pace the apartment. It took me two hours in the bathroom, make-up, hair, nails, perfumed lotion—the works. Then I dressed with care in my gypsy skirt and a red top with a plunging neckline. Now I'm eyeing the buzzer, as if I can somehow will it to ring. At five to eight, it buzzes, and I rush downstairs to meet him.

I link my arm through his and say, "Let's go." He smells soapy fresh as if he too has just stepped out of the shower.

As we stroll toward the beach, we hardly speak. I sense his sadness over Eldora. He squeezes my hand and releases it.

It's dusk. Apricot clouds float above the sea line and a balmy glow tinges the landscape. People on blankets chequer the grass by Kits Beach. The air is muggy but warm. A black Lab lifts its head in slow motion, then slumps, closing its eyes. Bronze bodies frolic in the sand by a volleyball net. A bongo drum sounds in the distance, as partiers hover around picnic tables. A breeze carries the whiff of barbecue bricks.

As we stroll, I break the silence. "Our medical care in this province is excellent. Eldora should take the treatment."

"She does not trust the medicine here. She sips Carpenter's Weed tea, and this makes her feel better, but for the full cure, she needs *chuvihani* charms. No one in Vancouver can help with that."

We head away from the beach crowd, west of the swimming pool, along a dirt walking path that hugs a steep rock wall. Above us, the swank houses of Point Grey loom, but we are alone on the trail—the grate of gravel, the only sound. I think of the night Leandro rejected me, told me that his body could wait? I wonder if it's still waiting, or has it forgotten me?

His arm weighs heavily on my shoulder. "We must leave Vancouver soon. Is only one gig left here. Then we make the bus up for sale, to pay for airplane tickets."

"You're selling the bus?" I knew it. They're not coming back. He turns off the path and leads me to the same place we sat before, a private nook surrounded by bushes.

"Yes." He pats the log. "Sit here, listen. You will travel to Andalusia with us. Is what I want."

"You want me to come?" The thought of going to Europe creates a shiver of excitement, but it's mixed with terror. Does he realise I don't even know where Andalusia is? Somewhere in Spain, I guess, but I couldn't point it out on a map.

"Is *baxt,* is meant to be." He reaches up and glides his fingers over my hair. "Eldora has read your cards. She says we belong to each other." The pendant resting on my collarbone pulses with warmth.

As if he can feel it too, Leandro touches it. "What is this gem? I have never seen it. Is so hot."

"The woman who claims she's my mother sent it, along with the letter. I think she added heat from Buenos Aires too."

"A talisman." He lifts the necklace and rubs the stone on his cheek.

We sit propped against a log hidden by bushes on three sides. Now, the apricot clouds have darkened to burnt orange. The tide is out, and the breeze carries a fishy tang. Seaweed-slathered rocks decorate the coastline, and the ocean begins a gentle surge of blue-black swells.

Leandro pulls me close and feather-kisses me. He starts at my temple, then grazes my cheek, my neck, and then presses into my cleavage. With every touch of his lips, I quiver. He whispers in my ear. "You and I, we have worried away too much time. We love together now."

At once, I'm aware of nothing but the peppery spice of his hair, the taste of his mouth, and the viral tremor that's spread to my sandalled toes. I don't want him to stop, even for the minute it takes to kick off my shoes and unsnap my bra. He tries to tug my top up and over my head, and I stiffen. Even at this secluded place, he mustn't see the patches on my back.

"Wait, what if someone comes?"

Leandro re-adjusts my pullover. He slips his hand up under it. My nipples harden and my stomach muscles roil like an ocean wave.

I tremble, unbuttoning his shirt. He fingers my waistband and then lifts my skirt and slides my panties off in one fluid motion. The sand is soft and still warm from the afternoon sun. Then he kneels and guides my hand to the fly of his Levis. When his penis springs out, I gasp. This is not an ugly stump like pictures I've seen in magazines. It's a fascinating appendage, alive and taut.

He wriggles out of his jeans and lies beside me, touching and withdrawing, touching and withdrawing—repeating this over and over and over until I can't stand it anymore. I struggle to pull him on top of me.

He pushes back. "I try not to hurt you."

"Don't push me away then. That's what hurts." I grip his shoulders.

Finally, he rises above me, but then pauses, restraining himself, running his cheek along my arm, groaning. I arch and tug at him again. The sky whirls and his face swims in the stars. At last he plunges, and I gasp.

He freezes. "Do I hurt you?"

"No, no, don't stop." I am, of course, lying.

It's a razor-sharp pain, but I knew it would hurt. I squirm, and his tempo quickens. A squeak escapes my throat, but now he doesn't stop or can't stop. A pebble pierces my left hip, and I remember something Eldora said when she read the tarot cards, 'A woman's best gifts begin with suffering.' I release my mind and welcome the hurt. Delicious pain. Exquisite pain.

He shudders and falls limp to my side. "I am so sorry. *Demasiado rápido.*" He wraps his arms around me. "It has been so long."

"Don't be sorry. It was lovely, lovely, lovely." I'm not lying now. Despite the pain, I'm incredibly alive. I reach and touch the tender spot between my legs.

We lie quiet for ages, cocooned in each other's arms.

"You will love Andalusia," Leandro says, right before his breathing changes to the deep, slow pattern of sleep. It's odd, but fitting he should fall asleep out here on the sand.

I'd rather not think about Andalusia, or Eldora's illness, or anything. I jitter with energy. I reach for his hand and run one finger over the deer-soft veins above his knuckles.

After a while, I lift his wrist and ease out of his embrace. "Sleep tight."

I take a moment to enjoy the view. He's fast asleep and twisted sideways, muscled buttocks pressed clam-like into the sand. I squat and pick up his jeans and drape them over him. As I pad to the shoreline, sand works up between my toes. The sky is dark, the water black and motionless. Human voices pierce the silence, and I sniff a campfire somewhere along the beach.

My legs prickle in the icy water as I wade in up to my knees, skirt balled at my belly. Before rinsing myself, I pat the sticky blood inside my thighs. My fingers smell of the briny sea. A few stars glint on the western horizon as I splash myself clean while hum-singing a Kopana song.

"Sa me amala oro khelena

Oro khelena, dive kerena"

Leandro is still asleep when I return. I sit cross-legged and watch his face glimmer in the light of a distant street lamp. Later, I raise his arm and snuggle against him.

Fast Track

The next day Leandro lies sprawled at an angle on my bed, covers thrown off, sleeping. The midday sun streams in. Wriggled into my comforter, while listening to his deep, steady breathing, I admire every perfect inch of his tawny skin.

I slither out of the comforter, and he doesn't open his eyes. I tiptoe naked to the bathroom and glance in the mirror. The white patches on my back don't revolt me this morning. I twist, step closer, and study them. They resemble the decorative fabric in a Klimt painting. I grab my housecoat.

Everything feels different. The yellow wall in my kitchen is brighter. The red comforter is a richer crimson. Light refracts off the hallway mirror, shooting around the room, vibrant and vivacious. I turn the radio on low. "Hallelujah" is playing, and Leonard Cohen's deep, tender voice transcends the everyday world.

Curled up on the corner of the bed, I glide one toe over to touch Leandro's bare arm. He wakes, kisses my toes, tugs off my housecoat, and pulls me under the covers.

After we're both sweaty and spent, we prop ourselves against the pillows and talk, genuine talk, the kind I've always imagined true couples have.

He tells me of his home, the famous Caves of *Sacromonte* in the city of Granada, and how his people have lived there for centuries. I find out he was one of the last *Roma* born in a cave, a dwelling built into the side of the mountain. He says the caves are nightclubs now, a place where they perform flamenco. It sounds exotic.

I tell him he'd get along with my dad and what a great guy he is. I do my best to describe the house I grew up in and portray Mother as well as possible—her sternest and obsession with quiet. I say, "I was afraid to sing or even hum."

It shocks Leandro that anyone could hate music.

He explains how the caves were once the heart of the *Romany* culture, and I sense his pain.

"But now is all gone for the dog. A tourist trap." His eyes flash with resentment when he talks of his childhood home turned into a fancy hotel. "But Eldora once worked for the man who manages the hotel. So, at least we have a place to stay."

"When I was a boy..." His hand shoots out to indicate child

height. "... We transform the sleeping room in front of our cave house into a stage. Each night we move beds to the kitchen in back of our living quarters. Eldora sings and dances. Adan, Felipo, and Mendez play. All our time, the band we spend together. These are happy days." His chest heaves up from under the comforter. "Other *Gitanos* put on shows at the Caves, but our *Zambra* is best."

"Did your parents play too?" He's never mentioned his mother and father.

"*Si,* they did. We are all *Lautari*. But I have small memory. I am only three years of age when *mamá* and *papá* get killed on a motorcycle."

"I'm so sorry."

"Eldora took me as hers. I was *un niño pequeño*. She was, to my *mamá,* how do you say, *la prima*? Eldora's *mamá* and my grandma were sisters."

"The English word is cousin." I think of my meagre family and an ache engulfs me. At least Leandro knows who his cousins are. I have none I know of, not even from my adopted parents. "What made you choose Canada?"

"Is a long story." He gazes up and becomes quiet. He must miss his home.

The tuft of hair above his belly button is crying out to be touched, but he presses his hand over my fingers. I stare at his wineberry nipples, the same colour as mine. Last night, after three AM, we woke on the beach. Then we came back here. My mind reels with the memory, his hot skin, the sensual dance, and the unbelievable pleasure.

I lean over and rest my cheek on his arm. "So, you were adopted, too. You were lucky. Eldora is sweet and kind."

Leandro sits up straight and claps his hands. "Your *papá,* I must meet with him." He stares with purpose at the far wall. "Your *mamá,* too. Is necessary, I think."

"Why?" After what I've told him of my mother, why would he want anything to do with her?

"Maybe is not the same here. With our people, parents have much to say about the marriage."

My breath stops. He wants to marry me? My entire body trembles. Does he notice I'm shaking?

He continues on as if we're having the most natural conversation in the world. "When *Roma* kids are young, ten or eleven, their *padres* will promise the girl or the boy."

"Arranged marriages?"

"Yes, but is sometimes an *enorme* error. Love smokes up with another person." He pats my arm. "You remember, Vandlo's daughter?"

I nod, recalling how he teased Athalia that her mother had a nice *Roma* boy picked out. I never imagined he was describing arranged marriages.

"Then, the lovers, they need to run away. They must disappear until, how do you say, until the heat lies down?"

"But they still have a choice."

"*Si,* but to leave means no celebration, and you miss the best part. The *Romany* wedding is *fiesta fantástica.*"

I smile. It's always a party with the *Romany*.

Leandro throws one arm over my shoulders and gives me a squeeze. "Also, we prefer to see our parents happy. Is good, Eldora and Adan approve of us."

"Are you asking me to marry you?" Man, I wasn't expecting this.

"Is unnecessary. Last night, you became my wife." He fingers a curl of my hair. "Before we leave for Andalusia, we must tell to your *papá*."

He believes we're married? I go rigid. He assumes I'll pull up and traipse off with him to foreign lands. A fume of fresh coffee wafts through the open window. Leandro is so certain of everything. I love the confident set of his jaw. He's convinced he can snap his fingers *flamenco* style and we'll be off to Spain. I study his face and think he might be right.

"In Andalusia, we celebrate. Such a party—you will not believe." He grins and draws a circle with his finger on my arm. "If your *papa* wants to make a ceremony here, we must hurry. Today Eldora buys us plane tickets."

"Today?" This brings me back to reality. I reach for my housecoat, put it on and stand. On top of the fridge, there's still a pile of unpaid bills. Dirty dishes are piling up in the sink again. "She's not buying one for me, is she?"

"Yes, for all of us." Leandro cocks his head, shoots me a confused look. "Next week we leave."

My thoughts are in a flurry. "Next week is impossible. I have no passport. Why didn't she ask me first?"

"We will go to the passport office, explain the urgency to them." He slaps his hand on his leg as if this takes care of everything. "They have what they call fast track. I will pay the extra."

"You don't understand. I applied for my passport, two weeks ago. It takes four to six weeks." I pace across the room and back again.

He reaches for his jeans on the floor, digs in the pocket, pulls out a wad of cash, and fans a couple hundred dollars in the air. "This makes fast the paperwork."

"Things don't work that way here. Besides, that's not the only reason I can't leave next week." I step over to the sink, run water, and rinse out a cup. "My natural mother could be here any day. She's coming all the way from Buenos Aires to meet me. I can't go before she arrives."

"She says she is your mother, but do you know is true?"

For a moment, he makes sense. What do I know of this mystery woman? And I don't owe her a thing. But now the necklace is heating again. It's crazy, and no doubt a figment of my imagination, but when I reach up to touch it, the stone is as hot as a fresh-poured cup of tea.

"I can't go." I try to stay calm, but my voice twitches.

He looks heartbroken. I wish had something different to tell him.

"You need to stop Eldora before she buys my ticket." I take his hand.

He swings his legs off the mattress and stares at the wall.

The phone rings, and I step away to answer it.

"Hally." It's Dad. "There's been an accident. It's Mother." His voice sounds shaky.

I almost drop the receiver. "What happened? A car accident? Is she okay?"

"No, it happened at the dress shop. She's alive, but you need to come, and I will explain when you get here. I am in the Vancouver General Hospital emergency room."

I hang up and gawk around for my clothes. "That was my dad. He's at the hospital." I find the skirt half way under the bed and my top crumpled under the pillow.

Leandro jumps to his feet. "What happened? Your father is sick?" He pulls his jeans on.

"No, it's Mother. She's had an accident, and it sounds serious so I'd better get over there."

He wraps his arms around me. "I must go with you."

"No, you don't want to meet my dad for the first time like this." I nuzzle into his neck for a moment, then scoop up my skirt and blouse, and head into the bathroom to dress.

"Okay, now I should leave." His tone is confident again. "I will tell Eldora about the plane ticket. Tonight, at her party, we can iron up a plan."

I hear the door close and can't help wondering if Mother has the second sight, zeroing in on every fleeting moment of happiness I have, poised to snatch it away.

Poison Gas

I hurry from my car to the emergency entrance of Vancouver General Hospital. Near the doorway, a guy in a wheelchair with an IV bag strung beside him, basks in a triangle of sunlight. He puffs on a cigarette with one hand and adjusts his nose tubes with the other.

Inside, at reception, I get directions to intensive care where they've moved Mother. I dash past an elevator and through a labyrinth of corridors to reach her ward. The hallways reverberate with the sickening hum of tiny malfunctioning speakers, and the medicinal odours are belly wrenching. After checking in at the nurse's station, I tiptoe into her room. At this moment, I'd rather be anywhere else.

Dad stands next to a bed where Mother lies immobile, swaddled in a tight, white sheet. Her eyes are closed, and she's wearing an oxygen mask. She appears fragile, without a hint of her normal hostility.

I step closer. "Dad."

"Hally, you are here." He hugs me. "They put the mask on her. She had trouble to breathe, but she fought, even as the doctor examined her, so he gave her a needle to sleep. No worry. They say she will wake up." His white eyebrows furrow. Through the transparent mask, Mother's lips are slack and slightly parted. Her face is ashen and her hair a tangled mess.

I glance at the monochrome chair against the beige wall. At least she'll be at home with the colour scheme. But I've never seen her so decrepit. Good thing they've knocked her out. She'd hate this.

"What happened?"

Dad stands stooped beside the bed. "Mary, from the shop next door, sniffed something funny and followed her nose to the bathroom of *Der Schwarze Koffer*. She found your mother collapsed on the floor by the toilet."

He shifts his weight from one foot to another. His steel-toed boots grate on the hospital linoleum, and he seems out of place here, his bootlaces plugged with sawdust. He'll be working on those shelves under the stairs—her birthday present—replacing the one he smashed the other day.

Dad tucks the blanket tighter around Mother's feet. "She should have run away when she smelled it, but you know what your mother is like, *Ja*? She would want to finish the cleaning. A half-done job, it will upset her every time."

"This happened when she was cleaning?"

"Yes, a chemical accident. Two liquids she mixed produced a poison gas." He moves to the other side of the bed, picks up Lieke's limp fingers and pats them.

The room has one other occupant near the window, with curtains drawn. I spot a single wilting rose in dirty yellow water on the windowsill. That'll give Mother a heart attack when she comes to. I walk over, pick up the jar, and drop it in a nearby wastebasket.

A young Afro-Canadian doctor arrives. "Hi, you must be the daughter. I'm sorry we had to sedate your mother, but she panicked when I put the oxygen mask on."

We shake hands. My skin is alabaster next to his. I guess that Mother was more upset over this man's black fingers touching her than she was about the mask.

The doctor checks Mother's pulse and tells us that chloramine gas fumes caused her lungs to fill with fluid. She mixed bleach with an acidic toilet bowl cleaner which produced a toxic vapour. They realise this because Dad picked up the two containers and brought them to the hospital. The doctor explains that she'll recover, but needs to take it easy for at least a month. He warns us, "If infection sets in, it could be serious."

After he leaves, Dad slumps into the chair beside the bed. "She's too crazy for cleaning." He tries to smooth Mother's tangled hair. "You know your mother, Hally. She sees two cleaning mixtures and reasons that two is better than one."

Then he bends and whispers, inches from Mother's ear. "I will take you home soon, *Schatje*." He fusses with the blanket, drawing it up close around her neck. "I will take over the cleaning, and you must lie and rest."

I can't help envisioning this scenario reversed, with Dad injured. "When was the last time she listened to you, Dad?" He doesn't answer, just waves a hand at me. "When was the last time she nursed you when you were sick?"

He shoots me a wounded look.

Flash back to when I was sixteen. One glance at Dad that morning, and I could see he was ill. He'd dressed for work, but had a grey face, rheumy eyes, and a raspy voice. I thought he should stay home and said so.

Mother in the kitchen, hands on hips. "Staying home will make him worse. He will lie in bed and brood about being sick and get more sick. And the men do nothing if he's not there." Lunch bucket thumped down beside his untouched plate of toast and eggs.

Well, Dad went to work. The weather was nasty, hammering rain with a bitter wind. Before noon, he collapsed in a pool of wet cement they'd just poured in someone's driveway. He ended up in hospital for two weeks with pneumonia.

I itch to ask him now as he sits beside her bed wagging his tail, 'Remember that time? How often did she visit you in the hospital?' But I don't ask. He's upset and worried and I've said enough. Dredging up old crap doesn't help.

His right hand tightens to a fist. "She should not be working in that shop."

"Are you saying it's my fault, Dad? If I hadn't quit, then this wouldn't have happened?" Angry tears gather. This has nothing to do with me. "If mother wants to poison herself with cleaning fluids, that's up to her."

"No, that's not what I meant. She should not have bought the store. You are not to blame." But he looks away as he says this and I wonder if he's being honest, if deep down, he thinks it's my fault.

He gets up, takes my arm, leads me out into the hall, and speaks in a whisper. "When she wakes up, I will tell her I have found someone to operate the shop. Who should I say?"

"Didn't she interview someone?"

"Yes, but she said the girl did not seem reliable."

"But, couldn't you call her and ask if she's still interested?"

"I don't even know the girl's name. Your mother takes care of such business herself." He leans against the wall and massages his temple. "If only Ulla was here. She would help. What can I do? There is no one. If I close the store, she won't rest." Then he smacks a fist into the palm of his hand. "So I will shut it and tell her a lie."

"You don't need to lie, Dad." I touch his arm. "I'm not working right now. I'll open the shop tomorrow morning and stay until she's better." He grins, that goofy smile I love so much. He hugs me and I remember what Leandro said about how good it is to make our parents happy. So why is it that I have this sinkhole in my gut?

Back in the room, the oxygen mask makes a wheezing sound with every breath she takes.

"Want to get something to eat, Dad? It looks like she'll be asleep for a while."

"No, I'll remain with her. You go." He sits again, lifts her hand and cocoons it between both of his. "Tomorrow morning. See you at the shop, at ten o'clock? I will bring the keys."

Mother hasn't moved and still looks pathetic, but this isn't the first time she's duped me. What made me say I'd return to that damn dress store? Even comatose, the woman has wangled what she wants. She'll drag out her recovery too—anything to keep me there as long as possible.

I hurry along the corridors, in and out of the elevator—eager for fresh air. Dad's a grown man, and he can put up with her abuse, but I shouldn't have to.

Outside, I flee to my car.

When I get home, there's a piece of paper stuck in my door. In black felt pen, the letters fill the page:

RENT IS OVERDUE — TOMORROW MORNING —

10AM.

I step in and toss my purse on the table. I have the rent covered, so why did I agree to return to the shop? "You stupid girl," I mutter. From her hospital bed, and even while she's unconscious, Mother has me hogtied.

I glance at my watch. It's ten to seven. Leandro said he'd call at four. As this thought pops through my head, the phone rings.

"Where have you been?" Leandro asks. "I have phoned three times."

"At the hospital, with my dad, remember?" I hold the receiver away from my ear for a moment. Did he forget already?

"How is your *mamá*?"

"Mother will be okay." I sink into the sofa.

"Good, I come to bring you now, for the party."

"No, please don't. So much has happened today. I can't face a party."

"Eldora has just returned from downtown, and she bought the plane tickets."

"She'll need to cancel mine, then. She should get a credit, and I can use it later." He needs to understand. "You could use yours later, too. Why not stay? Ask Eldora to cancel your ticket too and we'll both go later."

"Is not possible. The band needs me in Spain. We must perform and win enough to pay expenses. I wish this is different." He sounds as if he means it.

"I would go if I could. You realise that, don't you?" I curl my legs up under me on thc sofa.

"But you will join the party? I'll come to get you. Rosario's cafe —the *Boro Coro* is on Main Street, is on the way."

"That's near Club Combo, isn't it?"

"Yes, the dinner is eight o'clock, but before seven, the others arrive."

"No, I'll skip tonight, but you go and have fun."

"What do I say to Eldora? I said to her, you will come."

"Well, you can say to her, I will not come." He's silent for a couple of moments, and I regret my bitchy tone.

"Okay, I understand you prefer not to see me. I'll sleep back at the bus." His voice is barely audible. The receiver clicks.

Singing Bird

I arrive at the *Boro Coro* for the going-away party just before seven. When Leandro hung up on me earlier, I immediately felt awful. This might be my last chance to be with him before they leave.

I've not met most of the crowd here, but Eldora spots me and strides across the room. "Sit, sit. I am so happy you come." She kisses me once on each cheek. "Leandro tells me you can't travel to Spain with us right now. Don't worry. Join us when you can." She shows me to an empty chair. "I will get us a drink." She heads over to a corner table jam-packed with bottles and stemware.

I scan the diner for Leandro. Through a window into the cafe's kitchen, I spot a young female chef in a black cap and apron. That must be Rosario.

Eldora returns with two flutes glasses. "You will love this. We call it *rebujito*. Is *Fino* and Seven-up."

"What's *Fino*?" I hope I won't be wasted after a single drink.

"Is only white wine, but from Jerez, fantastic Spanish wine."

I sip it and hardly taste the wine. "Where's Leandro?" I expected him to be here, still peeved at me, brooding in a corner somewhere. I have a sheepish speech all planned out. In the car, I practised a look of naughty innocence in the rearview mirror.

"Is with the others. They will be back soon."

"Where did they go?" My confidence was high a few moments ago, imagining instant forgiveness, but my courage is waning.

"A *gadje,* who owns a bar we play in once, wants to buy musical instruments.We sell him old things, purchased before we had money for the good stuff. We tried to tell them they're old but he still wanted to buy them anyway." She points to a stage set-up in one corner, band equipment propped against the wall.

A burst of laughter erupts from a group of children decked out like 1950s kids at a wedding—dark-haired girls in too-short dresses, boys in white-collared shirts and black pants. They're leaned over something on a table chattering. "That's so cool." "Give it to me. Let me try." "I'm first. You promised."

"Nintendo." Eldora rolls her eyes and pulls up a sheer wrap that's slipped down her bare arm. She's thinner than the last time I saw her.

I'm glad I wore my gypsy costume tonight instead of jeans. Eldora's ankle-length dress of sizzling blue hints of a 1920s jazz star.

"You look incredible." I hug her. "Will you sing tonight?"

Eldora stares at her fingers. "Adan makes me promise not to. Is scared over the cancer." She puts one hand on her throat. "So difficult for me." She presses a fist to her chest. "When I hear the music, my insides blow up like accordion bellows. Sometimes it feels I'll smother if I don't sing. But my husband worries, so I do as he asks. May be not so bad tonight. They play a *juerga,* or how you say in English, a jam session."

"Is it possible they won't play tonight?"

"No, they must." Eldora smiles. "What kind of party would it be without music?"

The traffic noise of Main Street and a cool breeze blow into the cafe as the men burst in, laughing. Adan waves a fan of bills over his head and shouts. "Can you believe it! He buys everything, even the old *zurna,* with the cracked-up stem."

Leandro, wearing his fedora, saunters in—an actor taking his stage. No wonder girls at the clubs vie for his attention.

His face lights up when he sees me. "You come." He strides over, pulls me up out of the chair, kisses me, and then draws me in for a rib-crunching hug. He's not angry or pouting—no apology expected. The evening promises more hope. I smile and gulp back my drink. "You need another *rebujito,*" he says and plucks the glass from my hand.

A few more people arrive and before long everyone has lined up to fill their plates from a table heaped with tapas: cherry tomatoes with black olives, *empanadas,* clams in a red sauce, creamy salads on leaves of lettuce and three or four different shapes of deep-fried fish. A cedar-planked salmon is the feature dish. It all looks and smells enticing but I'm not hungry and take only a small helping, but I guzzle the fizzy drink.

"You are not eating?" Leandro asks when he's finished his food. He puts one arm around me. "You need your strength... for after." His chuckle tickles my ear.

Adan hollers. "Leandro, enough *choom.*" Bawdy hoots erupt. He hoists his violin up by the neck, pumps it in the air twice, and feigns a scolding grimace. "Is time to kiss later."

I raise my glass and grin. Then Leandro and I kiss—drawn out and deep. Everyone claps. While Felipo blows a few notes on his horn, Mendez gives his accordion a squeeze, and it wails out a single long bellow.

After a few minutes, the first song begins. I've never heard it before, but it's amazing. I press on the tops of my legs to stop them dancing, and spy Eldora near the kitchen with a forlorn expression, fingertips touching her neck.

And then everything changes. The band plays my favourite Kopana tune, the first one I learned by heart, the song that freed me from singing in the shower. I can't help myself. A few words escape my throat.

Cantando la pena
la pena se olvida
'Singing the pain
the pain is forgotten'

Then my voice rises to blend with the music. I sing, oblivious to anything or anyone in the room. My core shatters into a kaleidoscope of musical particles, wavering, floating with each guitar strum, pulsing with each pipe of the horn. It's as if my body has fused with the sound.

After the song ends, the café comes back into focus. I'm on my feet, but I can't remember standing. Everyone in the restaurant is gaping at me. Leandro's mouth is open. Adan is statue-still, with a shocked expression.

Leandro breaks the silence and moves toward me. "You tell me you only sing in the shower."

Oh, God. He hated it, and he's embarrassed. "I'm sorry. It's just I don't understand the words. I meant no disrespect." Why did I knock back that second drink on an empty stomach? Now I've made a complete fool of myself. I want to turn and run, but Leandro's gaze holds me rooted to the spot.

"This voice, you never mention." He beams at me. "This singing —you waste it on shower tiles?"

I stare at him and step away. "You liked it?"

"No, I love it." He addresses the gathering, raising his index fingers like a conductor. "Is she not *fantásticá*?" They applaud.

I glance at the floor. My cheeks sizzle and I realise even my brown skin can't hide the blush.

"Have we heard a ghost?" Adan slaps his chest. "Is the voice of Kopana." He clutches Eldora's arm. "Remember that time, the concert in London?" He points at me, his finger shaking. "Kopana's tone—her energy, flows out from you, Hally."

"I learned it off her CD."

Eldora gazes at me. "*Si*, Hally, you are blessed. *Baxtalo.* What luck." She crosses the floor and hugs me.

Adan pinches his white beard to a point. "You must sing with us at the Club Combo this weekend." Titters of agreement circulate throughout the room. Then his eyes spark up and he claps his hands. "Is the perfect solution. They will pay for a five-piece band. The extra money helps with the hotel in Andalusia."

He chuckles. "We share with you too."

"But, I only know the Kopana songs."

Leandro throws his arm across my shoulders. "You must sing her songs then, in the final set." He grins. "Is our last gig here, and after they hear you, no one forgets us, never."

"What if I can't? I've never sung on stage, and I might mess it up." I realise that performing with real musicians on an actual stage won't compare to what just happened. Then all they'll remember is an awkward girl with stage fright.

"Not to worry. You will be *fabulosá, el pájaro cantor."* Leandro nods at Eldora. "Is she not a singing bird?" He picks me up by the waist and twirls me. "To chase away the fear, you must rehearse with us tomorrow."

"Is settled then." Adan starts to sing and clap, a song I'm unfamiliar with, but everyone else here knows it, and they join in.

I tug on Leandro's sleeve. "Can I talk to you in private?"

He stops clapping. "*Si*, of course."

He follows me along a hallway and outside through the back door into an alley. Leandro's face glows from the light of a single street lamp.

I whisper, "I can't rehearse with you tomorrow, because I'm going to work in my mother's shop." He'll understand. "It was my dad's idea. I couldn't say no. He's so worried about Mother. I've never seen him so upset, so I said I'd come and work at the dress store until she's back on her feet."

He looks perplexed. "Why, when you hate that job?"

"I promised. He's meeting me at ten with the keys."

"Does he need the money?"

"No, it's not that. He's worried Mother won't get better if she's fretting over the business."

"He should find someone else." He cups my chin in his hand. "Without the rehearse you could still sing. But if it makes you unhappy, don't work in the store."

At this moment, his words make perfect sense. "You're right. Dad doesn't need the cash." The world won't end if he closes the shop closes for a few days. He can lie and tell Mother whatever he wants to.

"I will stay with you tonight." He winks and smiles. "In the morning, I can help explain to your father." He wiggles my earlobe, kisses the tip of my nose and leads me back inside.

The adults are sitting at tables near the entrance now, drinks in hand. The proprietor has taken off her chef's cap, revealing a wavy mane of gorgeous dark hair. Leandro leans over next to her and laughs.

Everyone is speaking *Calo* or Spanish, or whatever mix of the two languages with the odd word of English thrown in, but I can't catch the gist of the conversation. They must think I understand because I sang the Kopana songs. The giddiness from earlier has worn off, and my head is pounding.

I get up for a glass of water, wondering what Dad will think of Leandro. I've never brought a guy to meet him. Eldora said Hollanders detest gypsies. What if they hate each other?

I need a plan. I could try to keep Leandro up tonight as long as possible, tire him out so much he'll be fast asleep in the morning when I leave? This thought sends a quiver through my body. My headache dissipates, and another blush incinerates my cheeks.

A Different Song

The next morning, I slip out of bed, tiptoe to the closet, get my clothes and sneak into the bathroom. Leandro's still sleeping and should be. We kept each other awake until the wee hours—not that I'm complaining.

I work to make myself myself presentable. After putting on black pants and a black sweater, I step back from the full-length mirror and admire my empowered look. It's true. Black gives you backbone. I am more than ready to meet with Dad.

I give the door a gentle push, trying to be quiet, but it creaks. No matter—Leandro's already up and dressed, and he's hanging up the phone.

"Good morning." I force a cheery tone. "Who are you calling so early?" Of course he's welcome to use my phone, but a brief flash of something—is it guilt?—skims his face.

He grins, and whatever it was, melts into his perfect smile. "I tell Adan we may be late for rehearse." He strides across the room, pulls me close, and cups my butt cheek. "Last night, hmm, you and me, *exquisito,* no?"

My hands trail up under his t-shirt. With my nose burrowed in his chest, I breathe in the spicy scent of him, stronger than ever from our nighttime antics. I ache to lure him back into bed, but I promised to be at the shop in a half hour. And he can't join me this morning. Letting Dad down is my job.

I reach up and stroke his face. "I don't think today is the best time to meet my dad. He's still worried about Mother. When you two meet, I want it to be perfect." I trace the edge of his ear with one finger.

"Okay." Leandro kisses the top of my forehead, saunters to the table, picks his fedora up and pops it on. "Maybe is best. I must return to the campground and pack. The man who buys the bus comes for it soon."

I trudge to the kitchen counter. This is another reminder that he's leaving in three days, and one more reason I can't let Dad pressure me into coming to Mother's rescue. I need to spend every precious minute with Leandro.

He grabs his jacket and plants a kiss on my cheek. "I will go now. At noon, we rehearse. See you then."

The next thing I know, I'm alone in the apartment clutching the coffee pot. I didn't expect him to give in so easily. So, what's changed? Last night he was determined to meet my father. And why did he rush off?

I push these questions away and concentrate on my spiel for Dad, because Leandro is right. I'd perish if I returned, even for a week or two.

The fifteen-minute hike from my apartment to *Der Schwartz Koffer* gives me time to think. Why not offer to interview candidates for the job? That way, I don't leave Dad in a lurch. I start along Arbutus Street. It's a quiet morning and a fall chill has settled over Kitsilano. Chickadees chirp out from a hedge.

I hear a rap, rap, rap and glance up to the source of the racket, a second-floor balcony of an older apartment building. A seagull, perched on a wooden plant stand, is hammering its beak against a glass door. It's a handsome bird and reminds me of Leandro, all boom and bluster.

An old man, head bowed as if sleeping, sits in his rocker, only a foot away. Rap, rap, rap. The bird is persistent. The clack is loud enough to wake a corpse, but the old guy doesn't move a muscle. Is he deaf, or, oh my God, what if he's dead? A shudder ripples through me.

Stepping off the sidewalk and onto the grass, I peer up. The seagull's tenacious. Rap, rap, rap, and then it backs off for a minute, cocks its head, and peers inside. A courtly gesture—another of Leandro's traits. When I crane my neck, I catch sight of the old man's face, but he has no features. It's a cloth face, a life-sized dummy in that rocking chair. What sort of person keeps that on their balcony?

The sliding glass door skids open and answers my question. A skeletal guy slips out onto the deck, a plastic bag in hand. He's bare-chested except for a snake tattoo winding from his waist to his neck. His pants are slung so low that even at this angle, I spot pubic hair. He scatters a few chunks of bread and steps back into the apartment. The seagull gobbles up his booty. Persistence pays off, and that bird has it figured out. I turn and stride toward the store with new resolve.

From the end of the block, I make out two figures inside the shop. That's not good. If it's a customer, Dad will expect me to take care of her, and he may even try to leave before I've talked to him. As I get closer, I can see Dad behind the counter. The other person is unmistakable, and I can't believe my eyes—it's Leandro.

I hurry into the store.

"Do you know this man?" Dad asks in a strained voice.

I should say, 'No, who are you?' It would serve him right for lying. He's supposed to be at the campground packing.

But instead I say, "Yes, I know him." I swivel to face him. "Why are you here?"

"I try to explain to your father about us." He takes my arm and leads me toward Dad. "I get the picture when you tell me not now, but don't you see how important it is we meet?" He flashes Dad a pitiable grin. "You are a little angry, Sir, and I do not blame you. Long before this, I should ask permission for Hally."

Leandro has underestimated the situation. Dad is more than a little angry. He's stock-still, with an explosive purple face.

Leandro's shoulders slump. "Let me make it up to you, Sir."

Dad ignores him and beads his attention on me. "Is he telling me the truth, that you plan to marry?" He grips the counter so hard the skin on his knuckles turns shiny.

"Yes, I do." I keep my tone breezy but watch him. Will he fly into a rage, throw things?

Leandro takes my hand. "You want my information, Sir? I am a musician. In my culture, they call us *Lautari*. We are famous for our music, well known and always have work. I will take good care of Hally, promise." He squeezes my fingers. "We return to Andalusia next week, so is important to meet with you now."

Dad stretches himself to his full six-foot-two and leans across the counter. "So, you go back to Spain. Why, when you have so much work here?"

Leandro presses on as if he hasn't noticed the sarcasm. "The wife of our band leader is sick and must see a *Roma* healer there. Hally joins us when her passport comes."

"*Roma*? What is this?"

"*Roma* is my culture. Hally too, at birth. This is no guess, Sir. We look the same, no?"

"*Roma*, you mean *Romany*, the same as gypsy? You are a gypsy? This story goes from bad to awful." Dad steps out from behind the counter and places a hand on my shoulder. "We need to talk." He gestures to the back room. "Alone."

I don't want to go into that room. I shouldn't even be here. Why did Leandro have to show up?

Dad's fuming, and we haven't yet discussed the shop. I'm tempted to tell Leandro to leave.

Chimes sound and the shop door chirrs open. A tall, well-dressed woman enters. She has the blackest skin I've ever seen.

Leandro claps his hands together. "Ah, here she is." He trots over and ushers her inside. "Sir, this is Zuri." He turns to me. "Zuri has moved here from Toronto. A friend of Rosario, at the cafe. Rosario tells me about her."

"Nice to meet you, Sir." Zuri puts out her hand and grins, exposing large, white teeth. Dad ignores her, and her arm drops. I cannot believe his rudeness.

Leandro says, "I bring you Zuri to make up. She needs a job and you have the opening here, no? Zuri has much experience. She sold dresses in Toronto, at a *bueno* shop." Leandro smiles and nods. "Is what you call a win, win."

"There is no opening here." Dad scowls. "Hally will mind the store until her mother is better."

"That's where you're wrong, Dad." My words snap out. Leandro's done nothing to deserve Dad's snarky tone. "I can't work here again—ever." I step back and bump into a rack of blouses. The hangers rattle and several garments fall to the floor. "I just can't, damn it." This last bit comes out as a shriek. My eyes sting.

Leandro looks stunned, and Zuri's expression says, 'I want to flee this scene.'

Dad comes up behind me, takes my arm, leads me into the back room and shuts the door. When he speaks, his voice is gentle, like my very own dad. "Do you understand what you are doing with this man?"

"Yes. I love him." There—I've finally said it out loud. "The first time I saw him, I knew."

"And when was that? How long since you met him?"

"Not long—about two months." It's been thirty-four days, but Dad doesn't need the details. "But I'm old enough to know what I want."

"Old enough? Are you?" He shakes his head. "I'm not so sure. And your mother will not approve."

"I don't give a damn what Mother thinks." Why does he always bring her into it? This has nothing to do with her.

"He is a musician, Hally." Dad's tone is pleading now. "His job will never be stable, and he's a gypsy. They wander, never settle." He strokes my arm. "You'll wish for a child one day, and roots. Do not trap yourself into a disastrous marriage."

"Why would it be so terrible? If we make each other happy, what else matters?"

"Do you believe that happiness will continue in Spain, in a different culture, away from your family and everything familiar?"

I clench my fists. "Were you happy when you got together with Mother, when you moved here to Canada?" I look him in the eye. "How long did it last, Dad, because I've never seen it?"

He rubs his temples. "How do I explain this to your mother?"

"Tell her, Hally found someone to run the shop, or you found someone. Hell, I don't care what you say."

"That woman is Negro. Your mother... well, you know your mother."

"You're right. Sadly, I do. But is this about Mother's bigotry, or yours, Dad?" I fling open the door and storm out.

Leandro and Zuri stand rooted—dumbfounded.

"Come on. Let's go." I take Leandro's hand and lead him to the exit. "Zuri, my dad will be out in a minute to discuss the terms of your employment, assuming you still want the job."

"Your father." Leandro stops at the entrance. "We should not leave like this."

"Yes, we should." I yank on his arm and he follows me.

Map of Andalusia

At noon, Leandro and I slip in the back door of Club Combo, into a narrow corridor, and walk toward a blasting horn. This is where we met, and I prickle with nostalgia. The cavernous taproom smells of stale beer, and it's seedy in the light of day. The red leather seats, which seemed elegant by candlelight, have seen much better days. Dust motes hover above empty tables with lazy brilliance. A sandwich board propped inside the entrance announces hours of operation: 5 PM to 3 AM. We have the entire afternoon to rehearse.

I tell myself this is only a rehearsal, but I'm a-jitter with panic. Halfway across the room I tug on Leandro's arm. "Can we just watch for a minute?"

The amplifiers jeer at me. The tiny stage is a hazardous-looking podium with a snarl of cords waiting to trip me up. Eldora stands there now, behind a microphone, her feet planted in that jungle of cable. In her jeans and chequered shirt, she looks twenty years old.

Adan sprints off the platform. "Okay, is time for the sound check."

Eldora taps the mike and a hollow tu, tu sound fills the room. "Test, test, test."

Fifteen feet off stage, Adan scratches his white beard. "Sing a few words. Only a little. Do not work your throat too much."

Eldora raises her arms, tips her head, and delivers a few lyrics.

♩ ♫ ♪ *Yo mate a mi dulce dueno*

I killed my sweet master

♬ ♪ *Con veneno que le di*

With the poison that I gave him

She stops, sticks her tongue out at Adan and steps aside from the microphone.

"Good, sounds good," he says.

It's more than good. It's spine-tingling. Only two lines of a song, and Eldora has bewitched me. I'll sound flat in comparison.

Maybe Mother had it right. In the ninth grade, I signed up for music as one of my school electives. She barged into the Principal's office and demanded he move me to a course that would, 'actually teach me something.' The two of them settled on Family Studies. I had no aptitude for cooking or sewing, but the class did teach me something—how to handle humiliation.

I glance at my trembling hands and then back to the stage.

Leandro studies my face with an amused expression. "You look scared. Have you seen a ghost?" He tweaks my chin. "To be nervous at rehearse is good. We always say, shaky now, perfect later."

I clunk my forehead against his chest. "I've never used a microphone."

"I will give a lesson. Come." He takes my elbow and leads me toward the open.

"What if I miss my cues and screw it up?"

"This is why we rehearse. Not to worry. Tomorrow night, you will be *estupendá*." He stops mid-room. "I remember when Adan first lets me play. Only age of five but for a year I already practise. On stage, that first time, is like my fingers turn into toes. He says, 'Forget your hands and listen. *Escuchar la música*. Let it fill you up. When that happens, your fingers, they know what to do.'"

"Hally." Eldora waves. She picks something up off the back of a chair and heads toward us. It's a garment covered in dry-cleaner film.

Holding up the hanger, Eldora says, "See, my lucky costume, I bring her for you." It's a sari-like, crimson dress with shiny golden trimming.

"It is gorgeous." This is no lie. I love the elegance of it, but the sleeves are short and won't hide my blotchy arms.

Eldora smooths a hand over her waist. "Is tight for me now, but for you, is perfect." She lifts the plastic film and fingers the fabric. "You put her on tomorrow night." Her eyes sparkle. "Every time I wear this, we make double the tips." She reaches in her shirt pocket and pulls out a photograph. "See, I bring this."

It's a younger Eldora. She's standing in an ornate doorway wearing that costume—a haughty pose, a *flamenco* stance. In the picture, Adan has black hair, not white, and he's on one knee beside her.

"A club, very famous in Granada." She smiles at her husband with a far-away expression. "Such a time it was—*Una diversion maravillosa*."

Leandro takes the dress and drapes it over the chair. "Lessons, microphone, now." He guides me to the stage.

Adan, Felipo, and Mendez quit tuning their instruments to watch. Leandro flicks one hand at them. "Go back to what you were doing." He positions the mike and blows into it. His puffs echo in the empty room. "Adan, turn the volume low for now."

Adan makes a few adjustments. Leandro blows again, and it's quieter. "Some say back away from the mike. We say, put your lips close and keep them close." He leans into the microphone and sings, "Ayh yaaah, ayh yaaah, ah yah yah yah." Then he steps aside. "Our songs catch all human sound. We want it *íntimo,* but strong, like wind on a mountain top. Here, you try." He plucks the mike off its stand and hands it to me.

I breathe in deep and mimic his notes. My voice thunders.

"It may be, you do not need the microphone." He laughs, leans over, and kisses my neck. "You have the built-in amplifier."

"We should start." Adan picks up his mandolin.

"Leave the Kopana songs for now. Give Hally more time." Leandro winks at me. "I want to show you something." After grabbing the mike, he begins singing *a cappella*—Spanish lyrics charged with emotion. Even though I can hear his breath suck in and his voice crackle, it takes nothing away, but adds to the song. I listen, unable to move, and afraid to breathe. He moves his head from side to side creating a wobbled sound.

Eldora claps with delight when he's finished. "You have not blessed us with that *canción* for years." Leandro bows and grins.

Then the music begins in earnest.

I can't keep track of how many tunes they play before the first Kopana piece, but when they start it, I'm up at the mike clapping and snapping my fingers. I am more than ready to join them, anxious, in fact. The microphone grazes my lips. Then the room echoes with those Spanish lyrics I don't understand but can somehow sing with absolute confidence.

We rehearse all thirteen songs. We begin with the tune I know best, a soothing ballad. The third is my favourite Kopana piece, with a strain of majestic sadness. Already the microphone feels it belongs in my hand. The fifth song is one I struggled to learn. I practised it over and over to get the tone right, and now I don't miss a beat. It's as if each band member, each instrument, has synced with my vocal cords. Then the tempo picks up with a robust tune, followed by a rousing piece. I dance and sing.

Perspiration drips off the end of my nose as we do the last song. I drink in an image of each of them—Mendez crushing the bellows of his accordion for one final blast, Felipo wrenching his lips off the horn. Adan, closest to the window, his beard aglow in a beam of sunlight, is tap, tap, tapping on the wood of his mandolin. Leandro's hand caresses the neck of his bass. I touch my windpipe and experience what they do.

It's the same for me. I am *Lautari* too.

When we finish, the bartender gives us an enthusiastic round of applause and brings over a tray of beer. The band members cluster around me when I spring off the stage.

"Pretty and talented too." Felipo grabs me and squeezes both arms.

"As good as, maybe better than Kopana." Mendez lifts me off the ground with a hug.

Leandro takes my hand, presses it between both of his and smiles.

"See." Adan points to his glistening eyes. "What your voice has power to do."

I look over at Eldora, assuming she'll take me aside and give me pointers.

She strides toward me, beaming. "You sing like the archangel."

Is it possible? Yes, she loved my performance, too.

The conversation turns to plans for the last gig. After that, they discuss the upcoming flight to Andalusia and I wish I could be a part of that discussion. I excuse myself and set off for the Ladies.

There's a billboard in the hallway advertising the Festival of India. A woman wearing a red sari smiles, striking a traditional pose. Her arms snake over her head, and I marvel at the intricate henna design covering her hands and arms. I've seen a place on Main Street where they offer hennas.

Eldora's costume comes to mind. I'll go home and give the shop a call—ask them to henna over my white blotches. I pray they can fit me in before tomorrow night.

When I return I say, "I'm going now. I need to make an appointment."

"I'll join you." Leandro stands.

"No, stay and have fun, but come to the apartment when you're done." I pick up the costume and hand him my spare keys, in case he arrives before I get back.

As I drive along 4th Avenue, I rewind our rehearsal in my head, trying not to focus on the upcoming gig, just on how well the practice went. Near my place I circle the block to find parking.

I spy a man on my street who resembles the Spanish translator, and I slow to look, but it's not him. When will I have news of the mystery woman? It's been over three weeks now.

I parallel park in a tight space, cut the engine and get out of the car.

A grey sedan pulls up beside me—Dad's car—and I lean to greet him. The window grinds down and I'm face-to-face with Mother, sitting in the passenger seat, her white skin whiter than normal, her face stony and stern. What's she doing out of the hospital? The doctor said he'd keep her in for at least a week and it's only been two days.

"Hello." I back away. "I thought you were still in hospital."

Her head pushes through the car window. “How can I stay put when I discover what you are up to with that man?” A flash of light hits her green eye. “Your father told me.”

Dad grips the steering wheel as if he is holding on for life. Why would he tell her? He said he didn’t want to upset her. Unless he’s come to his senses at last, and is trying to kill her off.

He leans across the seat and looks up at me. “I couldn’t allow you to make such a mistake. Your mother, she knows what to say.”

“So, what do you say, Mother?” My hands curl into fists. I am not, not, not willing to let this woman ruin my day.

“I say you are an idiot and always have been one.” Spit flies out of her mouth. “Years ago I knew. Before you could even speak. You were a stupid girl then and still are now. The first man who comes along, you will run off with him and break your father’s heart.”

I’m struck dumb. Dad continues to gape at me, squirming in his seat.

Mother clenches the inside frame of the car’s window. “I tried to tell your father we should return you to the nuns, years ago, before we even moved to Canada. But he wanted to help you. He felt pity for you—a little, brown, homeless girl.” She stops yelling and starts hacking so hard I step back, expecting her to vomit. But she catches her breath and continues in a raspy voice. “I was right all along. You are useless. Go, marry your dirty gypsy boy. We wash our hands.”

“You know what?” My words come out with a surprising level

of control. "I don't care what you think, and haven't for a long time. You're a small-minded, petty, wicked woman."

Her expression remains fixed in anger, but her eyes go round, giving away her shock.

I bend and stare at Dad. "And I feel sorry for you." I can't read his expression, because he's still gripping the wheel and gawking at his hands. "Why do you put up with her?"

All I note before marching away are the whites of their eyes. Once inside my apartment, the tears erupt. A few drops splatter onto a notice of registered mail as I bend to pick it up off the floor. It must be my passport come early. I stuff the thing in my purse. Instead of phoning for a henna job, I spend the next hour on the bed sobbing and hugging a pillow.

That's how Leandro finds me, and I calm at the sight of him. He runs one knuckle over my wet cheek. "What is wrong?"

"My mother was here." It's all I need to say. He pats my shoulder as if he knows and doesn't pry.

Later, after we've made love, he turns on the bedside lamp. I tense. His gaze travels over my naked body. "You are fabulous." He plants light kisses up and down my arm.

Then he brushes one finger over the biggest white blotch on my side and I cringe. He tenderly traces an outline of the patch. "Wow, is a map on your skin. I think is Andalusia. This is fantastic—a sign that tells for sure—you are meant to come home with me."

I say nothing. But if my passport has arrived, it's true, I can go with him. I feel light enough to float. And this affliction of mine isn't vitiligo. Leandro's just confirmed it—it's a fragment of the world that's stamped on my skin.

Enigma

"I'm sorry if I woke you, Halca." Roberto, the translator, is in the hallway outside my studio apartment shuffling from side to side in his signature black suit and a pair of dazzling white sneakers. "I come to tell you right away. She is here, in Vancouver."

Excitement and anxiety do a tango in my stomach. I tie my housecoat tighter and wave him inside.

Leandro comes up from behind and rests his hands on my waist.

Roberto stands in the doorway like a puffed-up politician. "She asks me to organise the reunion and requests this evening, for dinner." After glancing at my unmade bed, he averts his eyes and fiddles with his tie. My red lace bra sits on top of the pillow.

"No, tonight, for us is not possible." Leandro gives me a one-arm squeeze. "We have a gig."

Roberto's eyes fix on my face. "She is eager to meet you, only you, and did not suggest anyone else should come."

I don't back away from his intense stare. "If she's here, why didn't she join you?"

"I'm told she could not, and you must go to her." He breaks the eye-lock. "Putrika says you'll understand this later."

I pinch my throat. "We play at Club Combo tonight."

"No way we can make it," Leandro says. "We start at seven."

"What about now?" I suck in a deep breath. This is what I've waited for, information on my roots, my birth, anything. "You wait downstairs. I'll get dressed." The words tumble out of my mouth.

"No, she says, not before tonight." Then Roberto fixes his gaze on Leandro. "Ah, I remember you now. You are the bass player in 'Bloodfire.'"

Leandro grins. "You have heard our band?"

"Yes, many times." Roberto claps his hands. "In May, I saw you at Nightkat. Your music *es fabulosá*." He holds out his hand.

Leandro gives it an enthusiastic shake.

"An older woman, she sang with you." Roberto rubs his chin. "Last time, she was not there." He turns to me. "Did you take her place?"

"Yes, she's ill. Tonight's my first performance." An embarrassed squeak escapes my throat.

"You should come tonight. A treat for yourself." Leandro cuffs Roberto on the arm. *"Can tute rakker Romanes?"*

He nods. "Some, but I speak English and Spanish better. For most of my life, my father was a Spanish diplomat to Argentina, but we move to Canada five years ago. My mother strives to fit in here, so at home we speak only English. But she is Romany, born in Buenos Aires."

Leandro shoots me a smug look. "You see, what I tell you? One *Roma* always knows another." He clenches his hands together and brings them up to his chin. "So, the mystery mother. She is *Romany* too? I guess she is."

"Yes, she is." Roberto glances out the window.

"*Si*, right again." Leandro grins wide enough to split his lips. "I knew it." He kisses the top of my head.

I eyeball the translator. "Why this secrecy? Why won't she see us now?"

"So sorry. I don't know why." He pinches the bridge of his nose. "Okay then, tomorrow. We'll meet her at lunchtime."

I grab a pen and notepad off the kitchen table. "Where's she staying? Is it close?"

"Is an apartment, near Stanley Park, on Georgia Street." He reaches for the notebook. "Let me write the address."

"She's not staying in a hotel?"

"No, she requests an apartment. So I arrange to rent it for her, by the month."

"Will you be there to translate? Will Putrika be there?"

He writes something and passes the notepad back. "Yes, Putrika will join us. I'll come too, but no need for my services. Your mother speaks English."

"What sort of person is she? Do I look like her? Is that why you're so sure she's my mother?"

"I'm sorry. I cannot tell you. We have not met." Before he

opens the door to leave, he gives me instructions to meet him outside the building the next day at noon. Then he stops and lowers his voice. "Putrika has asked you keep this secret from your adoptive parents."

"Why?" I have no intention of talking to them, especially since yesterday, but what a strange request.

"Just do not mention, please. She says is important."

After Roberto leaves, Leandro and I return to bed. We make love, speculate on the mysterious woman, and then nap. A while later, we wake up and do it again in the same order. But the second time I can't sleep—not because of the gig. The woman's stuck in my mind, and I'm vibrating with fear and expectation. If she's come so far, there must be some link, or truth, or story.

Part Six

Travel Pass

This morning, following my debut performance with Bloodfire, I'm awake at 8AM, too wound up to sleep. As I sneak out of bed, Leandro rolls over, grunts, and then slips back to his dreams. After grabbing a pen, I sit crosslegged on the sofa composing a letter to Erin in my head.

I should describe the night in vivid detail. I will tell her how it was the final set before the band called me to the stage, and how surprised I was when the anxiety didn't paralyze me like I expected. It did the opposite—waking up an energy that added fire and clarity to my voice. Ten minutes into the set, I forgot to be nervous. I'll report how the audience stopped dancing at the start of my set, and how this worried me at first, but then I noticed that everyone who had been sitting, were standing. They were agog—paying full attention—over a hundred pairs of eyes on me.

I remember each moment as if it just happened. The music is still playing in my head. We performed all thirteen tunes I'd learnt. When Adan said goodnight, the crowd clapped and stomped for more. The audience held up lighters and candles off the table as if we were a famous rock band. We repeated four songs, and as we did the encore, people dropped money into Adan's open violin case—tips. Over two hundred dollars, when we counted later. The guys were ecstatic. We stayed in the club, drinking, chatting and laughing until 4AM. That's why Leandro can't wake up this morning.

Our first time performing together—it makes me tingle. Leandro and I will share this memory forever. We'll hone and perfect the story to tell our children and grandchildren. I think of mentioning this to Erin, and I try to imagine her expression when she reads it, but I can't. I cannot remember her face anymore. The necklace I'm wearing, the one sent to me by the mystery woman, the one with a stone that heated up when I kissed it, suddenly feels cold against my breastbone. I reach up to touch it. My fingertips turn to ice. As I ponder this, the pen slips out of my other hand and rolls across the hardwood floor. It's suddenly clear that I won't write to my dead friend now or ever again—that there's no room for a corpse in my future. I have a lover now, to share things with. Also, today I'll face the woman who may be my birth mother. Even if she isn't who I hope she is, Leandro wants me with him in Spain. Travel, adventure, and love—what more could a girl ask for?

The postal notice is still in my purse.

The fact that I have registered mail and it might be my passport—I've kept that a secret. Because, if my travelling papers are here it changes everything. I'll be free to leave with the band, and Leandro will insist I go. So I can't mention it yet. Who knows how this mother stuff will play out?

The post office opens at 9AM. I quietly dress and slip outside.

I walk uphill on Yew Street, mail notification in hand, trusting that the world is unfolding as it should. If this is my passport come early, it's a sign, and I will know what to do. Traffic is thin. I catch my reflection in an apartment building window. How different I look today compared to last night. Dressed in Eldora's costume, I was a spectacle, a real *flamenco* performer. Today I'm a city urchin huddled under my hoodie.

A light drizzle dampens my face. The morning is dreary, darker than it has been for weeks. I pull up the hood of my jacket. In the backyard of a vintage house, water-laden sheets hang on a clothes line. The kitchen lights are on, a yellow splash in the grey setting. A man with Einstein hair wields a spatula over his stove. His window is open, and I catch a heavy draught of bacon.

Minutes later, I'm waiting for a green light across the street from the drug store/post office.

There's a hand-written poster taped to the streetlight. It says:

Psychic Readings by Louria

Find Love

Master your life

Gaze into your future

I'd love to gaze into my future, but what's missing from the poster is a phone number, address, or any contact information. You'd have to be a psychic to get the help Louria has promised.

A gaunt man unlocks the drug store entrance as I approach. Inside, it's warm and smells of medicine. Pushing my hoodie back, I wend through the aisles to the postal outlet.

A girl with a brush cut takes my notice and asks for ID. I show her my driver's licence. She leans forward and scrutinises the picture, second-guessing the likeness. It was taken during my dress shop days with my hair in a bun, an absurdly proper-looking me. I tuck a woolly clump of hair behind one ear. She squints at me, hesitates, then rifles in a drawer, and hands me a packet. It's from the passport office. A frog of excitement leaps in my throat.

After signing for it, I take the booklet out and check the picture page. That's me. That's my freedom. My fingers graze over the embossed lettering on the cover. Then I insert it deep into the bottom of my purse. Outside, I drop the empty envelope into the trash.

Walking home, I imagine telling Leandro right away, as soon as he wakes. I need to tell him. I want to tell him. I can imagine his delight when I tell him, but we must meet with the mystery woman first.

There's a coffee shop on the corner. I duck in and order two lattes. Does Leandro like a latte? God, I don't even know something this basic about him.

It's 10AM when I arrive back at the apartment.

Leandro is sitting up in bed, bare-chested. "I woke, and you were gone. I thought you must be a dream." He lifts a pillow to his face. "Your scent, it stays here, so I decide is no dream." He gives me a teasing look, one thick eyebrow raised, his hair adorably tousled.

"I went out for coffee. It's raining." I pass him a cup, put mine on the table, and pull off my jacket.

He throws the covers aside and pats the space beside him. "Come back to bed."

I point to the bedside table clock. "We're meeting the woman at noon."

"I will be quick," he says with a grin.

I tumble into bed with him. A flurry of cast-off clothing and the sweetest skin on skin comes next.

Later, in the shower, the upcoming meeting gnaws at me. Dread and excitement seesaw in my gut. The translator said the woman speaks English, and I hope she's fluent, because I have so many questions. In her letter, why did she mention a stolen baby? Or is that a lie? Is she afraid to admit that she abandoned her child in a train station? Why is she so sure I'm her daughter? This meet-up might be a colossal mistake. A needle of panic sucks away my breath. There are DNA tests. Should I suggest we get tested? What if we do and she isn't my mother? Then I'll be back to knowing nothing.

I have to look on the upside. If the meeting flops, I'm free to go to Spain. It'll be clear then too, that finding my roots was never meant to be.

Face to Face

Leandro and I walk down Georgia Street toward Stanley Park on our way to meet the mystery woman. The rain stopped and the day has turned sunny but sultry. A few clouds float overhead like bubbles in bathwater. Traffic whizzes past. Across the road, a group of teenage girls giggle as they try to mount their rented bicycles. I squeeze Leandro's hand.

"He said Georgia Street, didn't he?" I squint left. "Did we get it wrong? These places are swanky."

Leandro pulls a piece of paper out of his jeans pocket. "No, this is right. The number is 1930." He points to the main entrance of a high rise with a Japanese-style garden.

I stop and point. "Look. There she is—Putrika." Surreal as a Frida Kahlo portrait, she sits posed on a low wall wearing her colourful poncho and smoking a tiny pipe. "She's the one I told you about."

Leandro chuckles. "She is like an old *monishi* from the upper caves of *Sacramonte*. See her scarf, how she ties it? They wear it that way and always smoke the pipe too."

Intent on her curl of smoke, Putrika doesn't notice us approach.

Roberto, the translator, appears down the block. He waves, hoofing it up the sidewalk, his black suit jacket flapping in the breeze.

As we get close, Putrika notices me and a wide grin bedazzles her face. She taps her pipe out on the cement, stands and comes for me with open arms, her grin growing bigger with each step.

Leandro steps between us and offers his hand. He says something in *Romany*, or Spanish. I'm never sure what language he's speaking. Putrika pumps both of his hands, nods her head and laughs. Her elfin face disappears in a thousand lines.

I nudge Leandro. "What did you say?"

"I tell her that only a *debla chachi* prefers to sit outside a place so fancy."

"What's a *debla chachi*?"

"Is a *Roma* goddess, genuine, the real thing."

Roberto arrives, puffing. "Sorry I'm late. I had to park blocks away."

Putrika chatters and flaps her hands. She's not laughing anymore. Her bright eyes dart from his face to mine. I can't be sure if she's talking to me or the translator. Then she reaches in a pouch around her neck, pulls out a hundred-dollar bill and gives it to Roberto. He looks crestfallen, turns, and trudges away.

I tug Leandro's shirt cuff. "What did she say? Why did she give him that money?"

Leandro leans close and whispers. "She pays him for his translation service. Now she asks him to go. She says he is no longer needed, that your mother is waiting for you, but not for him."

Putrika continues to yammer in her strange tongue. Her message is unmistakable—Leandro should leave too.

"I want you to stay. Tell her." My heart slams into my third rib. I can't do this alone.

Putrika keeps on with her babble.

I sense we're being watched and look up. On the fourth floor, someone is standing in the window. Is it her? A moment later, the figure disappears. I nudge Leandro, get up on tiptoes, and whisper in his ear. "I'm scared."

Leandro gives me a quick hug. Putrika nods in agreement and then continues to jabber.

There's a young girl across the street, chasing a balloon, squealing and running ahead of her father.

Putrika is still yammering, incomprehensible, but insistent. Leandro gawks at her. Then his eyes widen. "*Kek tacho.*" He turns and grabs my hands. "You must go with her now."

"You're not coming?"

Leandro squeezes my fingers, amazement spread across his face. "She explains your mother fears people, that it has taken all her strength to do this, to travel here. She says that later I might meet her too, but she worries will be too traumatic for your mother." Leandro pinches my chin. "Go—I'll wait here. If this woman is who she says..."

"Who? What did she tell you?"

"She says a *flamenco* singer, *muy* famous, hides for over thirty years from the world."

A hundred bottle-flies are attempting to escape from my palpitating throat. Leandro's shocked expression lingers. He wiggles his fingers in a half-wave and steps aside.

I take Putrika's outstretched hand and allow her to lead me into the building. In the lobby, she clasps my wrist and pulls me into the elevator. Moments later, I know we're going up, so why does it feel like we're plummeting down? I wipe a bead of sweat off my upper lip and try to ignore my mind's hubbub... if she's who the old lady says... a famous *flamenco* singer.

I've no idea what to expect. The woman could be some wild-eyed recluse. I've read horror stories of people meeting their birth parents, and they hate each other on sight. I concentrate on breathing in and out—slow and steady—in and out.

Putrika won't let go of me when the lift stops. We get out, and she tugs me across a wide corridor.

Then she opens the door and ushers me into a spacious room

where I'm blinded by a wall of blazing sunlight. I can make out a female shape floating toward us, backlit by the glare. She says something, but it's muffled. Putrika squeezes my hand, lets go of it and steps aside.

I strain to fix on the woman's face, but a halo of dazzling light conceals it. But I see her clothing, and this is no *flamenco* singer. She's dressed like a well-heeled housewife in a shock-blue, button-up shirt. For Christ's sake, she's wearing tights. Her fingers sparkle with rings, but she has no bracelets. A gypsy would have bangles, wouldn't she?

After a minute or two my eyes adjust, and I notice that she's browner than I am. But is that a trick of the light—a motif of mottled white on her cheek? If the blotch on my ribcage is a map of Andalusia, the one on her skin is Italy—a long narrow boot up her neck and onto her face.

She steps closer. She's right in front of me now. Tears cascade over her bottom eyelashes. "How many years I dream of this." Her voice is husky, and she has a Spanish accent.

I recognise her. It can't be, but it is. It's the face from the CD cover, older yes and spattered, but the same. "Kopana?"

What runs through my body is not a tremor—it's a quake.

"Are you Kopana?" I'm paralyzed.

She blinks, releasing a stream of tears. "You wear the necklace."

"Yes." I reach up and touch the pendant. The stone feels hot again, as it did when I first put it on.

"I learn that you sing my songs." This woman studies me as if trying to memorise each feature on my face. Putrika grins so hard her eyes disappear.

I should say something, but what? I don't know. The room is air conditioned and my feet are freezing. I glance at my sandals. "You heard me sing?"

"No, but my friend Joyce, she attends where you perform last night. She hears you and brings me news."

What sad eyes she has—big sad eyes that gobble me up. I avert my gaze to an abstract black-and-white print covering the entire wall.

"Thirty years it is, since I sing those songs or even listen to them."

Now I'm confused. Maybe this lady only resembles Kopana. Surely she'd listen to or sing her own songs. But why say that if it's not true? And what is this about a friend? I inspect the dim hallway. Is someone else here?

"Sit, *por favor.*" The woman motions to a white leather sofa. I can't help thinking that my adoptive mother would approve of the decor, the cream carpet, the pallid walls, the extreme absence of colour. One thing Mother would not approve of is the flamboyant Putrika. Ablaze in primary colours, she settles on a straight-back chair near the window and fans out her multi-layered skirts. Sunlight dazzles off her earrings and zings off the three heavy strands of gold chain hanging to her waist.

An intense silence goes on and on as Kopana continues to gape at me. I struggle for something to say. "This is a nice apartment."

She cocks her head. "You think so? Is terrible to me, no colour.

And I ask the man for trees, but they're distant, like a postcard." She flicks her hand at the window. "I prefer trees to reach out and touch."

"Yes, trees. Me too."

"Still, Vancouver is a beautiful city."

"Yes, people always say that."

Then she shifts in her chair, taking her eyes off my face and peers off into space. Now she's the spitting image of the confident *flamenco* performer on the CD cover. She may not be wearing the costume, but the profile is identical. It removes all doubt. This is Kopana—the Kopana.

Holy bejesus, I'm sitting across from a legend, a legend who believes she's my flesh and blood. Goosebumps erupt on my arms.

I sit up straight on the saggy sofa. "I love your songs. I can't tell you how much they move me." My heart seizes up, and I'm finding it hard to speak. "When I first listened to your CD, it was as if I've known the music all my life, like I was born to sing those songs. Why don't you sing them anymore?" I think of Eldora's cancer and how awful it is for her not singing. "Did something happen to your throat?"

"No, my throat is okay." Her eyebrows scrunch together—bushy eyebrows, identical to mine. Kopana runs one hand along the arm of her silky shirt and lowers her voice. "After what happens to my baby, to you, my joy dies. I never sing again."

Teardrops sting my eyes.

A woman enters with a tray. "I thought you might fancy tea

and biscuits." She's about seventy, matron-shaped, sporting a ball of white hair, and speaks with an English accent. She smiles to display a delightful set of crooked teeth.

"This is Joyce." Kopana's voice takes on a tender tone. "She works as my nanny when I am a girl. She stays with me all these years, my forever friend."

Ah, this explains why Kopana's English is so clear.

Joyce sets the tray down. "We've been through the mill together, we have." She lifts the lid on the teapot and stirs before pouring. Turning to Kopana, she holds up a plate piled high with cookies. "They have oatmeal in them. Healthy, they are. You've hardly eaten in a week." She glances over at Putrika. "How about you, Gran? Tea?" Putrika shakes her head. Joyce shifts her attention to me. "I was proud of your mum. T'was truly a feat for her, leaving the house in Buenos Aires. We've not left that place since the year your dad died."

I hear her words, but they don't register right away.

I'm on the verge of believing this might be my birth mother, but now a dead father? Pressure mushrooms up behind my eyes.

My shock must be obvious, because Kopana says, "Please leave us, Joyce."

"One thing before I go." Joyce passes me a cup of tea. "I saw you sing last night." Her voice cracks. "My heart almost stopped, it did. You were smashing. It was just like seeing your mum up on stage thirty-five years ago." She shoots me an intense look, then shuffles out of the room.

Kopana focuses on me again. "You have many questions. Joyce

should not tell it to you, about your father. I'm so sorry."

"It's okay. You're right. I have questions, but I don't know where to start." My head is threatening to explode. I pinch the bridge of my nose to relieve the pressure.

"You must learn the story." She slides forward in her chair. "Yes, my name is Kopana."

"You're Kopana, *the* famous Kopana." A tremor runs through me.

She squints at me. "You hear of me. You perform my songs, forgotten long ago. But that's not why I travel here to you. Before we come, I did not know you sing."

"Why are you so sure I'm your daughter?"

Kopana's eyebrows shoot up. "Do you not see it?"

I see it. Her face is my future face. My stomach quivers. It's not just thc vitiligo. Kopana's hair is straight, not fuzzy like mine, but she has the same arched nose, and the mole above her lips is a carbon copy of my own, almost in the same place. What are the chances of that? One in a million, I bet, even between mother and daughter.

"My parents said someone found me abandoned in a train station in Roosendaal, in the Netherlands. That's the other side of the world from where you live in South America. My mother, the woman who raised me, believes some girl who didn't know what to do with her child deserted me. Is that what happened? Did you go to Europe and leave me at a train station?"

"No. Do I seem like a woman to do that?" Kopana's eyes go round. "Besides, I lived in Spain then—not Buenos Aires—but I could never desert my baby. Children mean everything to *Roma* people." She leans, digs in a leather briefcase beside her chair and draws out a wad of papers. "I will tell you what's true."

She explains how the genealogy detective broadened his search when he couldn't find clues in Roosendaal, and how he put it together when he read about the stolen baby in Amsterdam that same month. His theory, Kopana tells me, is that the kidnappers boarded the train to Roosendaal. Then they became frightened, gave up plans for a ransom, and left me at the station.

She shakes her head. "But, his story of abandoned at Roosendaal makes no sense. Where is his evidence? Also, the city is only a hundred kilometres away from Amsterdam, and all the peoples of Europe read news of the kidnap. So why would no one tell us they found you?"

"But Mother said she adopted me in Roosendaal, at an orphanage run by the nuns. She has an adoption certificate."

"You have seen this certificate?"

"Yes." But now I'm blustering. "It's in Dutch. I couldn't read it, but she translated. She also said the orphanage had a flood that destroyed the church records, and that's why Mr Vanderburg couldn't find any details."

Kopana twists a cluster ring on her index finger. "Would she lie to you?"

"I don't think so... hmm... I'm not sure."

"I will not say bad of her, but I know you are my Kali and someone stole you from me, and the detective's answers are wrong." She spits this out with fierceness.

I love how she pronounces that name, like a Cala lily but with an ee at the end. It sounds so right. The name Halca has never been me.

Now, she looks determined. "Could be they bought you. That used to happen, and would explain why no one asks for ransom. The kidnappers would have made money by selling you. You should request for a copy of the certificate, to prove the story they gave. Is easy to check out fake papers." Her words are gushing out. "Many criminals in Europe make phoney documents. So, try to get a copy—it would be a way to know for sure."

Is it possible? Could my adoptive parents have bought me? It is true they haven't been up front with information. If they paid for mc, it would explain why I didn't have a birth certificate until I was five. But why would they do that and keep it a secret? Because it's illegal to buy a child... A skewer of pain bores into my temple. No, they couldn't have.

I flash on Mother's drawer in the study, where she keeps her important documents locked away. What would happen if I demanded my adoption certificate? I can tell her I need it for my passport. Mother will say no, of course. There's no doubt about that. She'll refuse to even let me in the house.

But she hides the key to her desk inside the mantel clock, and I know where Dad keeps a spare key for the front door. I just need them out of the house for a while. They are my adoption papers, and I have every right to them.

Kopana thumps the heel of her hand on her forehead. "Could also be the people who kidnap you get attached and decide to keep you. If this is how it goes, give them thanks from me. So many years, I believe you are dead."

Then Kopana picks up Mr Vanderburg's report and stuffs it back in the briefcase. "Is no matter now. What's important, you are here." She leans forward and puts out her hands. I hesitate for a moment and then touch her fingers. She bends to kiss my palm, and I hold back a torrent of tears.

"Joyce said my father is dead. What happened?"

Her face crumples in pain. "Let's talk about him later." She pats my hands. "For now, we'll get to know us."

"I'm sorry to be so blunt."

Kopana smiles, a sweet, forgiving smile.

Putrika stands and speaks to Kopana. It's a jumble of foreign words fired with hand gestures. As she talks, she withdraws a miniature pocket knife from the leather pouch at her neck. Then she stops her jabber, pulls out a thatch of white, silky material and a twist of red thread wound around a stick of cardboard. I watch, fascinated, as she sits on the carpet between us, places these items on the coffee table, and pries one shiny blade out of the knife.

"What's she doing?"

Putrika's expression is serious.

"Is a spell." Kopana says this as if it's the most natural thing in the world. She leans over, and Putrika slices a lock of her hair.

Next, I'm beckoned to tilt forward.

"Does she want a snip of my hair too?"

"Yes."

I do as she asks. The little knife must be sharp. I barely notice the snip.

Putrika tugs her long, grey braid over one shoulder and shaves the wispy end of it off. With gnarly fingers, she attempts to straighten my fuzzy hair next to the straight dark strand from Kopana and the wiry hunk of her own. She gives up and pinches the centre of the three strands together and then deftly wraps the red thread around her bundle.

"She wraps eight times," Kopana says. "For June eighth, the day of your birth."

"That's my birthday?" Blood pounds in my ears. "I've never known the actual date." I used to tell myself it shouldn't bother me, but it does matter, and now I'll never have to celebrate on June 15 again.

Putrika ties a knot in the thread and creates an envelope for the hair with the square of white silk. When finished, she encases the package in her fist and kisses it.

"What's the spell for?" I pray it's meant for me to help dispel the mumbo-jumbo of emotions roiling in my gut.

"Is to bring family togetherness." She points to all of us.

Putrika hoists herself up off the carpet and mutters.

"She must bury it now or the spell will lose potency. She asks me to tell to you, she'll come back soon." Kopana flits one hand at her mother. *"Kair hekta."* Putrika nods. Kopana smiles at her. "Is a mystery why my mother speaks no English. She never says a word, but she understands. Don't you, *Daia?*" Putrika nods and heads for the door.

After she leaves I have so many questions I'm struck dumb.

Joyce enters the room carrying an empty tray. She pats Kopana's shoulder and looks at me. "T'was my idea, you know, to go to Buenos Aires, just for a while. When she lost you, and then your dad too, your mum was so sad. I thought it would help her." She turns to me. "There's tango dancing in the square a few blocks away from where we live and lots of *Roma* folk."

Joyce stands at attention. "But she hid, refused to move off the property and has never met a single soul. Still, she insisted we stay."

Kopana slumps. "After a while, just the idea to go outside the yard makes it hard to breathe. So we purchase the house."

"We did." Joyce's forehead wrinkles. "At a fabulous price too, but I think we should've gone back to Spain."

"Joyce says I have the agoraphobia sickness and always tries to get me to visit a doctor." Kopana points to a laptop on the desk. "She spends too much time on internet searches."

"Humph." Joyce gathers empty dishes from the coffee table.

"But she is mistaken. When my mother tells me about you, all I want is to hurry here and meet you. Nothing can stop me."

Joyce steps away, cups and saucers jingling on the tray. "It's never too late now, is it? We could go home to Spain again."

As Joyce leaves the room, she whispers, "Is a lovely garden at our place in Buenos Aires, full of carnations. I plant them to remind me of Spain and simple times of childhood. Come there with me."

I panic. "You're not going back right away, are you?" She can't leave when I've only just met her.

"No, never, until you're ready to join."

I should tell her. At this point in time, a trip to Buenos Aires is out of the question. There's Leandro—there's the band and Andalusia.

The door flies open and Putrika steps in with something cupped in her hands. She grins and speaks to Kopana.

Kopana winks. "She says your boyfriend is playing music in the garden. You have a boyfriend outside?"

Leandro must have gone to the car for his guitar. "Yes, Leandro. Putrika told him I should meet you alone."

"Please go now and invite him up." She pats my arm, and hands me a key card for the elevator. "I want to meet this friend."

This prompts a huge smile from Putrika, who marches over to where we're standing, grabs my wrist and scoops a finger of mud that's pooled in her other hand. She massages it into the centre of my palm. Then she does the same thing to Kopana.

On the elevator ride down, I finger the mud. It's warm as gravy with a rich earthy smell. The heat spreads up my arm and through my body. And all I can think of is the glint of delight in Putrika's eyes.

The Story

On the lawn next to the building, Leandro sits cross-legged in a puddle of sunlight, focused on his guitar, strumming a mellow song. I find his jawline hypnotic. He taps a beat on the wood. I could stand watching him forever, but I won't. He'll be so excited to hear about Kopana.

I scamper across the grass and squat in front of him. "She's asked to meet you."

He stares at me, and then his eyes bulge. "She wants to see me? Really?" He blinks several times."Wow— I can't believe it. Did she say how she locates you? Does she still believe you are *familia*?"

I lean over and kiss him on the forehead. "I'll tell you everything later." Then I tug on his sleeve. "Let's go up."

The elevator opens with a ding on the fourth floor. Kopana's waiting near the open door of her apartment and she runs to us, pulls us into a hug, kisses us both on the cheek. Then she steps back, puts a hand on each of Leandro's shoulders. "You are Kali's *novio*. And *Lautari* too. Her grandmother tells to me. I am so happy to meet you."

Leandro looks stunned.

She says something I can't understand. An excited grin

replaces his dazed look. He claps twice and replies in the same tongue.

"No, we should speak in English. Kali does not yet know our language." Kopana shoots me a tender smile and my heart flies up through the roof.

Inside the apartment, classical guitar music purrs from a speaker in the corner. Sunshine pours into the room, setting the furniture and walls ablaze. Putrika sits planted near the window like a cactus in an English garden. Joyce is nowhere to be seen.

Kopana gestures to the sofa, and we sit. Leandro grips my fingers with one hand while clutching his guitar case with the other. Kopana perches on a leather chair, giving him her full attention. She inquires of the band, who are the members, how many instruments does Leandro play? He answers her, describing the musicians—explaining they are his family. Kopana studies him as he speaks but keeps glancing over at me, smiling.

Kopana wants to hear about his love for music, how it makes him feel, does he ever sing the *seguiriyas?*

"I play and sometimes sing." Leandro puts one arm around me. "Since I meet Kali, I'm not sad enough to sing the *seguiriyas*." He gives me a squeeze.

Besides Kopana, Leandro is the only person who's called me Kali. I'm thrilled with my new name.

Kopana's smile could warm the Arctic. "The music, the music, is in our blood for sure. Even Mama." She points to her mother, who nods and grins. "At home she plays her cimbalom every day."

"Your husband, Luca Laine, he was my hero." Leandro leans forward, eyes shining. "As a boy, I sat for hours and hours listening to his records. Still, today, I would die to play like him."

Kopana stares into space with a sad expression. Then she stands. "I have something for you. *Un momento*. I'll get it and then tell you the story of your *papá*." She hurries across the carpet and disappears into another room.

I glance over at Putrika posed on the slipper chair by the window, nodding, grinning, rubbing her legs and rocking—my grandmother.

After a few minutes, Kopana returns cradling a contoured leather case that's tattered and faded. She eases it onto the sofa beside me, unfastens the brass latches, and opens the case. She lifts out a violin. "Your *papá's*."

"My father played the violin too?" I squint at it. The rich, burgundy wood gleams as if someone's polished it recently.

"He could play anything."

"What an instrument. Look at her." Leandro leans toward it squinting. "*Fantástico.*"

Kopana places the violin on my lap. "Yes, is his first. His *padre* pass it to him, and his *padre's padre* pass it to him. We can only guess how many *padres* pass it along before then, and now I give it over to you, Kali."

My fingers shake. I pick it up and get a whiff of old, musty books and furniture polish.

"I don't know what to say." It's a family heirloom, my family heirloom. I have a family. I had a father, and his name was Luca

Laine.

Kopana sits erect, her cheeks slick with tears. She's no legend, but a flesh and blood mother—my mother. Putrika gets up, walks behind the sofa, strokes my hair and croons.

Leandro squeezes my wrist. "Never do I see such a violin."

I run my fingers over the smooth instrument. I can imagine my father as a boy, intent on his playing, the red wood tucked under his chin, but I don't deserve this gift.

"You shouldn't give this to me. I can't even play."

"I will teach you." Leandro makes it sound so easy.

Kopana sits up straight. "You must accept. Is your violin. You will learn fast. Is in your blood." She smiles, winks and circles a finger in the air above her head. "Also, the spirit of your *papá* will haunt me if I fail to pass along."

Leandro nods. "Is true, what she says."

"Okay, I'll learn how to play." Confident words, but my faith is iffy. I return the violin to its case and close the lid.

Kopana plants her hands on her thighs. "Now, I tell your *papá's* story."

Before she begins, Putrika returns to her slipper chair, and stillness settles on the room as we lean forward to catch her every word.

Kopana gazes above my head for a moment. "Is a story will break your heart, and it starts the day they steal you." Her voice is matter-of-fact. "We have just been to visit your *papá's* peoples in Yorkshire, for a wedding."

"My father was English?" This must be why my skin is lighter than hers.

"Yes, he is born in England, but when we marry, he comes to live in *Málaga* with me. That is my home, in the south of Spain." Her face softens. "Is true what Leandro says. No one plays the guitar like my Luca, not even in Andalusia famous for Spanish guitar. The first time I hear him play is at a party in Cumbria, and I fall in love with his fingers." She raises one hand and stares at her own fingers.

Leandro's eyes fix on her face. "He was, for true, the best guitarist of our blood, of the world."

"Ah, and he could sing, too. And so *guapo*." Kopana has a wistful expression. "Kali, you have his curly hair. I think also, you have his eyes."

"So, my father was *Roma* too?" A surge of gypsy blood gushes through my veins. I marvel at Leandro's wisdom. He never once doubted it.

"*Si*, yes. Otherwise my *papá* will never let me marry him. The old people, they are like that. Even after I am rich and famous, still *papá* has the power to choose my husband. But he never tries to arrange it. He wants me happy." She smiles. "He dies the year before you were *born*. A heart attack." She pats her chest. "But he was old already, not young like your papá." One thin hand comes up to rake through her long dark hair.

"How did my father die?" This may sound callous, but it is the reason I've been after information on my birth parents. What genetic disorders, illnesses, bats in the belfry? Then I realise the story can wait. "I'm sorry. This must be hard for you. We don't have to talk about it."

"No, no—you must hear." She lowers her voice. "Please understand, your *papá* takes the blame on himself for everything that happens." She pauses, as if collecting her thoughts.

Kopana hugs herself and leans forward. "It begins at the train station in Amsterdam. We had just played in Berlin and were travelling to Madrid next for the Paloma Festival. Joyce stays in England to visit relatives. Since you are a tiny baby, only two moons old, your *papá* and I have you with us."

I'm holding my breath.

"Is a problem with the tickets and I go to sort it out. Your *papá* stays with you. You are in your basket on the bench beside him." Her gaze veers off as if she's re-living the scene. "He has been awake all night with his crazy friends." She shifts and her knees bang against the coffee table. An empty teacup shakes and rattles in the saucer. "There's a huge line-up at the ticket counter. It takes longer than it should—over an hour. After they fix the problem, I come back. Your *papá* is asleep on the bench, but where is your basket?"

Her eyelids flutter closed. "I don't see it. Did he put it behind the bench? I walk around. He is still asleep and then I scream, 'Wake up, where is Kali?' I shake him. 'You ask someone to watch her, tell me yes you did.' He sits up. His eyes spin around wild. He jumps to his feet."

"For the next hour, he runs over and over every corner of the station ten or fifteen times, searching. I stay near the bench. I circle the bench. I cry, 'No, no, no.' I kick the bench. I stand up on the bench and search over the heads of peoples, but no one has a basket. No one has a baby. I scream and kick the bench. You are simply gone... *Oh Dios*."

She slaps her chair's arm, and it hits my ears like a gunshot.

"Later, the police, they drive us back to the hotel and tell us wait there for a ransom note." She shivers and hugs herself. "Maybe we should act another way, contact the newspapers, plead with the kidnapper to please bring you home." The heel of her hand rises to thump her forehead.

She pats the leather briefcase beside her chair. "*Señor* Vanderburg reports they find you at the Roosendaal station. At first I thought if only we break the story when it happens, someone might connect it up." She lowers her head, shaking it side to side. "But we stay quiet and wait like the police ask."

My gypsy blood is no longer gushing, it's erupting in my veins.

Kopana shrivels in her chair. "The police, they come every day. They say a ransom note will soon arrive. We tell them we have money, more than we can spend. No matter how much the kidnapper asks for, we can pay. So we wait." She pauses. Her shoulders collapse.

Leandro and Putrika both look on the verge of tears.

I'm dizzy. My head swirls. I struggle to concentrate.

Kopana clasps her fingers together. "We were crazy with the waiting. I paced the room. I walked outside. Nothing helped, but there was nothing we could do. Then one day, weeks later, the police decide there will be no ransom note." Her speech begins to drag now. "They say has been too long, and tell us, go home. They promise to continue the search. But the officer in charge, we see no hope in his face. This is when your *papá* picks up the whiskey bottle." She twists a handful of her hair. "Even though I never blame him, he hides in drink for months. After that, he starts to heal and I have him back, but not for long."

The apartment goes blurry. Kopana is still speaking, but her words don't register. It's as if I'm in a corner, shrunk to the size of a gnat. I can see my body's slight movements, the tilt of my head, but the burr of her voice is mixed in with the clamour of my dead ancestors.

She begins to describe my father's airplane, and I snap out of it. Kopana tells us of his passion for flying and how he died on a bright summer day when his plane crashed into the Mediterranean near their house.

She stomps her foot and scowls. "He is sober too, but the reporters say he is drunk."

I reach for Leandro's hand and grip it.

Putrika stands, steps across the room, massages her daughter's shoulders and hums in a way only mothers hum.

Kopana wrings her hands. "Suicide, the police decide, but one thing I am sure of—my Luca, your *papá* would never leave me on purpose like that."

Putrika returns to her chair and Kopana goes on. Afterwards, she says, the newspaper people camped outside the door, reminding her every day of her missing baby, of her husband's death. They wrote articles, calling them terrible parents, and claiming they neglected their child, as all *Gitano* do. They had decided her husband couldn't live with his guilt and took his own life.

Leandro raises one hand. "No Roma ever thought suicide."

She shoots him a grateful smile. "I hope is true, but I was *vacío*, scared, and afraid to step outside the house. So Joyce arranged for us to leave."

"Where did you go?" Leandro asks.

"To Argentina. We travel to Buenos Aires from Casablanca by freighter. It takes a month."

I try to imagine a month on a boat.

Her face crumples in sadness again. "No airplanes—never again, after what happens to your *papá*." She closes her eyes, pinches the bridge of her nose, and then shakes her head to regain composure. "Also, it was easy to take lots of money on the freighter. No one questions my trunk or tries to inspect it. I use my birth name, Isabel Flores."

"So, is my name Kali Flores?"

"Yes, Kali Flores." Kopana continues to explain. "You see, your *papá* and I marry Romany style, no official papers, so is my legal name. Not many know that name, and those who do promise to keep it secret."

"We find a house in Buenos Aires, in the San Telmo district, the old section of town. She is a big place, on a quiet street, surrounded by a jungle of trees. It feels safe."

Leandro shakes his head. "In 2001 our band travels to Buenos Aires. That was before we move to Canada. We try Argentina first, but find riots everywhere, people walking around, banging pots and pans, setting fires. From what we see, is not so safe."

Kopana brings one knee up to her chest and hugs it. "I remember that time, but we stayed home, and saw no violence happen on our street, so I was not afraid. But a bigger fear keeps me inside, that someone will recognise me, and I would die if reporters come to hound again."

"Do you miss Spain?" There's a hint of nostalgia in Leandro's tone.

"I try to forget. Do you?"

"Yes, all the time. We return next week."

"Back to where?"

"To Andalusia."

"Why Andalusia?" Kopana gets up and paces.

"Eldora, my adoptive mother needs to visit a healer there. Is our home."

I stand. I have to tell her. "They've asked me to go with them."

Kopana slumps. It's as if an invisible folding machine has landed on her spine. "Next week?" She squints up at me. "Do you have to leave so soon?"

"I don't know. It's hard for me to focus right now."

I reach out and take her hand.

Kopana's face oozes compassion. "Such a lot of news for you at once." She squeezes my fingers.

"Yes, you're right. I need to be alone for a while to think."

She nods. "I understand." She stands and hugs me. "Come back tomorrow? We'll talk more then, okay?"

I wonder how much of our conversation Putrika understood.

She rushes toward us as Kopana, Leandro and I move for the door. Then she pulls us in close. The violin case is between the four of us, pressed up against my chest. I grasp the solid muscles of Leandro's back. Kopana smells of lavender. Pipe smoke lingers in Putrika's hair. I feel light, as if a slight wind might lift me to the ceiling. For several minutes we stand that way, not speaking, swaying, the violin centred like a fulcrum.

Mantel Clock

As we walk away from the apartment on Georgia Street, I glance up to see Putrika and Kopana in the window waving. I hug the violin case and return the wave. I have an urge to run back and kiss them both, a thousand kisses.

"Kopana—is so hard to believe." Leandro's eyes flash. "I can't wait to tell Adan and Eldora. We should go now, to the campground." As we hoof to the car, he's speaking excitedly, holding fast to my arm. "But first, we pick up the van. Adan needs it today."

An idea strikes and I check my phone. It's five minutes past three. Mother should be out this afternoon. I need that adoption certificate, and this could be my only chance. Now is the time to make sense of it all.

Traffic has backed up on Georgia. Heatwaves shimmy above car hoods, distorting the tree-scape of Stanley Park. As we stride alongside the line-up, my plan takes shape.

Mother goes to the Chinese Garden on Sundays and never gets back until at least four-thirty. It's also the day Dad drives to Steveston for fresh fish from the wharf. There's a good chance the house will be empty, but to get that certificate, I'll have to break and enter.

It's crazy—planning to sneak into my family home, but Mother took my keys away years ago when I moved out. She said if I wasn't living there, I shouldn't have keys. I didn't care. She's never known about the spare key Dad has stashed in the front yard, but I do. I've never had reason to use it before now.

If I hurry, I can make it. When Mother showed me the adoption certificate, it was in her desk. Many moons ago, I saw her hide the key to the desk drawer inside the mantel clock. If I sneak in, grab the paper, and get out, they won't even realise I was there. After I snatch the document, I'm not sure what I'll do with it. But some government body should be able to verify its authenticity.

On Denman Street, where we parked the car, I want to blurt out my plan, but Leandro mustn't know. He'd insist on coming and if something goes wrong, he might be implicated.

The car shrieks when I turn the key.

"Shit. Damn." I pound on the dashboard and try again. When

the engine sputters to life, I slap it in gear and zip down the street. We zigzag through the West End, over the Burrard Bridge, and pull up next to Leandro's van near my apartment building. "You go to the campground. I'll follow in the car. I have to do something first." My brain is urging me to hurry, hurry, hurry.

"Okay, but try to come quick." He jumps out and throws me a kiss.

Within ten minutes I'm on Arbutus motoring toward Marpole.

The homes on the street where I grew up are 1970s split level structures with modest well-kept yards. My parents' place sits smack in the middle of the block. I slow the car, but don't stop. Mother's Volvo is not in the carport and Dad's Subaru is nowhere in sight. Yes! I thump the steering wheel with the heel of my hand. Mrs Parker's blinds are closed as usual, but the old snoop is always home, and she has bat ears. It's not that she'd think it odd to see me go into the house, but she would mention it to Mother. That woman prattles on and on endlessly, about everything and nothing.

So, I turn up a side street and park. A neighbour's lawn mower is whirring, but the only person in sight is Mrs Lutz bent over in her garden. I speed-walk past her. She's intent on her flowers and doesn't notice me.

I spot the Browns' Dobermann Pinscher, Kubla, and slow my pace. He's come to the end of his run, his pointy nose pressed through the chain-link fence. "Please don't bark." That would bring Mrs Parker out on her front step in an eye-blink. I try to keep my movements fluid, to fool the dog with my nonchalance, but he eyes me and raises his snout, priming to yelp. Then his ears perk as another dog howls in the distance. He loses interest in me and lopes away.

At my parents' place, I dash up the driveway, eyes on the yew tree. With any luck, Dad hasn't moved the key. But why would he? It's been there forever, on the wooden ledge along the back of a birdhouse he built years ago. I get to the tree and stand tippy-toed, pretending to peer in the hole. It may be an unnecessary precaution. I'm out of sight now. Thank God for summer leaves that block the view. I slip my hand around the rear of the birdhouse and snatch the spare key. Then I hear a rustling and freeze. A squirrel scurries out of a boxwood hedge that circles the yard. When he sees me, he screeches to a halt, looking more scared than I am. Then he turns and bounds away.

I vault up the four steps to the front entrance, insert the key, unlock the deadbolt, slip in and shut the door. I don't think anyone saw me. While leaning my head against the doorframe, I do a *Pranayama* breath to slow my heart.

Motionless, listening, I gaze up past the stairwell into the living quarters. The house is eerily silent, except for the tick of the mantel clock. As usual, the air reeks of furniture polish. I peep at my phone. It's only three forty-five, so there's plenty of time.

I kick off one shoe, stop, and put it back on. Why should I take off my shoes? They won't make noise on the carpet. They aren't dirty. This place could use a smudge of dirt, anyway. I mount the stairs without even checking behind for marks on the cream-coloured shag.

The door to Mother's office is open. The tick, tick, tick of that clock is unnerving. It sits on the shelf above the fireplace, and I head there. When I open the tiny door beneath the clock face, it squeals like a terrified rabbit. I freeze and listen.

My fingers fumble for the key and find it left of the pendulum. I pad over to the den, stop at the entrance, and peek in. The room is empty, but Mother's presence permeates every square inch of this house, so I need this to be quick. As the key jiggles in the lock, I pray she hasn't moved the certificate.

The drawer slides open to reveal a stack of paperwork: passports, a black leather cheque book, a small metal box with thumb tacks and a wad of loose documents. I rifle through the pile. The paper crackles like a forty-foot bonfire. Near the bottom of the heap, I spot an official header stamp, slip the document out, and hold it up to the light. Yes, this is it, the adoption certificate. Then I rearrange the papers and slide the drawer back in. She'll never suspect I was here.

Just as the lock clicks shut, I hear a thud. It sounds like it's coming from the living room, but it can't be. I clutch the certificate to my chest. My heart hasn't flapped this hard since I watched *Friday the 13th* in high school and almost died of fright. There's another sound—a creak. I rear backwards in slow motion, my whole body convulsing.

Mother looms in the doorway.

"What are you doing?"

She's in her housecoat, rumpled and sleepy-eyed.

"I thought you were a burglar. Are you trying to send me back to the hospital?" Her tone is sharp—not sleepy at all.

"Your car isn't in the driveway."

"It's in the garage." She shoots me a quizzical look.

"What do you have there?" She steps close, peers at the document, scowls. She thrusts out her hand. "Give me that."

My heart takes one more leap to the ceiling, but then I recover. I have every right to be here. "This is my adoption certificate and I need it." I clutch it to my chest.

"It is not your property." Her words snap, and her face reddens. "You come here like a thief. What else have you taken? I should call the police." She looks lively now, but clownish, with a thatch of hair poking straight up from her bangs.

I pause and try to regulate my breath. I am not doing anything wrong.

"This is all I came for." I step to the window and hold the certificate up to the sunlight. "And I don't think you'll phone the police, will you? If I asked them to examine it, what would they find—that it's a fake?" I'm taking a leap here, but I pay attention to her face. It's quick, almost indiscernible, but a flicker of terror grazes her expression. This woman I've called Mother for my entire life is hiding something huge.

She steps toward me. "You understand nothing about nothing." Her voice spews venom. "Give it to me."

I step back, holding the paper away. "No." I'm not afraid of her. I'm truly not scared of her for the very first time.

Why did I ever fear this woman? She's a pathetic old hag. Every belittlement she's administered, every slight she's imposed, every cruelty she's inflicted pours up and out of me in a single storming breath. I am free of her, once and for all. My shoulders relax, and I smile.

She steps back. "Now Halca. What do you need that paper for? You have your birth certificate." Her voice is compliant, pleading, a tone I've never heard from her.

"Yes, my birth certificate—how many lies did you tell to get that document? I noticed they didn't issue it until I was five."

Even my birth certificate is in question.

"It's a fake, isn't it?" Is every single piece of paper that documents my existence counterfeit? "You bought my birth certificate, didn't you?"

Lieke crosses her arms and puts her bulldog face back on. "Don't be a stupid girl. Go home and read it. Feel the seal. Take it to the embassy. It is genuine. Let them tell you." She walks to the desk, realigns the pop-up calendar with a leather notepad and then thrusts her hands into the pockets of her housecoat. "The dress shop is open again, no thanks to you."

I've waited my entire life to get answers from this woman, and I will not let her change the subject. "So, you bribed someone at the embassy. Is that how you got them to issue a birth certificate? How much did that cost?" Lieke seems calmer now. She sneers.

"No, I didn't have to bribe anyone. But you're right—it was expensive. They charge almost nine hundred *guilder* for lost certificates. Over one thousand Canadian dollars I paid to acquire legitimate papers for you."

A flush of bitterness interrupts my normal breathing. "So you told them you lost it? What did you have? A photocopy of a fake birth certificate?"

"No, it was easy back then," she says with a smug expression. "They only asked for a photocopy of the adoption papers."

"So you used this adoption certificate to get official documents from Holland?" My hands are sweaty, and I wipe my palms on my jeans. "So, if I take this to the embassy, they'll tell me it's genuine?"

"Put the document back in the drawer." She knots the belt on her housecoat. Our eyes lock, and she steps forward. Her hand darts out to snatch the paper from me. I hold it away from her, over my head.

A few moments pass. Then she backs off, and her expression turns muddled as she speaks in a lower tone. "The nuns were not skilled with paperwork. In my letter, I explained this to the officials. The sisters did not bother to apply for a birth certificate. I told them this. Then, a flood destroyed all the orphanage records. They only had to check. That was a true fact."

"Answer me. Is this adoption certificate genuine?"

She looks up, stunned, as if addressing an audience in the ceiling. "When we came here... Janz and I, our papers were in order." She fiddles with a stub of her blonde hair. "They did not go through baby documents if both parents were travelling. At the airport, they didn't even inspect you or notice you were brown. They only checked single parents who might be running away with a child, understand?" Her head bobs. It's like she's speaking to herself and has forgotten I'm in the room. "I knew all of this. My cousin Bram worked in the customs." She walks over and slumps down on the office chair.

"So the certificate is fake?"

She sits up straight, her face hard again. "Yes, it is. But try to prove it." She tosses an imaginary ball of paper over her shoulder.

"So, you bought fake documents. What happened? Did they decide you'd be a rotten mother and refuse to let you adopt? Did you buy me?"

She chuckles. "No, you have it all wrong. This part is funny. No one even asked to see the adoption certificate when we brought you here. Back then, it was easy to immigrate. Canada jumped in joy for people from Holland. Your father was a skilled tradesman, a cement mason. They put their arms open wide for us. Not like today. They let all kinds in, from third-world countries, no skills, no brains."

"Are you saying you didn't buy me? Do you expect me to believe the nuns just handed me over to you, one less child to feed?"

She taps her fingernails on the wood desk. "Like I said, you know nothing about nothing. Everything was easy. They only asked for copies when we applied for landed immigrant status. And I didn't even need the story about a flood at the orphanage or how the nuns lost the records. I did a lot of research too—to find the flooded orphanage and then a person to make up the paper. All the planning, the worry, and the money—unnecessary. It was expensive too." She spins the chair around and stares out the window.

"So, everything you told me is a lie? You didn't even get me from an orphanage? You've been lying to me all my life? Did you steal me?" I step forward to see her face better. "Did you?"

She frowns. "I don't like that word, 'steal.' It was a rescue, from a negligent father. He was fast asleep on a bench in the train station. Anything could have happened to the baby."

My mouth drops open. "You took me from my parents? You kidnapped me? Why? For money?"

"No, not for money." She squints. "I needed a baby, to get your father back. Understand this, he was leaving me because I couldn't give him a child." She pinches her chin and nods. "What I regret is not looking closer at the man sleeping under his hat. I thought you were a white baby."

I hear footsteps and turn. Dad's standing in the doorway, his face drained of colour and his torso stiff. He's staring at her with his hands clenched, as if he wants to strangle her, but he doesn't move. I knew it. He didn't know about this. Relief floods through me.

"You promised." He croaks out these two words.

For a moment, I stare at him in disbelief. He's not looking at me or talking to me. He's speaking to her. "What did she promise, Dad?"

She gets up and strides toward him, shoulders square, head erect. "Halca has only herself to blame. I have always stuck to our story." She wags her finger at me. "Like a common thief she came in here, broke into my desk, took the adoption certificate."

"I did not break into anything." I wave my hand at the desk. "Is your desk broken? I took nothing that isn't rightfully mine."

"You are a robber, a dirty, gypsy thief. This is not your desk to take things from." Lieke flings one palm in the air. "Did I not warn you about her? I warned you she would turn into a thief. It's in her blood."

I eyeball Dad, who hasn't moved an inch. "Did you know she kidnapped me? Were you in on it?" He doesn't answer, but moves toward me, places one hand on my shoulder, his face overrun with guilt.

I slap his hand away. "I can't believe you were a part of this."

She pipes up. "I wanted to give you back, when I found out who your mother was. It was all over the papers, Gypsy singer loses baby." Her scowl is one I'm familiar with, eyes narrowed, scolding. "But you." She shakes a finger at Dad. "She bewitched you."

Dad looks stunned now. His head flops forward as if he's rehearsing his next line. Then he swings around. "Your mother acted on her own."

"Don't call her my mother." I spit the words out.

"The damage was done already. I swear I didn't know." He speaks each word as if reading a script. "By the time I found out... and... I had no plan... what to do. I cared about what would happen to your mother."

"I told you. She is not my mother."

"The police would have sent her to jail, and it was because I wanted a child." Now his body stiffens, and he sounds angry. "Before I knew what she did, she showed you off to the neighbours and told them we adopted you. They had no hint about the trouble between us. How could I walk out on my family then?" A blue vein pops up on his temple. He turns to her. "Why did you announce a baby to the world before telling me?"

She stamps her foot. "I told them before I knew who her mother was." She points at me. "You... I wanted to return you and get a different baby. He said, 'No more taking babies.' He said he wouldn't be a part of it, and then he blackmailed me and made me promise to care for you and tell no one or he would turn me in. So I was stuck with you. Those were his conditions. He promised to stay with me and say nothing if I did what he asked."

Dad shoots her a flinty stare, his body visibly vibrating with tension. Then he grabs a crystal paperweight off a bookshelf. He raises his arm and I think for a moment he's going to throw it at her. I picture her skull cracking open, blood spraying everywhere. Then he switches direction and hurls it. "*Hoerenjong.*"

There's an ear-splitting crack. The glass ball goes right through the plaster with a thud, punching a fist size hole in the wall.

The enormity of the situation hits me, as if the paperweight has canonballed my gut.

"How coldhearted and selfish are you two?" I glare at her and then at him. "Did you give one thought for the mother and father of the baby you stole, how you destroyed their lives? Did you think of me? I'm thirty-three and I've just met my mother, but not my father. He's dead and lived his whole life not knowing what happened to me." I'm shrieking at them now, but I don't care. Let the neighbours hear. I walk over to the open window. "Do you people out there realise what kind of sick people live in this house?"

"You talk of your mother and father?" She bangs her fist on the desk. "Gypsies, that breed like rabbits. You should see what I have seen in Europe; dirty little gypsy kids everywhere. You should thank me, that I gave you the chance for a normal life. You should count your lucky stars."

I glance from one to the other. My whole body is shuddering now. "You destroyed my life." I stomp up to Lieke, stand in front of her, nose to nose. She has sour breath and I recoil. "I despise you." I turn to Dad. "And it's worse, what you did, because I loved you." There's a moment of complete and utter silence. The mantel clock in the living room strikes four.

He speaks and sounds defeated. "If you go to the police, they will deport us or send us to jail, maybe for the rest of our lives."

I consider this. It is what they deserve.

But right now I only itch to get as far away from them as possible, in body and in mind. I see them as a stranger would, with their white hair and wrinkles. I realise I don't have the power to turn back time, to undo the mistakes they've made, but I can direct my future. It's like Eldora said... 'Life passes us by in a moment, so we must fill our days with *felicidad*.' My anger shrivels and dies.

The adoption certificate is crumpled between my fingers. I assess the situation and the document for a few moments and then tear it in half. After that, I tear it and tear it until the pieces are so small I can't rip it any more. A breeze shoots through the window, and the bits of paper take flight, whirling around Lieke and Jans like confetti.

Then I leave.

Outside, as I race to the car, tears sting my eyes. Then I turn my thoughts to Leandro and the band. They'll be at the campground, sitting outside, waiting for me, the men drinking beer, Eldora nursing a *demi*-cup of coffee. When I arrive, everyone will kiss me and I'll kiss them back. Leandro might be telling them about Kopana right now. And when they find out she wants to meet them, I shiver, sensing their excitement.

I can imagine my life ahead, like a delectable dream—standing outside in the salty air, barefoot on a Persian carpet, under a canopy of swinging pots, hushed *and* healed by my Romany blood. And one day soon I'll sing this song for my mother.

♩ ♫ ♪ *Con mis dedos hago el fuego*

With my fingers, I make fire

Epilogue

At just past six in the morning, Kali sits alone at a sidewalk cafe on the *Camino del Sacromonte.* The sun glows amber on the magnificent palace of the Alhambra. A silent sentinel of trees encircles the structure, as imposing and ancient as the fortress. The locals call this landscape *Valparaiso,* a valley of paradise, and it's been Kali's home for ten months.

It's as if she has always lived here. She gazes at the labyrinth of streets leading up to where she sits. The cafe isn't open yet. The roads are quiet, serpentine and still.

She had little sleep the previous night. Along with Leandro, the band members, and Eldora, she'd stayed up waiting for hours after the *Zambra* closed. Kopana had been due to arrive but didn't show.

Kali enjoys the morning serenity without the constant clatter of Spanish and the concentrated effort she must make to catch the gist of every conversation. This pleasure pricks her with guilt. She should be worried about her mother, but still, she senses no bad karma.

Reflecting on the past months, Kali's contentment rises along with the sun.

Halca Visser ceased to exist when she left Vancouver. She thought of herself as Kali straight away. If only Spanish could be so effortless.

Romany is easier. She can already follow the thread of a

conversation.

"Is simple to learn," Eldora explained. "*Romany* only has one-third the number of words as Spanish."

Kali finds some *Romany* words ingenious. The word for a television set is *dinnilos dikkamuktar* which translates literally as 'fools' looking box.' It makes her smile.

As soon as they arrived in Andalusia, everyone, including Leandro, began speaking Spanish most of the time with a few *Romany* words thrown in for spice. Except Putrika—she spoke English for the first time in her life. The old woman is not fluent. But with a spatter of words, a plethora of hand gestures, and emphatic body language, Kali is getting to know her grandmother. She's teaching Kali how to play the cimbalom, and where there's music, words don't matter.

Putrika returned to Spain with them to keep an eye on Eldora. She and Eldora's healer have been busy doling out remedies. The treatments are working—the herbs, the chanting, and a small leather pouch that hangs around Eldora's neck. Kali hopes it doesn't contain bat wings or mouse droppings. Eldora's voice gets stronger every day. She sang with stamina the other night at the *Zambra.*

Kali has been eagerly awaiting her mother's arrival, having only spent a few weeks with her in Vancouver.

One day last year, Kopana and Kali were outside admiring the Japanese garden beside the apartment on Georgia Street. Kopana said, "I need to visit my garden in Buenos Aires one more time. Joyce must line up the sale of the house. Please to come with us." Then she paused and kissed Kali's forehead. "But maybe you need to stay with Leandro. I understand new love."

Kali chose Spain and Leandro and hasn't regretted that decision. Kopana promised to join them soon. She should have arrived last night.

In Vancouver, Kopana and Joyce arranged everything—the train tickets for everyone, a luxury liner to Spain, and a bus at the port of Málaga that brought them here to the Caves of Sacromonte.

"No airplanes, please," Kopana pleaded. Putrika declared her daughter's fears warranted, claiming that a family curse hovers above the tree line.

They're lodged in a hotel at the Caves, up one street from where Kali sits now. All of them have rooms, except Putrika, who prefers to stay in a brightly painted caravan parked near the end of the street.

The hotel owner told Kali that, in the early 1990s, he joined nine of the original cave dwellings to create this luxury hotel. Colourful tapestries and fabrics hang over the furniture and decorate the doorways. Only the walls, round, bumpy with rock, and painted white, suggest that they're staying in a cave.

Next door to the hotel is the *Zambra* known as *Rosarios*. It was once Leandro's family home and still bears the name of his grandmother, the most famous *flamenco* performer ever born in the Caves. Eldora's second cousin runs the *Zambra* now, and Kali has performed there, with Bloodfire, every Friday night.

One night, Adan had an offer to play at a prestigious club in

Madrid. Leandro says the quality of the performances at the Caves has declined. He says it's become a Disneyland of *flamenco,* all for the tourists, and claims that serious artists play the venues in Madrid or Barcelona. Still, she suspects it was Leandro who persuaded Adan to refuse the offer. He hopes to restore the Caves's reputation to the glory of his grandmother's day.

Last night everyone sat at the sidewalk cafe eating tapas, waiting for Kopana to arrive. After a few hours, Eldora asked Leandro, "Do you remember, many years ago, when we expected Kopana here? Remember how excited we were, that someone so famous would visit our *Zambra*?"

"*Si,* a faint memory."

"You were only four years of age. She never made it."

As sunlight breaks bright over the Alhambra, Kali again fixes her eyes on the empty roads that bring cars up to the *Camino del Sacromonte.* From behind, she hears footsteps.

Putrika places one hand on Kali's shoulder and says, "Not to worry. Bad luck does not visit us today. A black cat visits the *vardo* this morning. Is *cushti bokht,* a sign—and lucky. Your mother is only late."

Bio

Laurel Mae Hislop was born in Saskatchewan, has resided in various towns and cities in Western Canada, and now lives and writes in Vancouver, British Columbia. She's obsessed with all things artistic—words, poems, and stories that cultivate and uplift.

This is her third book. Her previous two books, "Chitchat" and "f-Holes of Melancholia," were both shortlisted for the Whistler Independent Book Awards in 2016 and 2020. Her fourth book, "Fresh as Dew Renewal Retreat," will come out soon.

For more information about Laurel and her writing, visit her website: https://mannamarkbooks.com

Acknowledgements

The following books (among others) contributed to my understanding of the Romany people: *Bury Me Standing—The Gypsies and their Journey* by Isabel Fonseca; *¡QUÉ GITANO!—Gypsies of Southern Spain* by Bertha B. Quintana & Lois Gray Floyd; *Gypsy Jib—A Romany Dictionary* compiled by James Hayward; *American Gypsy* by Oksana Marafioti; *LAVENGRO—The Scholar, The Gypsy, The Priest* by George Borrow 1851; *The Romany Rye—A Sequel to Lavengro* by George Borrow 1857. The poetry of Federico García Lorca inspired the emotional charge of the prose.

This book is dedicated to my dear, late friend Raquel Garcia Varela who was a creative, brilliant, beautiful person. She encouraged me from the beginning and assisted with my Spanish phrases. A deep thank you to everyone in Scribblers for all your help with early drafts. And for their gentle nudges and wickedly keen editorial assistance, I thank Elizabeth Boyd, Lara Sleath, and Nancy Baye.

Love and thanks to my family—my daughter, Lesley and my son, Lochlin—for your encouragement and enthusiasm. To my husband Karl, without your patience and understanding, this book would never be.

Manufactured by Amazon.ca
Bolton, ON

21731935R00153